MURDER
ON THE
WATERFRONT

MURDER ON THE WATERFRONT

A BILL DONOVAN MYSTERY

....

MICHAEL JAHN

THOMAS DUNNE BOOKS / ST. MARTIN'S MINOTAUR ❧ NEW YORK

THOMAS DUNNE BOOKS.
An imprint of St. Martin's Press.

www.minotaurbooks.com

ISBN 0-312-27857-8

First Edition: October 2001

10 9 8 7 6 5 4 3 2 1

FOR ELLEN

Author's Note

New York City's 578 miles of coastline include wildlife refuges, family and nude beaches, yacht havens, and mafia "swim-with-the-fishes" locales in addition to the expected tar-sodden commercial docks. As dramatic as some of the outer-borough coastline may be, however, if you think of New York City waterfront, you're standing somewhere along Manhattan's West Side docks staring at the Hudson piers and mumbling Marlon Brando's lines from *On the Waterfront*.

Scrupulous readers of the Donovan series know that Bill has dabbled on the docks before. He spent a summer with Marcy aboard a wooden boat docked at the Seventy-ninth Street Boat Basin, pulled a corpse or two from the Hudson, and every night drifts off to sleep with the salt air spilling into his bedroom window fifteen floors above Riverside Drive near the Soldiers and Sailors Monument. There's a lot of my family history behind Donovan's occasional return to mother *mer*. I come from a family that has managed to spend a few hundred years (that I know about) on or near the sea. One ancestor was a whaleship captain based in Sag Harbor, on the other end of Long Island. Another was a career Navy man who went to Japan with Perry and served in the Civil War with Farragut, appropriately, for a Brooklyn man, as gunner aboard the U.S.S. *Brooklyn,* before rounding out his career as storekeeper at the Brooklyn Navy Yard. A third forebear ran a dockside saloon in a landmark building alongside the Brooklyn Bridge. One way or another, we managed to stay wet.

So it was inevitable that Donovan would investigate a murder on the waterfront, on a rustbucket freighter docked for several fateful days between a mammoth luxury cruise ship and the *Intrepid* Sea-Air-Space Museum. While the freighter is fictional, the setting is real enough. Visitors to the city can view the approximate scene of the crime by walking west on Forty-second Street until swimming becomes a possibility. View the *Intrepid,* the other historic ships, and the pastel new cruise ships a dock to the north; maybe take a Circle Line cruise around Manhattan, and if you close your eyes you can hear Brando's voice from half a century ago, rasping, *"I could have been a contender."*

Michael Jahn
May 3, 2001

To read more about the Bill Donovan Mysteries and/or to contact me, visit **Michael Jahn's Book Pages** at http://home.att.net/~medj.

Murder
on the
Waterfront

1. AN EAGER YOUNG MAN APPROACHED, PREDATORY, GRINNING LIKE A HYENA.

Donovan hated the new look of the Hudson River waterfront, which was trending toward upscale eateries and scrubbed tourist attractions, not the least of which was the pastel and crystal palace of a cruise liner called the *Trinidad Princess*. At the least, Donovan was deeply suspicious. He liked his city seasoned and fun for folks with just a few bucks in their pockets. He liked the fast-disappearing days when you could get a flat fixed for three dollars or buy a hot dog for a solitary buck. And if the tabloids screamed about the "headless body in topless bar," such as the *New York Post* did once, famously, the possibility of danger was one of the city's attractions, what got the tourists pouring off the planes from Dubuque, along with the lights and the Sinatra tunes. Looking up at the outline of the *Trinidad Princess* looming over the concrete ramps and ramparts of the passenger ship terminal like a floodlit peach palace, a Third World dictator's notion of splendor, he said, "This is what happens when you get a mayor who wants to be president of the United States."

"What, the traffic jam breaks up?" his driver said, joining

the line of limosines dropping off swells outside the immense ocean liner.

"No, he wants to impress his buddies nationwide, so he throws a ten-thousand-dollar-a-plate bash. But in order to get them here, he has to spend eight years turning the city into Minneapolis, only bigger."

"What do they make in Minneapolis, Cap? Beer?"

"That's Milwaukee. In Minneapolis they make twenty-mule-team boredom. Such as my wife and I are gonna experience tonight."

"If you don't insult the host and get us thrown overboard," Marcy offered.

"Not a bad idea. I may do it just to get out of there," Donovan said. "So anyway, the mayor turns the City of New York into one of those well-scrubbed Midwestern towns where there's no litter on the sidewalk and poor people are required by law to stay out of sight where their Kmart slacks and vinyl belts won't offend the wealthy. He does this so his rich buddies will come here and not have to suffer the humiliation of seeing a normal working person who actually sweats, farts, and crosses against the light."

"Calm down, honey," Marcy said.

"No. As I was saying, to make sure the event is uneventful, the mayor stages the event in a place that does not look for even half a nanosecond like it belongs in New York. Going on board the *Trinidad Princess*, I bet, is like walking into the atrium of one of those big Marriotts—gigantic, better lit than a tanning booth, and you can walk into one in Houston and not be able to tell you've left Boston. After all, you can't entertain all those out-of-town fat cats at a normal New York City spot. Too big a risk of running into a New Yorker."

"Tell the sandwich story, William," Marcy said.

"This is a good one," Donovan announced, warming to the task. "Moskowitz and I were having a snack about one in the morning at a sidewalk café on Second Avenue. We were sitting outside and at the table next to us was this middle-aged couple who must have just hopped off the bus from Topeka. They were sitting there feeling sinful for being up at one in the morning, and along comes this homeless guy. He walks up to the male half of this couple, eyeballs the half-eaten sandwich on the guy's plate, and says, 'Can I take that for you?' The man thinks he's a waiter, you know, dressed up in authentic Gotham costume, and nods. So the homeless guy takes the plate and goes and sits down at a table and eats it. And this man and woman are staring at each other and I feel like saying, 'Well, folks, I guess you realize you're not in Kansas anymore.' "

"Did you arrest the guy?" the driver asked.

"Which one?" Donovan replied. "The homeless guy for being poor and pushy . . ."

"The mayor has outlawed it," Marcy said, speaking at exactly the same time.

"Or the guy from Kansas for being a dope?" Donovan concluded, squeezing Marcy's hand.

"What you're saying is that after the mayor cleaned up the city tourists could come here and still think they're in the heartland," the driver replied, driving up a ramp that led to the passenger ship terminal's VIP debark area.

"The joint is getting to look like Kansas City," Donovan said.

"Not only Kansas City, but a floating palace on the Mississippi . . . or whatever river they have in there," the driver said.

"The Missouri," Donovan told him. "Although it's been many moons since I explored that quadrant of the galaxy . . .

and I ain't entirely sure I ever did. You know what ticks me off more than anything?"

"What?"

"Hizzoner ain't even showing up. His advisers told him at the last moment that Bennett was the wrong horse to back. So guess who gets to greet him? Me."

What the mayor had done was something he had done before—ask his most highly decorated and famous detective to stand in for him at a public affair. Previous such events had included museum openings, college colloquia, borough political events, and, naturally, the street fairs where a city official shakes hands with its prominent local citizens. But what caused the mayor to think that Donovan would bond with the rich white conservatives gathering that summer evening on a luxury liner docked at one of the Hudson River piers to raise money for the presidential campaign of Pete Bennett, senator from Alabama?

"Why couldn't the mayor send Pilcrow?" Donovan moaned, looking out the front window in growing despair as the traffic jam seemed a few minutes away from dissolving.

Deputy Chief Inspector Pilcrow was Donovan's immediate superior and longtime nemesis. He was a starchy black conservative and by-the-books guy who resented Donovan's success and feared that the loose-cannonism that marked Donovan's career during his drinking days would return to cause a mammoth embarrassment.

Pilcrow was, overtly, the obvious choice to represent the city at a Compassionate Conservative Party fund-raising event. He was *profoundly* conservative, though not especially compassionate so far as Donovan could tell. Pilcrow perhaps hoped that his political utterings would, coming from an African-American, convince the law-and-order white mayor to appoint him the next police commissioner. So far no dice.

"Pilcrow's black," Marcy offered in explanation of the man's absence both from the commissioner's office and the evening's fund-raiser. "Bennett is a cracker."

"And white southern conservatives are desperate to associate themselves with like-minded blacks—the few they can find," Donovan replied.

"Pilcrow must not have known that Bennett was in town," Marcy offered.

"With *his* cadre of yes-men and spies? If he's not at the conservative party tonight, there is only one explanation. He's dead. If so, I must have been dozing when the all-clear alert sounded."

The limo pulled into a VIP lane, painted red to suggest a carpet, that ran alongside a broad indoor plaza that actually *had* a red carpet spread across it. Red, white, and blue balloons were bunched like grapes into a gigantic cargo net that was tied to the ceiling. Similarly colored crepe paper was wound around every vertical structure; patriotic Ace bandages, Donovan thought. Those young and pretty hostesses . . . ever-smiling Miss Kansas runner-ups, or so it seemed . . . in red, white, and blue blazers worn over white blouses and navy-blue miniskirts who weren't bustling around carrying trays of champagne carried trays of silver-dollar-sized buttons that bore the legend PETE FOR THE PEOPLE. Here and there among them stood eager-looking young men . . . larval game-show hosts, Donovan thought . . . expensively suited and perfectly groomed, who were helping funnel the Brooks Brothers–and–bejeweled guests from the red-carpeted reception area onto a red-carpeted gangplank. The destination was the *Trinidad Princess*'s promenade deck, the pastel railing and interior walls of which were sprinkled with balloons that glared, somewhat aggressively, in the light of the floodlamps.

The driver stopped the vehicle and hurried around to open the door, straightening his uniform as he did.

Donovan took the hand that the driver extended to help him out of the car. The help was unnecessary and, to a less secure man, would have been insulting. But Donovan was happy with himself and, while he no longer got into pickup basketball games in Riverside Park, still worked out three or four times a week and jogged when he could. The driver said, "Cap, I was noticin' you squirming around back there and you don't seem to feel so good."

"His cummerbund shrank," Marcy said, slipping out of the limo and onto the red carpeting as if it were a move she had practiced for years, the sheath riding up her long legs and then slipping back into place with a rustle of nylon.

"Gotcha."

"And he doesn't like rich people."

"I'm with you on that," the driver said agreeably as Donovan pulled at the offending strip of fabric.

One good thing about the glitter and finery of the luxury liner and the fancy-dress party going on adjacent to and aboard her was the smell of salt water. Donovan inhaled some, then smiled with a very basic and deep satisfaction and said, "Next Friday is dads' day aboard the *Intrepid*. I'm gonna take my kid."

"Good deal. Hey, is he walking yet?"

"Soon."

"Kinda young to be going to museums, isn't he?" the driver said.

"You're never too young to go down by the waterfront with your dad," Donovan said. "My own used to bring me to the water's edge all the time. We'd sit on the rocks near

Eighty-sixth Street and watch the candy-bar wrappers, condoms, and dead fish float by . . ."

"And the occasional cadaver," Marcy added.

"And dream we were on the Grand Canal in Venice. There's nothing like it."

"Those were the days, eh?" the driver said.

"Maybe it's not so bad how the mayor's turned around this city," Marcy said, straightening her husband's jacket and bow tie. She added, "You look wonderful and I adore you."

Donovan looked over at the assortment of hostesses and young conservative aides eager to greet him. Beyond them, vaguely recognizable conservative politicians—most of them from the tristate area of New York, New Jersey, and Connecticut—held court amid knots of adoring supporters below the swollen cargo net holding the balloons.

"I don't see the great man himself," Marcy said.

"I'm sure he's waiting to make an entrance," Donovan said. "At this point in the festivities, all we have to deal with are his minions, who suggest a cloning project ran amok in the heartland."

"Come on," Marcy said. "Let's go mingle."

A burst of helium-filled balloons popped from a net that party planners had anchored to a crepe-paper-swathed litter basket. They rose to the immense ceiling as a group of matrons standing nearby made an "oohing" sound, after which a banjo band burst into its version of "The Stars and Stripes Forever" and began perambulating around the reception.

Donovan grimaced and held his wife's hand, forcing a smile as an eager young man approached, predatory, grinning like a hyena. This one was not so young as the others . . . the many with the Glen Campbell look of golf pros . . . perhaps thirty-five years of age . . . and his eagerness was tempered by the deliberate nature of his movements. He also was conspicuous for having slightly longer and more expensively cut hair than the others as well as a snappy, red, white, and blue bow tie and no HI! I'M . . . name badge. Guests were presumed to know who he was; of course, Donovan was among them.

"Rob Ingram," the captain said, letting go of Marcy long enough to shake the man's hand, noting the manicured fingernails.

"Yes!" the man replied. "And you're . . . ?"

"Captain and Mrs. Bill Donovan, representing the New York Police Department," Donovan said grandly.

"Captain! So good to meet you at last. The commissioner said you're a much better conversationalist than he." With that, Ingram snapped his fingers and said, sharply, "D." Within seconds, a girl appeared carrying a platter of snap-on ID badges, the names on which began with "D." Ingram plucked the ones he wanted and handed them to the captain, who thanked him.

Ingram turned his attention to Marcy, and said, "Your father, now, is not a conservative, but a great man and we admire him immensely."

Ingram added a silly grin.

Donovan said, "Justice Barnes's wisdom transcends politics."

Ingram nodded, but without much conviction. Marcy thanked him for the compliment anyway.

"I saw you on *Larry King*," Donovan said.

"How did I do on my first national TV appearance with the campaign?"

"You were good."

"Thank you. Look, Captain and Mrs. Donovan, thank you *so* much for joining us tonight. If you'll excuse me, I have to run off."

"Go right ahead," Donovan said.

"But I hope we can talk again later. I hear you know every inch of New York."

"Is this your first visit?" Marcy asked.

"Oh, I was here as a kid, but not since. It's very exciting."

Ingram looked around, taking in the pastel of the ship and the red, white, and blue of the decorations.

"Wow! New York!"

"Approximately," Donovan said.

"I'm staying aboard the ship, but I'd love to see the town. Maybe you can direct me to some of the interesting spots?"

Perhaps it was something in the way he said "interesting" or in the way his eyes narrowed yet sparkled, but the effect was to make him appear like a novice falcon about to try out its talons.

Donovan grasped the man's hand and gave him a solid shake as well as a conspiratorial grin, the "cops-know-everything" look that was but one manifestation of the truism that cops and robbers were different, but clearly equal, sides of the same coin.

"I still have friends in low places," Donovan said.

"Just what I'm looking for," Ingram said, slapping the captain on the arm before rushing off to greet the next guests.

"I'm never gonna forgive the commissioner for this," Donovan said.

"Young buck on the prowl in the Big Apple," Marcy commented.

"Let's send him to Brownsville on the L train. If he survives that, I'll get Mosko to take him to CBGB for a night of slam dancing."

"Who *is* that guy? Did you really see him on *Larry King*?"

"I really saw him," Donovan said, helping her put on her ID badge and adjusting his own before leading her across the red carpet, slipping around knots of celebrants, ignoring offers of cocktail franks skewered on red, white, or blue plastic toothpicks but accepting a glass of champagne for her and a bottle of Kaliber for himself.

"Where was I?" Marcy asked.

"Sleeping with the baby."

"What is he, an aide or something?"

"Pete Bennett's campaign manager," Donovan replied.

"Oh, so he *is* important."

"Very."

"He's very young," she said.

"He's the new conservative *wunderkind*, a present-day Lee Atwater."

"The Reagan guy who played guitar and died?" Marcy asked.

"Yeah, him. Antichoice and bigoted. Don't believe the smile and the glad-handing."

Marcy looked down in distaste at her hand, where Ingram had shaken it. Then she shook her hand as if to fling off the germs. "I'll pay his fare on the L train," she said.

Donovan continued, "Rob Ingram is the hottest young political operator the conservatives have these days. If Bennett gets into the White House, Ingram is sure to be named attorney general."

"Is there any way we can prevent this?" Marcy asked.

"I don't know. Bennett has a solid lead in the early polling. This is Ingram's doing, I guess."

"Can we kill him?" Marcy asked.

2. "IF IT'S WINE, WOMEN, AND SONG YOU'RE LOOKING FOR, I SENSE ALL THREE LURKING BELOW," DONOVAN SAID.

At that moment, the strolling banjo band stopped playing in the middle of "Swanee" to make way for an announcement. The dinner was about to begin and all were encouraged to move from the reception area to the liner.

Donovan and Marcy held hands as they slipped into the crowd and followed it up a broad, red-carpeted gangplank over which hung a gigantic banner that read SET SAIL INTO THE FUTURE OF AMERICA.

What they stepped into was a fairyland of color and convenience, a floating Mall of America in which the pastel decor was marked every few yards by a dark-tinted boutique window and the bright, reassuring red and orange globes of a MasterCard logo. The promenade deck of the *Trinidad Princess* had neither sharp edge nor disturbing hue. A broad promenade circled the ship, offering guests a vinyl-covered, padded rail so they could rest their arms, without fear of abrasion, while pondering either the peaceful Caribbean or whatever waterfront was on the agenda, at that moment the New York one. On the other side of the promenade was a shopping mall. A hundred small shops, it seemed, lined the promenade, selling everything one would expect in the suburban mall experience that played such a large part in most cruise-goers' lives—Victoria's Secret nighties, Beanie Babies, J. Crew blouses, Borders self-help books, Crabtree & Evelyn scents, Body Shop soap, and faux-Cuban cigars sold with the help of blowups of Arnold Schwarzenegger chomping a stogie.

Interspersed among the boutiques were cafés and small plazas leading to the central court, itself a Marriott atrium that was even more of an imitation crystal palace than the average Marriott atrium. There was a courtyard restaurant seating perhaps five hundred people at round, twelve-person dining tables. Just behind it . . . or "aft," in the nautical parlance that Donovan recalled from his several teenage summers spent sailing while staying with his aunt on Long Island—he suspected that nautical parlance was not much used aboard the *Trinidad Princess*—was a casino. Several dozen slot machines were clustered to one side of a small array of keno, blackjack, poker, and roulette tables. Waitresses in red, white, and blue leotards worn over black fishnet stockings circulated, smiling ceaselessly, with platters of champagne.

This modest and highly middle-American den of iniquity, which could be used under normal circumstances only when the ship was at sea and beyond the twelve-mile limit, was bustling with gamblers who rushed to it from the crowd of politicians, spouses, and fellow travelers.

"How can they get away with that in New York?" Marcy asked.

Donovan pointed out a sign that read:

THIS LAS VEGAS NIGHT BENEFITS THE
SAVE THE UNBORN OF
NORTHERN NEW JERSEY FUND

"That way," he said.
"Are they who I think they are?"

Donovan nodded. "That group that brings unlawful-death lawsuits against women who have had abortions, purporting to represent their unborn fetuses," he said.

Squirming, Marcy said, "I think my cummerbund is getting too tight, too."

"I warned you."

Looking elsewhere around the room, Donovan took in the grand staircase that led down from the deck above to the side of the plaza restaurant. Doubtless the night's honoree would make his entrance down those steps. Donovan also pondered the balance of the periphery of the plaza, which contained a long, black-leather-topped bar, currently swarming with people, a bandstand from which a pop quartet backed up a Tom Jones-ish singer who warbled, of course, "New York, New York," a lounge with comfy chairs and small sofas arrayed around cocktail tables, and a gift shop that sold T-shirts and shot glasses bearing the likeness of the *Trinidad Princess*, among other items. Centered over the plaza restaurant was an immense crystal chandelier that dangled from a three-deck-high ceiling emblazoned with lights meant to suggest the constellations of the night sky. Slender wire tethers kept the chandelier from swaying and reminding passengers that they were on a boat. Two decks' worth of balconies looked down on this seagoing Marriott atrium. Behind each, Donovan assumed, was a passenger cabin.

"Let's sit down," Marcy said, and the Donovans walked to the lounge area and plunked themselves down into adjacent easy chairs.

They sipped their drinks and talked quietly—to the extent it was possible—while watching the crowd drift in and get settled. Donovan could see more clearly then that the men and women were nearly all middle-aged and white, with two or three black faces as well as a thin, white-haired man who arrived late, a nervous hand prodding along a much younger white woman.

Donovan was about the same age as most of the men, but Marcy was noticeably younger than most of the women. She drew a few stares, as usual, for being beautiful but also, from that crowd, for being multiracial. Donovan knew that there was something about being multiracial that offended white conservatives more than, say, being African-American. Perhaps the offendees saw in Marcy their fears of a future in which most Americans were sort of latte. That such a thing should bother those so clearly fond of pastel surroundings was unfathomable to Donovan.

After fifteen minutes or so, the band abruptly began playing "Orange Blossom Special," which Donovan understood to be the theme song of the Bennett campaign. It assumed the role "Don't Stop Thinking About Tomorrow" had in the first Clinton presidential campaign. Enthusiastic applause accompanied yet another release of red, white, and blue balloons as a dramatically floodlit procession began down the grand staircase. Flanked by wife, advisers, and key supporters, Pete Bennett descended as if a gift from the firmament depicted on the ceiling, waving to the left of him, waving to the right, smiling broadly while the pace of his footfalls matched the beat of the music.

Bennett was sixty-something and patrician, with soft pink skin that draped his face loosely so that the growing jowls rolled like the gentle, grassy hills of the heartland. Bennett had small eyes and thin lips, both of which narrowed into straight lines when he angered, a condition in which he found himself frequently during his younger years as Alabama's take-no-prisoners prosecutor. Walking by his side at the front of the pack of advisers and keeping perfect

14

pace, Ingram had on him the satisfied grin found on a cat that has bravely slaughtered a cricket.

Bennett's supporters rose and applauded more and some of the women squealed in an ovation not too different from the ones their granddaughters gave Ricky Martin. Donovan and Marcy exchanged glances. Her look was conciliatory, a sort of "when in Rome" resignation. Donovan's look was defiant, however. He was determined to stay seated, the way he did in high school during the late fifties when others in his class were required to recite the pledge of allegiance. But then Marcy patted him on the leg and he gave in, standing with her and even offering a perfunctory hand clap.

While the applause soon faded, the guests remained standing as Bennett and his party made the rounds. Ingram made introductions; Bennett pressed the flesh and gave pudgy smiles; his wife went off on her own, saying hello to select friends.

When at last he got around to the Donovans, the captain heard Ingram say the words that had become ritual at these political events: "Senator, meet Captain and Mrs. William Donovan, representing the New York Police Department."

Donovan smiled his political smile and grasped the candidate's hand, which, unlike the rest of him, was calloused and hard.

"Bill Donovan! I've heard about you. Read the book, too, years ago. How are you doing? Still catching them?"

"Every day," Donovan replied agreeably. Then he said, slightly by rote, "On behalf of the mayor and the police commissioner, I would like to welcome you to our city."

Smiling, Bennett turned to Marcy, who was radiant as always, and said, "So you're the daughter of Charles Barnes. How *is* your father?"

"Well, thank you."

"He's still on the bench? Hasn't retired?"

"Dad will never retire."

"Too much work to be done," Donovan added, tweaking Bennett a little. Bennett and Barnes were at opposite ends of the political spectrum, more opposite than was easy to imagine.

"My motto exactly," Bennett replied.

"Senator Bennett is a big fan of the job the NYPD had done in cleaning up this city," Ingram interjected.

"Magnificent job, absolutely magnificent," Bennett agreed. "If you don't mind my saying, twenty years ago crime was out of control in New York."

"My husband was only a lieutenant then," Marcy said.

"Now look at the place."

Bennett swept his arm around to suggest that the promenade deck of the *Trinidad Princess was* the City of New York.

"The city is a lot cleaner," Donovan said.

"I've got to go meet my other friends now," Bennett said, pulling back a little.

"The senator has a very busy schedule," Ingram added.

"But we'll talk again, Captain," Bennett said. "Maybe I can talk you into giving me the benefit of your expertise on how we can get the crime rate down nationally."

Donovan thought, but didn't say, "Provide education, training, and jobs; ban handguns."

What he *said* was, "I would be honored to help in any way I can." And he stuck his hand out again to be shook again.

"And, Mrs. Donovan, please give my best to your father," Bennett said.

"I will," she replied, lying as adroitly as her husband, Donovan was certain.

Ingram touched Donovan on the arm then, and said, "We'll talk later."

"Definitely," Donovan replied.

Bennett turned partially away, an action that was only half planned, then hesitated, returning his attention to the captain, this time his gaze inquisitorial and a bit harder. "I've met you before, haven't I, Captain? Many years ago?"

Donovan shrugged and said, "Not so's I recall."

"Ever been in Alabama?"

Donovan said, "I may have driven through it once. Would have been a long time ago."

"I must be mistaken."

"Lots of people mistake me for someone else," Donovan said.

When the entourage was gone, Marcy said to her husband, "I think you're being groomed for a spot in his administration." There was a twinkle in her eye.

Donovan smiled but said nothing. Instead, he picked up his wife's hand and squeezed it again.

"Wouldn't you want to be director of the FBI?" she asked.

"I would sooner have my flesh ripped by demons," Donovan replied, using a favorite phrase. "I'll tell you what, though. Finish your law degree and you can become attorney general in the Clinton administration."

"The Clinton administration?"

"The Hillary Clinton administration."

With another twinkle, Marcy asked, "Don't you want money and power?"

"I'm comfortable with the power I have now, and we have enough money."

"Don't you want to live in D.C.?" she asked, by now

sounding so deliberately provocative that it was hard for her not to laugh.

"No one lives in D.C. It's a Fig Newton of the general imagination."

"I might run for president one day," Marcy said. "Attorney general is not enough."

"You go, girl. I'd like to be First Husband. In the meantime, can we go outside and get some fresh air? I'd like to see if some of the *outside* of this ship *looks like* a ship."

"Don't bet on it."

"Come walk."

They went arm in arm back out on deck, excusing their way past a pair of party faithful who appeared amazed that anyone would leave, however briefly, the presence of the man they were sure was the future president.

The promenade deck—the actual deck, the outside part, not the wine-and-dining area inside—was deserted save for one other couple. The white-haired man and the young woman Donovan saw earlier were leaning on the vinyl railing, apparently pondering the deck of the *Intrepid,* which was brightly lit and swarming with tourists, and staring at the harbor waves.

Not every patch of the *Trinidad Princess*'s promenade deck was illuminated, only those nearest the party area. Donovan and Marcy found a spot in shadow, one where they were spared the worst of the pastel assault. A cool breeze ruffled up off the Hudson, rattling the metal stays of a yacht that was docked at the U.S.S. *Intrepid* museum complex alongside the aircraft carrier, the destroyer *Edson,* and the submarine *Growler* as well as a host of smaller vessels and any number of private yachts that docked overnight for visits. There was a time when Donovan, as a single man in his thirties, counted himself as a World War II buff. But looking at the *Intrepid* that night he found himself thinking of the ship's preretirement role as the principal recovery vessel for NASA, plucking *Mercury* astronaut Scott Carpenter out of the ocean. There were so many better things, he knew, than to fight.

The wind made an odd thrumming sound quite nearby, and that caught Donovan's attention. As his wife leaned her head on his shoulder and his arm encircled her, he looked at the source of the noise—the topmost part, sort of a crow's nest encircling a variety of gear, of a ship's mast. The crow's nest of this other boat swayed gently a handful of yards away, close enough to throw a clam shell at with reasonable expectation of scoring a hit. Strange, Donovan thought, he hadn't noticed a ship floating in the darkness between the *Trinidad Princess* and the *Intrepid* complex. His eyes followed the mast down to the deck and there it was, a vintage freighter a fourth the length of the *Trinidad Princess*, a black and rusting vessel of a sort seldom seen since Indiana Jones skulked around one in *Raiders of the Lost Ark*.

Donovan knew this ship, had seen it anchored around and even been on and off it a few times. Indeed, it was hard to miss, for despite its appearance as either a movie prop or a poster child for nautical historic preservation it was often docked at one of the city's tourist spots. The name was *Sevastopol Trader*, which also conjured up the picture of a gnarled and bearded captain wearing oilskins and chomping on the end of a pipe while steering his battered but determined old barge into the teeth of a North Atlantic nor'easter.

The ship was a newly arrived legend of the New York City waterfront. Rusted, rotted, and relegated to a dock in Gloucester, Massachusetts, during the 1950s, it promptly sank and filled up with mud and barnacles. It was bought in the early 1990s by Dennis Yeager, a Floridian who had come north years before to pursue the life of an eccentric New York. He had fallen in love with the waterfront and wanted a dockside project that he also could live in. Donovan knew Yeager from the time that Marcy, then still Donovan's girlfriend, lived aboard an old yacht docked at the Seventy-ninth Street Boat Basin. *Sevastopol Trader* was moored nearby and the scene of frequent all-night parties. For Yeager had restored the ship in a manner befitting Manhattan cool. After buying the hulk and paying to have it refloated, he and dozens of friends shoveled out the muck, ripped out the old engine room, and installed a much-smaller diesel engine borrowed from an old truck. However, Yeager left in the barnacles. The idea was to create a sunken-ship atmosphere that he and his friends promptly augmented by decorating the *Sevastopol Trader* with yard-sale furniture, antique lithographs and photographs, and gewgaws (such as Depression glass, Pixieware, and a Frankenstein's-lab assemblage of old and apparently nonfunctional electric gadgets culled from dozens of thrift shops). Moved to the Manhattan waterfront, *Sevastopol Trader* was both Yeager's home and a for-rental party space, serving community theater groups as well as the entertainment industry for use in chic parties and like events. The emptied-out hold was perfect for small theater groups or large and raucous private blowouts. Madonna was among the rock stars who shot music videos there, and every night following the presentation of the Grammy Awards a gaggle of Hollywood, rock, jazz, and blues stars clambered aboard the *Sevastopol Trader* for parties that ended sometime the following day or, on occasion, the day after, and were dutifully chronicled in the tabloid press. Donovan had been known to sit on deck and join Yeager in the occasional beer, back in the days when Donovan did that sort of thing.

He smiled and said, "Look who's moved to midtown."

Marcy peered over the rail and replied, "Is that Dennis's ship? I thought he was docked at South Street Seaport these days."

"They must have kicked him out again."

"*Sevastopol Trader* has been kicked off every dock in New York," Marcy said.

"I heard he's gone legit," Donovan said. "Made up with the Coast Guard and the harbor authorities and is negotiating to be given an old railroad pier down in Chelsea. He wants to create a respectable dockside theater space akin to Barge Music." Donovan referred to a Brooklyn institution, an old barge tied up at the foot of Fulton Street upon which chamber music concerts were held almost nightly.

"More like he's trying to compete with *Frying Pan*," Marcy added. That was a magnificent, fire-engine-red lightship that another mariner had restored and turned into a party space even more famous and desirable than *Sevastopol Trader*.

"I haven't seen Dennis in years."

"He appears to have plenty of company," Donovan replied. He pointed to the foredeck, where something was happening. Two women, one black and one white, both tall and leggy as models are, wearing wispy clothes that amounted to wearing nothing at all, were being photographed as they cavorted around the rusty ship's anchorcable winch, which sat on a frame near the bow. Atop the cabin, on the other hand, six or seven men and women swilled what appeared to be champagne, sitting on or hanging out around the several deck chairs and coffee tables kept there. And despite being covered with a blue awning, Donovan could get a glimpse of the afterdeck and the party that raged upon it. A jazz band played; he could hear bits of it if he ignored the banjos blaring behind him. Several canapé tables and a bar were set up, and several dozen people milled about.

"A party," Marcy said. "What a surprise."

"A high-powered one, too," Donovan replied. "Do you see who that is?"

He pointed back toward the bow, to one of the women being photographed, the black one. She was easily recognizable despite the distance, with her height—over six feet—and distinctive buzz cut. Marcy pressed a fingertip beside her eye to help her contact lens focus.

"That's Caren Piermatty," she said.

"The model."

"She's on the May cover."

Marcy referred to the cover of *Perfect*, the fashion magazine edited by her mother.

"Have you met her?" he asked.

"Sure. Two weeks ago at the party mom threw to celebrate the spring fashion issue."

"Where was I?" Donovan asked.

"Where else? At the Fulton Fish Market staring at a corpse."

"Oh, *that* night. What's she like?"

"Nice. A live wire. Sexy. You're not going anywhere near her."

Marcy smiled, and so did her husband.

"I think I've proven my faithful credentials by now," Donovan protested.

"That's true," Marcy allowed. Then she added, "Hey, I remember what's going on down there. Mom mentioned it. Caren's agent, Veronica Cascini, is launching a perfume line."

"And of course is doing it on Dennis's ode to nautical

decay. I love it. What's the name of this perfume, Shipwreck?"

"Cascini," Marcy replied. "Mom is hoping it will catch on and make things easier for Veronica. Her agency has been struggling lately."

"Maybe it will," Donovan said. "Let's crash the party."

"Can you get away?" she asked, the possibility of being with a more interesting crowd tantalizing her.

In reply, Donovan took out his cell phone and dialed a number. To whomever answered, he said, "Call me back in half an hour and tell me they've found another body at the Fulton Fish Market." Then he listened to the reply and said, "It's none of your business what I want to get out of! Just do as you're told."

He put the phone back in his pocket, and said, "We'd better get back inside and take our places at the dining table. I want witnesses when I'm called away on an emergency."

"You think of everything," Marcy said.

"A man who's in the public eye must always be equipped with excuses." He was about to turn away when he spotted Yeager, clambering up the vertical ladder that led to the roof of the cabin, accomplishing this feat while holding a glass of champagne.

"Hey, Dennis!" Donovan yelled, startling the man and his companion who stood farther down the railing. Donovan also waved at Yeager, but the man apparently heard or saw nothing.

"We could almost jump to the mast and shinny down," Marcy said, gauging the distance and reaching out toward the crow's nest.

"In *that* outfit?" Donovan said.

"I can do anything," she replied.

Donovan turned away again, and this time ran smack into Rob Ingram, who slid up to the rail alongside and pressed his pointy elbows into it.

"Hi," Marcy said, peeking around her husband's chest.

"Aren't you supposed to be shaking hands?" Donovan asked.

"Pete's much better at that than me. And Ree came back to help him, so I split."

"Who's Ree?" Donovan asked.

Suddenly a bit flushed, Ingram said, "Valerie. Mrs. Bennett. Ree is her pet name. Sorry. Anyway, I wanted to catch you before the sit-down dinner started."

"You caught me."

"Tell me where I can go later. Someplace that's not in the tourist books."

"What are you in the mood for, wine, women, or song?"

"Oh, I don't know. Let me pick from the menu once I get there."

A mischievous look came over the captain's face. He said, "There's always the Shining Path Poet's Café in the East Village."

"I *heard* about the East Village," Ingram said. "But . . . what did you say the name of that place was?"

Donovan smiled, and said, "On the other hand, maybe that's not your crowd. Performance artists who smear themselves in apricot butter and read *Das Kapital* in the nude."

"Not tonight," Ingram said, forcing a smile.

Donovan thought for a moment, then said, "There's a great chicken joint on Seventy-first and Second. Middle Eastern. Tabouli. Israeli salad. The Arab cab drivers go there. You can buy a bumper sticker that reads 'Allah is Great.' "

"In Arabic, of course," Marcy added.

"You want to see New York, and this is it in the raw. An Arab chicken joint that features Israeli food."

"Israelis go there, too?" Ingram asked.

"Yeah, they and the Arabs sit around and watch soccer on a black-and-white TV and argue. Everyone has a ball. I highly recommend it, but one tip—try the red hot sauce, but not the green. You get a blast of the green hot sauce and you're gonna be pushin' up cacti in the Negev."

"I think I'll pass," Ingram said.

"We'd better send him to Tavern on the Green, honey," Marcy suggested.

"No way. I got the spot—try Boot Hill on Amsterdam and . . . where it is, Sixty nine?"

"I think it went out of business," Marcy said.

"Nah, no way. Great joint. Very sexy. Western motif. Everyone in there is young and hot."

Donovan was smiling in that way he got from time to time when he was up to no good. Marcy recognized the look and said, "Rob, I have an idea for you."

"What is it?" Ingram asked, relieved at the hope of a sensible suggestion.

"Down there," she replied, pointing over the railing and down at the *Sevastopol Trader*.

Ingram craned his neck and peered over the railing. "What's *that*?" he exclaimed.

"That's the *Sevastopol Trader*," Donovan replied.

"What is it, an old freighter? It looks like something from a Humphrey Bogart movie."

Donovan explained how *Sevastopol Trader* came to be what it was. When the explanation was over, Ingram said, "So she's a party barge, eh?"

"For very chic parties. Such as those attended by super-models. Look more closely."

Ingram scrutinized the ship more closely, as instructed, and then said, "Is that . . . ?"

"Caren Piermatty," Marcy said.

"Wow, a supermodel! That's great."

"If it's wine, women, and song you're looking for, I sense all three lurking below," Donovan said.

"And close enough to the *Trinidad Princess* that I could get away with sneaking over once the dinner is done," Ingram said. "Do you think they'll let me in?"

"The owner's name is Dennis Yeager," Donovan said. "That's him on top of the cabin in the captain's hat pouring champagne."

Ingram looked and nodded.

"Just tell him you're a friend of mine and he'll let you in," Marcy said.

"You can get me into the party?"

"My wife can do anything," Donovan said.

"I've met Caren. She's very nice."

"How do you know her?" Ingram asked, surprised to hear that the wife of a detective and the daughter of a state supreme court justice was hobnobbing with jetset celebrities.

"She's on the cover of my mother's magazine."

"Your mother's . . . ?"

"Marcy's mom is Deborah Magid, editor of *Perfect*, the fashion magazine."

It became Marcy who Ingram was scrutinizing. Then he said, "I know who you are now. You're multiracial."

She replied, "Yeah, I got lucky early on."

"And you're also filthy rich."

"As my husband would say, 'slightly soiled,' " Marcy replied.

"I don't suppose you support conservative causes? No,

of course not. Sorry for even thinking it. I would hit you up for a donation. Well, thank you for coming to our party anyway."

"The City of New York heartily welcomes the esteemed candidate for the Compassionate Conservative Presidential Nomination and his team," Donovan said, slipping back into official mode.

"And I'm equally delighted to be here, Captain," Ingram said, turning to face the captain and pumping his hand again. "I think I *will* go to Tavern on the Green. My mom expects me to."

"You're not going to the party on *Sevastopol Trader?*" Marcy asked.

"Ah, you know how it is: too risky. If the press got wind of it, my career would be over. Besides, I don't think they'd like me very much on that freighter."

"Below us lays a nest of liberals," Donovan said.

"And, no doubt, some illegal drugs," Ingram said.

"That wouldn't surprise me, either," Donovan replied, sniffing the air in vain search of a telltale whiff.

"You ought to get after 'em."

"I ain't Sergeant Preston of the Lifestyle Police," Donovan said.

"If there's no body, he's not interested," Marcy added.

"If something does no harm and, like my father used to say, 'doesn't frighten the horses,' it's okay with me," Donovan concluded.

Ingram shook his head but smiled nonetheless. "A liberal cop," he said.

"A progressive cop," Donovan replied.

Ingram sighed. "Tavern on the Green it is. Thanks for the tips, anyway."

Donovan offered a gesture that said "I tried."

"Got to run now," Ingram said, easing away from the rail. "There's money to be made."

Marcy said, "Bye-bye," and waved the fingertips of one hand at the conservative activist as he slid back into the fund-raiser.

"I can't believe *you* were sending him to Dennis's party," Donovan said.

"And I can't believe *you* were sending him to a gay bar."

"Why couldn't the commissioner have assigned Pilcrow to shake hands on the *Trinidad Princess*?" Donovan moaned as he looked longingly below, the hint of a jazz band having wafted up from the freighter, finally able to be heard over the *Trinidad Princess*'s banjo band.

Marcy kissed him on the cheek, then grabbed him by the shoulders and turned him toward her.

"What?" he asked.

She hooked her fingers inside his cummerbund and pulled him along after her as she began to walk backward, away from the rail. "Come on, sailor," she said. "Let's go see if that band down below knows our tune."

3. BARELY ATTIRED BODY PARTS BOUNCED
AROUND TO THE RIGHT AND THE LEFT.

Unlike the gangplank that led to the *Trinidad Princess*, the gangplank that let the Donovans get from the *Intrepid* dock to the deck of the *Sevastopol Trader* was, well, a plank. No gang went up it, at least not all at the same time. Passage was strictly one at a time, walking uphill tenuously (more so in high heels). The handholds were iron chains strung between boat and dock, and they rattled ominously as the boat shifted. Unlike entrance to the *Trinidad Princess*, with *Sevastopol Trader* there was no way to escape the fact you were boarding a boat . . . and that only a thin metal plank and two rattly chains separated one from the harbor water, black and sinister-looking between the hull and the dock at that hour and at high tide. The fact that the passageway was poorly lit—the *Sevastopol Trader* was between and dwarfed by the cruise ship and the aircraft carrier—only added to the adventure.

Donovan was about to step onto the gangplank ahead of his wife, gallantly leading the way, when she put a hand on his chest and slipped by him. "Hey," he said.

"I'm better at this than you, honey," she said, nodding in the direction of the burly bouncer who stood at the other end of the passage.

Donovan dutifully followed Marcy as she went into "I have arrived" mode. He followed her in admiration, watching her behind undulate up the gangplank and listening as she said, in supreme confidence, "Marcy and Bill Donovan" to the man, who peered with the assistance of a small flashlight at a list on a checkboard. She made a "sign-me-in" gesture with three fingers as she brushed by.

"I don't have you," the bouncer said, a bit put off by addressing her back and her husband's shoulder as they passed.

"And you never shall," she shot back.

Donovan shrugged at the man, who was regaining his composure and about to say something else when he heard Yeager's voice, calling, "Marcy! Bill! Up here!"

The bouncer shook his head and went back about his business.

Yeager was still atop the cabin, still holding a champagne glass, which he waved at them.

"Hi, Dennis," she called back, pulling her husband up alongside her and walking with him down the dark deckway leading to the ladder. There was no vinyl railing on this ship, only an iron one long since rusted and painted over. No MasterCard decals punctuated shop windows. Occasional portholes, the metal frames rusted and painted over and the glass glowering darkly as if to discourage attempts at viewing, were separated by assorted pipes and stanchions and, on that night, by fashionably dressed . . . or nearly undressed . . . couples either engaged in deep conversation or halfway to coitus in the shadows, slender bare limbs climbing up thicker, expensively suited ones. A saxophone improvisation on "Bewitched" floated along the night air from the afterdeck along with sweet sometime whiffs of brandy and marijuana.

The Donovans reached the base of the cabin ladder and peered up. Yeager stood at the top, and looked straight down for a moment, waving and smiling giddily, before apparently being dizzied by the vertigo and pulling back from the precipice.

"Dennis is whacked," Marcy said.

"Imagine my surprise," her husband replied.

"Let's go up."

She took off her high heels and gripped the straps between her teeth and began up the ladder, her sheath all over the place but not, obviously, covering her legs. Donovan followed, amused by the whole thing but mainly relieved to be off the *Trinidad Princess* and back in an environment that he found darkly exotic and comfortable.

When Marcy reached the top she spun around and gave her husband a hand up. At the instant Donovan stood atop the cabin Yeager folded the two of them in his broad and sinewy arms, saying, "My friends! I'm so glad to see you! It's been years! You got married, yes?"

"Yes," Marcy said.

"I *saw* it. In Times Square on New Year's Eve!"

"I promised her a dignified ceremony," Donovan said.

"That was so fabulous. How did you ever arrange it?"

Donovan said, "A guy was trying to kill me. I chased him, into the spotlight, as things turned out. Half the world was watching. The mayor was there with a Bible. He married us, hoping to push us into genteel middle age."

"Did it work?"

"What do you think?" Marcy replied.

"I think that you're both absolutely mad and I adore you. Have a drink." Yeager waved over a waiter, who was a twenty-something man wearing a Hawaiian shirt, and said, "An Evian and a Kaliber, please."

"Sure," the man said, tucking a bare platter under one arm and starting down the ladder.

"We have a baby," Donovan added. "Daniel."

"That's great! How old?"

"A year and a half, nearly," Marcy said.

"A terrific age. Taking his first steps?"

"Soon," Donovan said.

"You've got to bring him here to visit. Let him get his sea legs. You know the old sailor's chanty, don't you?"

"It's been a while since I joined in the singalongs at South Street Seaport."

Yeager sang,

> " 'If you have a daughter,
> Bounce her on your knee.
> If you have a son,
> Send the bastard out to sea.' "

"*My* son is going to law school, like me," Marcy sniffed.

Donovan looked away, pondering once again the harbor water.

"Law school? Did you . . . ?"

"Go back? Yes. I'm finishing my degree next year."

"I remember you dropped out of Columbia when you took up with this guy," Yeager said, patting Donovan on the arm. "Say, I don't suppose you know anything about . . . no, too long a shot."

"What?" Marcy asked.

"Maritime law."

"Not me, but by husband knows everything because he reads everything."

"Do *you* know maritime law?"

"Sorry," Donovan said.

"Never mind. It's an unpleasant topic."

"What happened, are you getting kicked off another pier?"

"It's not me. It's this miserable hulk next door."

Yeager elevated a middle finger in the direction of the *Trinidad Princess*, which lurked over their heads like a gigantic pastel thundercloud.

"Oh, *that* ship," Donovan said. "Didn't notice her before. What's up?"

"Illegally dumping toxic waste into the sea," Yeager said. Then he added, quickly, "Hey, never mind. This is a wonderful evening and I have great guests. Come and sit down. Have something to eat. What are you in the mood for?"

"I'll take anything," Donovan said. "An egg roll would be nice."

Making a face, Yeager said, "Chinese food gives me the hives. We have *wonderful* things to eat here tonight."

A bit unsteadily, he ushered the Donovans to a chaise longue built for two. They sat on it, entwined as in the old days, looking up at the sky and the few stars that they could see through the mist of the harbor and the lights of the City of New York off to one side.

Yeager sat between their feet, stared at his empty champagne glass for a moment, then looked around for the bottle. He found it atop a glass table that sat near a cluster of five partygoers who were close together and engaged in soft conversation about something or another. Donovan heard the word "project" mentioned several times, and from that, their attractiveness, and their dress assumed a TV or motion-picture deal was being talked about. Yeager took a half step, poured himself another glass, and sat back down, unbuttoning his jacket. As ever, he wore his "captain's outfit." That was old black Dockers that a cardboard-looking belt held tenuously atop a wash-and-wear white shirt that clearly was more of the latter than the former. Over it was a navy-blue captain's jacket, authentic enough, bought at a secondhand store, with Coast Guard epaulets. On Yeager's head was a captain's hat that had seen better years, almost certainly at the St. Vincent de Paul Thrift Shop on Tenth Avenue.

"This is a good evening," he said, half sighing.

"You seem to be prospering," Donovan said.

"Oh, you mean my parties? Yeah, I do a lot of business ever since that writeup in *New York* magazine. Did you see it?"

"The next time I want to read about how hard it is to hire a maid I'll read *New York* magazine," Donovan replied.

"I get the parties that are too funky for *Frying Pan*," Yeager said.

"So Veronica finally launched her perfume," Marcy said.

Veronica Cascini owned the modeling agency that bore her last name, and in the years that surrounded the turn of the century had acquired much fame and fortune by managing the careers of her immensely successful supermodels.

"You know her?" Yeager asked.

"Oh, I know Veronica," Marcy said happily. "My mom does a lot of business with her."

"Your mom has made her a millionaire," Donovan added.

"I think that would have happened anyway," Marcy said. "It's hard *not* to be successful when Caren Piermatty is on your roster of girls."

"Caren is here!" Yeager said, his excitement level rising again.

"I know."

"Did you say hello?"

Marcy shook her head.

"Let's do that. She's down in the theater space, where we have a band about to go on. A Dallas group called Baboon. Sorry, Bill . . . it's rock and roll."

"I've grown more tolerant since finding that Daniel likes the Beatles," Donovan replied.

"All little kids love the Beatles," Yeager said. "Caren and Veronica are *both* down there. Come on, they're about to start shooting footage for a video. The two of you can be in the mosh pit."

"Exactly how I planned to spend my middle years," Donovan said. "The evening is progressing admirably. Who else is here besides a rock band and party guests?"

"The caterer and a video crew. That's it. What do you mean 'the evening is progressing admirably?' "

"What my husband means is that the reason we're in the

neighborhood was to stand in for the police commissioner at a Compassionate Conservative fund-raising event aboard the *Trinidad Princess*."

"Is that easier than staring at bodies?" Yeager asked.

Donovan shook his head. "The fund-raiser is for Pete Bennett."

"Oh, the Nazi. You got some life, *mi amigo*."

"But then we saw you and decided to cop out."

Yeager smiled, and said, "Let's go. There's something I want to show you."

"What?"

"You're fond of antiquities. What do you have in your apartment, the Aga Khan's dagger?"

"It was Kublai Khan."

"*That* must be worth a fortune."

"I'll have it appraised one of these days."

"God, I'd do it in a flash. Come with me."

Yeager stood, a bit too fast, Donovan supposed, for the man wobbled and had to extend a hand to the police captain, who helped him get his balance.

"Easy," Donovan said, a memory slipping in off the salty air. "Old times come crashing back."

"A drunken sailor never falls down aboard his own ship," Yeager replied.

Once stabilized, he straightened his jacket, went to the ladder, and started down. Marcy and Donovan followed, the latter noting the quaintly old-fashioned way that Yeager averted his eyes when Marcy descended, her sheath flying open. At the bottom, Yeager took the bottles of Evian and Kaliber from the returning waiter, then led the way below.

Donovan and Marcy followed Yeager down a brightly lit gangway, decorated with colorful found objects, leading to the theater space. They bumped shoulders with a succession of men and women, each thinner than the last and wearing less, some gabbing noisily, others, including a fashionably bored male model with blond hair the tips of which were frosted, gaping at Yeager's collection. Donovan, who counted *La Dolce Vita* as one of his favorite movies, immensely enjoyed sharing the decrepit and atmospheric hallway of the *Sevastopol Trader* with what appeared to be a casting call for a remake.

Descending into the bowels of the *Sevastopol Trader* was akin to entering an old coal mine that squatters had taken over and furnished thanks to frequents visits from the Salvation Army. The walls were dark with whole and crushed barnacle shells, rust, paint stains, oil, and too many other substances to list. Water pipes and electrical conduits of all sorts, equally ancient, ran here and there. Switch boxes that hadn't worked in decades served as platforms for candles and miniature flowerpots filled with fading satin roses. Seen from the inside, the portholes were even darker. But everywhere, tucked into even the darkest corners, were cheery decorations: framed photographs of Victorian children, old monkey wrenches painted red or yellow, needlepoint showing country cottages and church spires, and rag dolls, lots of rag dolls, some sitting prettily atop junction boxes and others hanging from limbs that were tucked behind cable conduits.

The one-time hold indeed had become a small theater, with a tiny, speaker-laden stage on which the rock band was setting up facing a round dance area that looked to Donovan like the inside of a gigantic pot-belly Franklin stove. Dance music played from speakers and two dozen or so revelers pranced and wiggled around below. Two video crews— Donovan couldn't see their faces but there was something about one of the men, an attitude, perhaps, that caught his attention for a moment—were shooting footage off in the shadows, apparently wide-angle shots of the crowd.

Yeager had led the Donovans out onto a narrow catwalk that ran smack over the middle of the dance area, about ten feet above it.

"I love this place," he bellowed above the din.

"I hate disco," Donovan said. "I forgot how much."

That notwithstanding, Marcy was beginning to move along with the music.

"Look at this," Yeager said, reaching up to unlatch the door of an emergency locker built into the roof above the cat-walk and used at one time to hold fire axes. From it he took a long . . . very long, about eighteen inches . . . knife with a wooden handle and a symmetrical blade. Donovan had never seen anything like it. To him it resembled the business end of an African spear.

Yeager handed it over, and Donovan hefted the thing in his hand. Unlike the ship in which it resided, the knife was old but lovingly restored, the wooden handle smelling of polish, and shining, too.

"I'm not into weapons," Donovan said. "They come to me in the course of my working day, but I don't go out of my way to find them."

"Me, either. This is the only weapon I've ever allowed on this ship."

"What is it, exactly?"

"A mincing knife," Yeager said.

"For onions? Awfully big onions."

"For whales," Yeager replied.

"Oh," Donovan replied, making a face and handing the thing to Marcy, who held it briefly and gingerly, as if it were made of pure evil, before giving it back to Yeager.

"I found it when cleaning up the last bit of muck from the after bilge. There was a big patch of goo to one side of the drive shaft. This is stuff that came in through a hole in the hull while the ship was sunk in Gloucester. She must have foundered on the site of an old whaleship wreck."

"Is this valuable?" Marcy asked.

"Only as a symbol of man's inhumanity to fellow mammals," Yeager said.

"Dennis, you're preaching," Donovan said.

"You agree with me," Yeager countered.

"Maybe, but I don't preach."

"I would like to take this and stick it in that Nazi Bennett, since you brought his name up," Yeager said.

Donovan made a show of inspecting the immediate surroundings.

"What are you looking for?" Marcy asked.

"Secret Service microphones."

"They'd never pick us up over the sound system," she said, raising her voice as the taped music suddenly became the Village People singing "In the Navy."

"I guess I'll just add this to my collection of curios," Yeager said with a sigh, putting the knife back in the overhead compartment.

"Is that the safest place to leave it?" Donovan asked.

Yeager thought for a fragment of time, then said, "I guess not. Later on I'll put it in my utility room backstage."

A voice drifted up from below, then another, both yelling "Marcy!"

The trio on the catwalk looked down to see Caren Piermatty and two other women looking up at them and waving excitedly. Marcy waved back, smiling, and Donovan did likewise, although he didn't know who the other women were.

"That's Veronica," Marcy said, reading her husband's mind. "And another one of her models, I guess."

He nodded.

"Let's go down and dance."

"Let's just go down," Donovan replied.

Following a return to the end of the catwalk and, then, down the same gangway as before, they found themselves pushing their way onto the dance floor. Barely attired body parts bounced around to the right and the left. Leading the way, Marcy hurried into the arms of Cascini and Piermatty and all squealed hellos. Donovan stood to one side, after a moment turning his head to look up at the stage, where Baboon was nearly ready to begin their set. A problem had arisen, with one of the group's road managers holding up a power cord and waving frantically to Yeager.

"Jeez, the wiring again," Yeager said.

"No juice for the amps?" Donovan asked.

"Not again!"

"What a shame."

"I better go fix it."

Yeager leaned over and kissed Marcy goodbye on the cheek, but she paid scant attention and the man careened unsteadily off through the crowd with no further exchanges. When once again Donovan looked at the women, he heard Piermatty say, in the tone of voice that celebrities use to flatter members of their public who are privileged enough to enjoy their company, "Hello, gorgeous. So you're the one who caught Marcy."

"Guilty as charged," Donovan replied.

"I'm Caren."

The woman leaned forward and gave Donovan a peck on the lips, a kiss on the lips being a celebrity meeting ritual that he thought the AIDS epidemic had done away with. He noted a fleeting wisp of a slightly floral scent.

"Bill Donovan."

"You must be very special."

Marcy said, "He is. You can't have him." And the women giggled.

Indicating the older of the two other women, Marcy said, "And this is Veronica."

"Hi," Cascini said, settling for shaking hands.

"Hi," Donovan replied.

"I'm going dancing," the other woman, a very young and striking one, said, slipping off into the crowd.

Cascini was much more conservatively dressed than Piermatty. Appropriate, Donovan thought, for a self-made millionaire who ran her own modeling agency. She was a born-again blonde of forty-some-odd years with a pile of curls that just covered raven roots—no attempt to cover the coloring job, perhaps in defiance of the opinion of others—and a cream-colored silk blouse with a high collar worn under a charcoal-gray miniskirt suit. An immense seashell necklace, more like a lei than a string of pearls, hung to her waist. Piermatty, on the other hand, wore *something* . . . Donovan couldn't tell what, exactly, at least not without the sort of closer inspection that would have gotten him in deep trouble. All he could tell was that it was dark, diaphanous, and approximately covered her breasts and below before disappearing into a series of ribbon-like panels that waved around as she moved. Donovan reflected on a sixties truism that it was impossible for a man to have a serious conversation with a woman in a see-through blouse, no matter how hard he concentrated. While talking to Piermatty he looked at her face, which seen up close was less beautiful than striking.

Cascini said, "You're what . . . director of special investigations for the police department?"

"Chief."

"I'm glad to have you here," Piermatty added. "There's crime *everywhere* on this ship tonight."

"I get that impression."

"It's really outrageous," she said, giggling again. "You'll have to call a bus to haul everyone off."

"The riot squad is on its way as we speak," Donovan said, sipping his beer.

"However did the two of you meet?" Cascini asked.

"I was teaching a seminar at Columbia Law and Marcy was one of my students. There . . . another crime . . . well, a breach of the political-correctness laws, anyway. We hooked up. Hey, it's a long story and we didn't come here to talk about me. You launched your perfume!"

"It's so exciting," Cascini said, her voice halfway between announcement and squeal.

"I think I just got a whiff of it," Donovan said, touching a fingertip to his upper lip where a spot of scent remained as well as a bit of lipstick, which lacking a handkerchief he wiped on his shirt cuff.

"Everybody had better be wearing Cascini."

"Congratulations," Donovan said.

"Yes, that's *great*," Marcy added.

"And it would not have been possible without your mom," Cascini said to Marcy. And, to Donovan, she said, "She's a very influential woman in the fashion world. And fashion leads to commerce, you know."

Donovan said that he knew.

"And her dad . . . I think he's some sort of a lawyer or judge or something. That's great, too."

Donovan nodded. Despite the presence of such internationally famous beauty, he found his attention drifting back to Yeager, who was up behind the stage trying to get the electricity working properly. Perhaps noting that male eyes had strayed, Piermatty suddenly let out a breathy "Hey," and grabbed Donovan about the waist and twisted him back toward her. Beginning to bob along with the music—now "Play that Funky Music"—her breasts bouncing in and out of the bit of fluff she was wearing, Piermatty said, "Let's dance!"

But Marcy took ahold of her husband's arm and yanked him back, saying, sharply, "He's on duty!"

"Dancing is against the mayor's new policy," Donovan added.

Piermatty pouted. There was no indication whether she believed Marcy or not. Then she said, "Oh well" and, after planting more kisses on Marcy and her husband—on Donovan's cheek this time—said, "Off to find another victim" and slid away, her hands fluttering high in the air.

"She's just a child," Cascini said with a smile.

"A six-foot-one, C-cup child," Marcy said.

"You're gorgeous when you're angry," Donovan said.

Donovan noticed that Yeager was gone from the area of the stage, apparently having solved the problem. The band had begun testing its amplifiers, sending both high crackling sounds and deep rumbles throughout the echo-prone belly of the freighter. One of the two videocameras recording it was being fussed over by a young man; the other was curiously unmanned.

"It's too bad that your mom couldn't make it tonight," Veronica said.

"She went with dad to a seminar on law and social policy at Harvard."

"Oh. She likes that political stuff?" Cascini seemed perplexed. Then she added, "I'm glad she gave you the invitation."

Marcy apparently didn't feel like telling the woman that she stumbled over the party on *Sevastopol Trader*, instead saying, "We would have come earlier but had to make a stopover on the way."

"I had to stand in for the police commissioner at the fund-raiser next door," Donovan said.

"Oh God, how could you *stand* standing in for him?" Cascini said, a hidden anger arising. "I mean, you seem like a reasonable man. Those politicians are all such vicious hypocrites. I'm surprised that Bennett had the nerve to show up in a progressive town."

"We stayed the minimum and then split," Donovan said.

"You poor guys, what an experience," Cascini said. "By all means, have some champagne."

"Thanks, but this is it for us," Donovan replied, indicating his Kaliber and Marcy's Evian.

The recorded music suddenly shut off, leaving the dancers in midhop. A few of them uttered sounds of complaint. Caren Piermatty, who had landed a few yards away dancing with another model, tossed her hands up in anguish and disappeared from the dance floor, heading up the port gangway.

Baboon began to tune its instruments. Even the sound of tuning was crashing, and Donovan began to shift his weight uneasily from one foot to the other.

"What do these guys play?" he asked.

Cascini said, "I guess you would call it hard rock. They're very hip."

"Played in the iron belly of a freighter? Who's on the entertainment committee, a hearing pathologist?"

Cascini laughed, and Marcy leaned toward her and said,

sort of conspiratorially, "His cummerbund is too tight. We'll have to go upstairs."

"It's called 'topside,' " Donovan said.

"Yes, honey."

Yeager reappeared, up on the catwalk this time. He was looking down at Donovan while seeming to feign listening to an older man, white-haired and full-bearded and wearing jeans that seemed wilted and wet, perhaps the result of an errant burst of champagne, who was talking animatedly in his ear. Donovan gave Yeager a wave, and the man quickly smiled and waved back.

"I've got to keep making the rounds," Cascini said. "Why don't you go enjoy the buffet. I'll get you some samples of Cascini and we have a wonderful layout in the, in the . . . back of the boat."

"It's called, 'aft,' " Marcy said.

Donovan smiled and patted her on the bottom.

"You must try the vegan roast beef," Cascini continued.

"Vegan roast beef," Donovan said.

"Oh, it's *wonderful*. Made out of braised tofu and . . . oh damn, I don't know . . . celery and seaweed and stuff. You'll love it."

"It sounds great," Marcy said.

"I'll get you the recipe for your restaurant."

"I don't do my restaurant anymore, at least not personally. I'm too busy raising David and finishing my degree."

"We hired a manager," Donovan said. "We drop in all the time to eat, though."

"I'll give him the recipe," Marcy said.

"It would be remiss for Marcy's Home Cooking not to have vegan roast beef," Donovan added.

"And if that doesn't sit well with you," Cascini replied, "there are twenty-four pizzas from John's Brick Oven."

"We'll see you later," Marcy said.

Donovan and she slid through the crowd and began back up the starboard gangway just as a thunderclap of guitar chords and a crashing of cymbals heralded the start of the rock band's set. The music did indeed turn the iron belly of the ship into its own amplifier, and by the time the Donovans reached topside Marcy was holding her ears.

"Wow, that's *loud*," she said, shaking her head as if to redistribute the neurons that had been jolted out of place.

"Rock, rock, rock and roll," Donovan said. "Lead me to the vegan roast beef."

"I had the pizza in mind."

"Me, too, actually."

The couple walked aft, in the direction of the buffet. What they found was a splendid array of meats, fishes, fruits, vegetables, cheeses, and breads in addition to the vegan roast beef and the pizza. Though the Donovans were late, the food was plentiful, perhaps, he thought, because the terminally thin party guests weren't eating. Whatever the reason, they skipped the pizza and filled plates with finer fare. Then they found spots on adjacent deck chairs alongside the aft rail and sat back and enjoyed their meals while the music in the belly of the *Sevastopol Trader* made the ship throb gently, like it had a heartbeat. And eventually the band stopped and the jazz quartet came back and Donovan and Marcy stayed and held hands and listened for another hour while watching the Circle Line tour boats come and go from their Forty-second Street pier. A small tender was tied to the rail of *Sevastopol Trader*, its bowline taut. A rope ladder, also tied to the rail, dangled down. The lapping of the waves made the bow of the little service boat go softly bump in the night against the hull of *Sevastopol Trader*, and that sound was fine, too.

The Donovans discovered that, following a rocky start, it had become a wonderful evening after all. They pocketed leather-boxed samples of Cascini and got home before midnight, kissed the baby, and snuggled the covers around his tiny shoulders. Then they climbed into bed and, wrapped around one another, slept peaceful sleeps and didn't think about politics or parties of whatever kind until seven the following morning when Detective Sergeant Brian Moskowitz called.

Donovan listened for a moment on the bedside phone, nodded grimly, and grunted a few times, then said, "Bring bagels" and hung up.

Marcy was looking up at him sleepily, accustomed to the routine.

"Another body at the Fulton Fish Market?" she asked.

"Rob Ingram should have listened to his momma."

Her eyes went wide, then back to normal. "Where'd they find him?" she asked.

"Dennis just found him in the middle of the dance floor in *Sevastopol Trader*, stabbed to death. He should have gone to Tavern on the Green."

4. "YOU WERE UP THERE, ON THE LOVE
BOAT? THEN YOU CAME HERE? TO
THE DEATH BOAT?"

Rivers and dawn aren't always romantic. Too often they bring not bright and wonderful awakenings, but bodies, and they also bring the ability to *see* them far too well. For police, rivers and dawns also bring the obligation to clean up the mess.

Several dawns found Donovan on the bank of the Hudson inspecting remains. One time someone washed up on a beach. Another time the corpse was snagged on a pier. This time the body was *in* a ship and not bobbing up and down alongside it, but still Donovan found similarities—the smell of oil, rot, and brine that is unique to urban waterfronts, the wail of seagulls, the lowing of fog horns, and the shuffling of spectators on the pier.

He parked his car at the *Intrepid* pier and walked over to *Sevastopol Trader*. As if oblivious to the tragedy next door, the *Trinidad Princess* was bustling. White-uniformed whatever . . . Donovan hesitated to call them "sailors" . . . moved about, with bottles of Lysol, the captain was sure, to polish the vinyl, hardly to swab the decks. Soon-to-be passengers lined up, luggage piled high on brass racks pushed by red-vested busboys. A line of taxis dropped off more.

Donovan walked past Howard Bonaci's crime-scene van, pausing just long enough to see that it was empty, and ducked under the yellow tape that barred entrance to the *Sevastopol Trader* pier, turning his collar up and moving quickly so that the horde of reporters lurking on the quay wouldn't recognize him. Seagulls squawked in protest and flapped off the pilings as Donovan walked past, meeting Moskowitz by the gangplank. The sergeant wore a blue Brooklyn Dodgers jacket over a Canarsie Gym T-shirt that was stretched tight over his bulging pectorals. His ubiquitous laptop was perched atop an old oil drum, the screen displaying showing the Special Investigations Unit logo.

"*Que pasta?*" Donovan said.

"Huh?" Mosko replied.

"That's Spanish for 'What's to eat?' "

"Oh yeah, how'd you know I'd be coming up Coney

Island Avenue past that bagel shop you're crazy about?" Mosko asked.

"A little birdie told me," Donovan replied, nodding at the seagull that was perched on a nearby piling, eyeballing the white paper bag that Mosko handed over.

"Here's your everything bagel with butter," Mosko said.

"Gracias."

"How come you don't do cream cheese no more?"

"The Irish blood missed butter," Donovan replied, taking his bagel from the bag and peeling off the white paper that surrounded it.

"There's something wrong with a guy who don't like cream cheese on his bagel. So what's your involvement in all this, boss?"

"We were there," Donovan said, using the bagel to point at the cruise ship, "and here," he said, while chewing, indicating the *Sevastopol Trader.*

"You were on that thing? Oh, that was where they were having the blowout you were so thrilled about going to."

"That's the place."

"Jeez, I guess it blew out. The deceased was Senator Bennett's campaign manager. I guess you know that."

Donovan nodded. "We talked to him. He was looking for some after-hours fun and thought we could point him in the right direction. Marcy came up with the idea that he boogie on down here."

"On this tub? What does Mrs. D. know about . . . hold on, this tub was full of cocaine and models last night, wasn't it?"

"I saw models," Donovan replied.

"And her mom hires models. Which ones did you see? Was Heidi Klum here?"

"Who?"

"Cover of the *Sports Illustrated* swimsuit issue."

"Don't read *Sports Illustrated*," Donovan said.

"Jeez, you're a strange man," Mosko said. "An Irish cop who don't read *Sports Illustrated*."

"I'm only half Irish. Hire a lawyer and sue me."

"So who did you see?" Mosko asked.

"Caren Piermatty," Donovan replied.

"The black babe who used to date your old pal Kurt Sharkey?"

"I only knew Kurt Sharkey because of a case," Donovan said. "He wasn't my pal, and I don't keep track of who he dated."

"Caren Piermatty was on this year's cover of the *Sports Illustrated* swimsuit issue, and in some fuckin' bathing suit, too," Mosko said. Then he added, "Wait, wait, wait. The coffee ain't hit yet, and I'm trying to focus. You were up there, on the Love Boat? Then you came here? To the Death Boat?"

"You're a bright kid, as I've said. You'll go far."

"What the fuck did you come here for?"

"We went out on the deck of the *Trinidad Princess* to get away from the politicians," Donovan said.

"I can dig that."

"We looked down and here she was. Yeager didn't tell you we were here?"

"Nah, he was just yelling for us to call you. Says you hang out with him at the Seventy-ninth Street Boat Basin. Wouldn't say nothin' to nobody else."

"He trusts me," Donovan said.

"So this is the barge you used to boogie on during the old days," Mosko said.

Donovan sighed, and said, "If you mean, is this one of the places I used to drink during the days I did that sort of thing, yes, this is it. I used to sit up on the cabin roof and drink beer. Can I call my lawyer before you slap the cuffs on me?"

Mosko smiled, and gave his boss a buddylike punch on the upper arm.

"Where is Yeager?" Donovan asked.

"In the wheelhouse, I think you would call it. Sobering up."

"He was four sheets to the wind last night," Donovan said.

"Yeah, well, he's got one bitchin' hangover right about now," Mosko said.

"Champagne has that effect."

"Is that what he was drinking?"

"When I saw him. But the evening was young and possibilities were endless."

"When will guys learn that no harm will come to you if you just act sensible and drink beer?"

"God has mandated that you're the one to teach them. What was Ingram stabbed with?" Donovan asked.

"It looks like a sword . . . dagger . . . whatever. Old and fuckin' gigantic, with a wood handle."

"If it's the weapon I'm thinking of, it was a mincing knife," Donovan replied.

"This murder weapon is too big to mince garlic with," Mosko protested.

"You use it to mince *whales*, son. Or used to, the practice having gone somewhat out of favor."

"Isn't this tub a freighter? How did whales get into it?"

"Dennis collected antiques. Old knickknacks, anyway. The mincing knife was one of them. He showed it to me last night."

"Oh, he *showed* you the murder weapon and then committed the crime?"

"Whoa," Donovan said.

"Whoa, bullshit! The preliminary estimate says that the murder occurred between four and five in the morning. Yeager was probably the only other one on the boat then."

Donovan patted his friend on the back, and said, "This is Manhattan, not Canarsie. The last time a party ended at four in the morning on this boat, the *Sevastopol Trader* was laying at the bottom of Gloucester harbor full of mud and barnacles. What makes you think Dennis Yeager would want to kill anyone, let alone a political presence like Ingram?"

"Ingram had to be the . . . what's that three-dollar word you use for 'opposite'?"

"Antithesis," Donovan replied.

"Yeah, that one. He had to be the antithesis of the cocaine-and-models stuff going on here last night."

"I didn't see any cocaine," Donovan replied.

"How hard were you looking?"

"I had a bottle of Kaliber and we ate. Get off my back."

"You're touchy this time of day, you know that?"

"I'm not so sure that Ingram was the complete conservative prude his reputation makes him out to be," Donovan said.

"Young man on the prowl?" Mosko asked.

Donovan finished his bagel and wiped his mouth on the paper bag it came in, not having been given a napkin. "There was a bit of Joe Buck in him."

"Who Buck?"

"Joe Buck. Didn't you ever see *Midnight Cowboy*?"

"I ain't into classic movies, boss," Mosko said.

"It only came out in sixty-nine . . . oh, never mind.

Handsome southern hick comes to the Big Apple figuring to become a professional stud. Winds up as something less than that."

"Happens every day. Check out the dudes coming off the Greyhounds at the Port Authority Bus Terminal."

"Where was the knife found?" Donovan asked.

"A few yards from the body."

"Which was where, exactly?"

"Flat in the middle of the dance floor."

"I want to see it. Is forensics done?"

"Not yet."

"Did you search the suite where Ingram was staying?" Donovan asked.

"Yeah, I just came from there," Mosko said. "It's in a pretty fancy row of expensive suites . . . I didn't know you could have a *suite* on a ship. Anyway, Howard and I went over it and came up with *bupkes*."

"Not a thing?"

"Nah, just the normal shit a guy takes with him when he's on the road. There were signs that a laptop had been plugged in . . . the cord was still in the wall . . . but the laptop itself was gone. I asked about that and was told it contained privileged campaign information and had no bearing on Ingram's murder. In fact, I'm now told that we can't get onto the *Trinidad Princess at all* without a warrant, and I for one am having trouble coming up with probable cause."

"I'm not sure at this point how badly I want to go send the lawyers into battle to get the laptop or onto that ship," Donovan said. "The laptop is probably what they say it is. Did they let you look into the other suites before the lawyers closed in?"

Mosko shook his head.

"Let's walk around the deck," Donovan said, leading the

way up there. He stepped lightly up the gangplank and, as he did so, was aware of a flurry of activity among the press assembled on the quay, especially the TV crews. He stole a glance in their direction, long enough to get a mental snapshot of the reporters. It was a Polaroid that caused an unpleasant memory to skitter in and out of his consciousness. When he set his feet upon the deck of the *Sevastopol Trader*, Donovan turned to his friend and associate and said, "That's the footage of the investigating officers going into the crime scene. It will be on the five o'clock news just before the sound bite of the mayor reassuring the citizenry that New York's Finest remains firmly in control."

"I'll tell my wife to tape it," Mosko said.

"And by the way, thanks for not wearing a T-shirt with the word 'fuck' on it today."

Mosko told his boss that he was welcome.

Donovan continued, asking, "Did you get a chance to look over that bunch of press guys before I got here?"

Mosko shook his head. "You're in charge of insulting reporters," he replied.

"I thought I saw an apparition, an evil thing, a specter lurking in the weeds."

"You got to stop hobnobbing with jet-setters and get more sleep. This lifestyle I see before me is no good for your corpsuckles."

Donovan made a sound like "mmmf" and turned aft, away from the bustling reporters on the shore. He led Mosko along the same starboard side he had walked with Marcy half a day earlier. Their feet scattered an array of rented wicker-and-glass party furniture upon and around which lay party detritus—empty and half-empty bottles of Opera Pia, Banda Azul, Pineau de la Loire, and Red Dog Ale, faux-crystal goblets of the sort delivered by A-list Manhattan caterers, ash trays speckled with the residue of Sherman's Ovals, tiny Treppchen plates upon which half-eaten finger sandwiches— portobello mushroom and mozzarella with pimento on ten-grain bread—lay a-moldering in the moist harbor air. And everywhere . . . on tables and chairs and on the deck propped up against bulkheads still resonant with the shells of deceased barnacles . . . were plastic bottles that once held designer water.

"This is what it looks like in the Canarsie Knights of Columbus Hall right after a first holy communion party," Mosko said, stepping around a canapé dish that had been left carefully balanced atop a wine bottle that sat midway between bulkhead and rail.

"They have crystal goblets at the K of C hall?" Donovan asked.

"You bet. You know, the plastic ones that ShopRite sells?"

"Oh, *those*. Sure. Hey, around here . . ."

Donovan led the way to where, the night before, he had noticed the tender tied up to the rail of the *Sevastopol Trader*. A few feet from the rail, he stopped Mosko with a hand to the chest.

"What?" the detective asked.

"I want Bonaci to go over this rail." Donovan swept his arm across, showing a roughly six-foot-wide stretch.

"You mean, like, jump into the river?"

"No, *schmuck*. I mean, get fingerprints and fiber samples."

"What's he looking for?"

"Evidence of a rope ladder and the people who may have tied it there," Donovan said.

"What rope ladder?" Mosko asked.

"Last night a tender . . . a little boat . . . was tied to the rail here," Donovan said, leading Mosko to a spot where they could look over without disrupting evidence.

"A tender," Mosko said.

"Yeah, a little motorboat. About twenty feet long, with an inboard motor and stick steering. No wheel. You push the stick forward to turn to port, and pull it aft to turn to starboard."

"What's the point of that arrangement?" Mosko asked.

"So you can steer standing up and with one hand, keeping the other hand free for handling ropes and fighting off pirates."

"That kind of steering has got to take some getting used to."

"It does. Yacht clubs and marinas have these things, at least *used to*. The style is kind of old."

"You saw one last night. So what?"

"Do you see it here now?" Donovan asked.

"Nope," Mosko said, looking down at the low tide swishing about the hull of *Sevastopol Trader*. Then he added, "Somebody came to the party in a boat. So what?"

"In the cocaine-and-models crowd, someone comes in a cruddy old marina tender and climbs up a rope ladder?"

"Oh. I get your point." He took a slender steno pad out of a back pocket and made some notes. Then he looked up, a thought prancing around, and said, "Why don't we just ask Yeager about it?"

"Because he lied to me last night. I asked who was there and he said only the party guests, the caterer, the band, and the video crew. He didn't say anything about anyone likely to come in a small boat."

"What about the band, the video crew, or the caterer?" Mosko asked.

"Do you want to haul a Marshall amp, a Sony digital

videocamera, or a platter of vegan roast beef up a rope ladder?"

Mosko nodded.

"Moreover, whoever arrived on that tender didn't intend to stay long," Donovan said.

"How do you know *that*?"

"They tied the bow line tight," Donovan said, his tone suggesting that Mosko should be able to get it.

"So fuckin' what?" the sergeant asked.

"The tide had only just begun to go out when we were here. But when the tide starts going out full blast you get swirling currents, and if you tied the rope tight the bow of your little boat is destroying itself against the hull of this ship. Or suspended half in midair."

"Oh," Mosko said again. He looked embarrassed, for only for a moment, long enough to fill in while his natural contrariness kicked in. Then he said, "Hey, I'm a New Yorker. I been on Circle Line boats and I was on an NYPD boat a couple of times looking for corpses and I took my kids flounder fishing out of Sheepshead Bay now and then, but I ain't no expert on boats. You're the one whose society babe girlfriend, now Mrs. D, used to live on a yacht."

"It was a wooden boat, not a *yacht*, and it was only for one summer," Donovan said.

"Oh, forgive *me*," Mosko replied.

"You're forgiven."

"I can't believe you noticed what *tide* it was. Weren't you partying?"

"Noticing things is fun," Donovan replied.

"What *color* was this tender?" Mosko asked.

"White."

"What were the registration numbers?" Mosko asked, his eyes carrying that I-got-you-now glint.

"I *was* taking it easy last night," Donovan said, then added, "I want you to . . ."

"Got it, boss. Search the harbor for this tender."

"Smart kid," Donovan replied.

"I'll have guys looking up and down the waterfront," Mosko said, making a note.

"Concentrate on *down* the waterfront."

This time Mosko's eyes appeared perplexed, like soft brown cat's-eye marbles. He hesitated for a second, stared at his boss with a look that had pleading in it, and exhaled softly in gratitude when Donovan replied, saying, "That little old boat could make maybe four or five knots. If she didn't leave before the tide got going full tilt in the direction of Venezuela . . ."

"Got it," Mosko said, smiling.

"Then the only direction she could have gone and *gotten anywhere* is downriver."

Mosko sang, badly as usual, " 'Come on, baby, let's go downtown.' What about Jersey? Could that thing have gotten across the river?"

"At high tide, sure. At low tide, no doubt. When the tide was going out full, figure on landfall somewhere in the Falkland Islands."

"I'll have the waterfront in Weehawken and Hoboken searched. You know, in that big marina next to the ferry terminal?"

Donovan acknowledged that it was a good idea. He added, "Once we find out who came to the party in that boat, we'll find out who helped him . . ."

". . . or her. You always tell me, 'Let's not be gender-specific.' "

"Arrive and depart. Do you know why he, she, or it had to have help?" Donovan asked.

Mosko held up a hand to stop Donovan from explaining. Then the sergeant leaned over the rail and stared at the water and then scrutinized the rail another time. "The rope ladder," he said.

"The rope ladder," Donovan replied.

"That's a chunk of feet between the water and the rail. Whaddya call that distance? You told me during Marcy's yacht days. Freestyle? Freemason? Free at last?"

"Freeboard," Donovan grumbled.

"Yeah, free room and board. Well, it's got to be a good fifteen, twenty feet worth of free room and board between the water and the rail. Maybe the rope ladder was there when he . . ."

"Or she."

"Arrived. But who took it down when he left?"

"That's the question," Donovan said.

"Or, I guess I should say, 'Who pulled it up?' "

"Exactly. Go find it. And when you do, have forensics look it over for whatever."

"Fibers from Dior gowns," Mosko said.

"I don't think that Dior is the designer of choice for supermodels these days," Donovan said. "And anyway, I'm sure that none of the party guests arrived by rope ladder."

"Caren Piermatty is strong enough, so says *People* magazine. I read it in the dentist's office last month. She does rock climbing."

"I suspect that her arrival and departure was duly noted and that it took place by more conventional means," Donovan said. "There was a bouncer with a checklist at the door. Find him."

Mosko nodded and made a note on his pad.

Donovan looked around, his back to the rail, scanning the bulkhead in the immediate vicinity. He saw a rattan table with a smoked-glass top that held half of a gigantic clam shell that someone had used as an ash tray. A Hoyo de Monterrey Churchill cigar, half smoked, the cocoa scent still wafting through a ring of lipstick, was tamped out on it. Nearby was an unopened bottle of Steamboat Ferry Inn Ale. The expected pipes and other conduits bisected the wall and the glass in a solitary porthole was just clear enough to reveal a ceramic Statue of Liberty birthday-candleholder. Donovan imagined that it played "America the Beautiful" once lit.

He raised his hands, palms up, in the gesture of "where is it?"

Mosko said, "The rope ladder?"

"Right, when you haul in a wet rope you leave it on the deck to dry out. You don't bring it inside and add to the killer humidity problem."

"Somebody not only went to the trouble to pull up the rope ladder, he went to the trouble to hide it."

"I would have rolled it up and hung it to dry from a hook or something." He squinted into the shadows where the bulkhead met the deck above, then took out his Maglite and shined a beam on a metal strap that had come loose from a long-disused conduit to make a nice hook. "Like from there."

"A lot of trouble went into this rope ladder thing," Mosko said. He looked around for a moment, then spotted something and walked a handful of paces down the rail— away from where the tender had been tied up the night before—and bent over to inspect a red-painted metal box that was riveted to the bulkhead near another porthole—this one completely impossible to see through. He opened a latch and lifted the cover, then shrugged and reversed his actions.

"Nothing?" Donovan asked.

"Zip. Not even cockroaches."

"We need that rope ladder."

At that moment, Moskowitz's cell phone rang. He plucked the instrument from its belt holder and spoke his name into the mouthpiece. Then he listened for a moment, his face increasingly grim. At last he said, "Try to hold 'em off."

As Donovan took an interest in the conversation and strolled over, Moskowitz said, "I don't know! Think like the captain! Stall a fuckin' truck and block traffic!"

Donovan smiled. "What's up?" he asked.

"Bennett is on his way here and Pilcrow is with him."

"Oh, *man*. There goes the directorship of the FBI."

"You were offered that?" Mosko asked.

"Definitely," Donovan replied. "Ask my wife."

"Hey, if you get to be J. Edgar Hoover, can I be your assistant?"

"What's your dress size?" Donovan asked.

"On second thought . . ."

"Why me? I just got to this party, and already Bennett is coming down to bust my onions for not arresting a suspect in the first thirty seconds."

"You got that right," Mosko replied.

"I should have never come back to New York. I should have stayed on the road."

"When were you ever *out of* New York?"

"I drove around the country when I was a kid," Donovan answered. "Those three years in the sixties you've been after me to talk about? That's what I did. Follow in the footsteps of Jack Kerouac and get in trouble. One night on top of a mountain in the Sierra Nevadas I swore I'd never go back to New York City. But here the fuck I am. So what can we do about Bennett and Pilcrow?"

"Block traffic," Mosko replied.

"Can we do that? What direction are they coming from?"

"From a breakfast meeting at City Hall. Up West Street."

"What about commandeering a garbage truck and stalling it across the road?" Donovan mused. "Nah, won't work—there's five uptown lanes. When will they get here?"

"Half an hour," Mosko said, glancing at his watch.

"We'd better go talk to Dennis now," Donovan said, starting off in the direction of the wheelhouse with Moskowitz closing his notepad and trailing behind.

5. "DOCTOR McCOY, REPORT TO THE BRIDGE."

As a longtime World War II buff and fan of old naval warfare movies—he had the entire *Victory at Sea* video archive in his den and was apt to blast the Elmer Bernstein score during moments of stress—Donovan relished the opportunity to spend time in the wheelhouse of a ship. And the wheelhouse of the *Sevastopol Trader* was especially atmospheric, and in the trendy-squalor way that Donovan liked. In fact, the reddish-brown residue of barnacle shell and Gloucester harbor mud as well as the spiderweb cracks decorating the large portholes that ringed the structure made the wheelhouse look like the bridge of the RMS *Hood* as seen in old movies as she took her fatal pounding from the big guns of the *Bismarck*. Donovan could imagine himself as a wartime captain barking orders as his sturdy vessel fought for survival, finally taking the wheel himself in a burst of last-gasp heroism.

That wheel was especially attractive, being four feet across and lovingly restored, all varnish and gleam. The ship's telegraph, which sat atop its pedestal to one side, was more like the rest of the room. It nobly reflected the bruises of time.

Yeager sat in the pilot's chair, slumped forward with his forehead against the cool walnut of the wheel, his hands grasping the spokes on either side. Uniformed policemen guarded the port and starboard entrances, and were an unsubtle reminder of how far down the social ladder he had fallen in a matter of hours.

Donovan waved the cops away and, standing in the port door, cleared his throat and said, "Permission requested to come on the bridge."

Yeager jerked his head up, and that appeared to hurt, so he sat back in the chair and clapped hands against both temples.

"Jesus . . . Christ . . . there's no way to hold my head that doesn't hurt."

"I seem to recall singing that tune in days of yore," Donovan said. "Can we come on the bridge? I ask because I like to observe formalities when ships of the line are concerned."

"Ships of the . . . ? Oh yeah, sure . . . permission granted. Bring your friend."

Yeager took one hand from his head long enough to waggle it at Moskowitz.

"This is Sergeant Moskowitz," Donovan said.

"My pleasure," Yeager said with a moan. His hand went back to his temple and he stumbled out of the pilot's chair.

"Yo, babe," Moskowitz replied, "need a hand?"

"No. I just got to get supine."

With that, Yeager lowered himself to the floor and sat with his back against the telegraph.

"I hear you and the champagne had a tough night," Moskowitz said.

"If it was just alcohol, I wouldn't be so . . ." Yeager's voice trailed off, and then he smiled sheepishly and said, "That's probably more than you want to know."

"We ain't the lifestyle police," Mosko replied.

The captain duly smiled.

"How old were you when you quit drinking?" Yeager asked Donovan.

"Forty and change."

"How hard was stopping?"

"Stopping was less of a problem than thinking about stopping. That took years."

"Man, I'm about ready. So . . . look . . . what happened last night? I passed out in my own bed like a gentleman and this morning there's a damned corpse in my ship. And I don't know what happened. I mean, I get up this morning and make coffee . . ."

"What time?" Donovan asked.

"Seven."

"Why so early?" Mosko asked.

"The caterer was coming back to pick up his stuff. After I found the body and called the cops, I had to chase him off."

"What time did you hit the rack last night?" Donovan asked.

"What a question! Why not ask me what time Mars set the night before."

"Take a guess," Donovan replied.

"I think around three."

"Why so early?" Mosko asked again. "I thought your blowouts didn't blow out until after dawn."

"Often enough they do. But my guests last night are people who get paid a lot of money to look good. They need their sleep. The party started to break up around two.

The band had gone and guests were drifting off. Caren was still here. So were Veronica and a couple of others."

"Ingram?" Donovan asked, helping himself to the pilot's chair.

"Never saw the man," Yeager replied. "I would have thrown his reactionary ass over the side if I had."

"As your friend and gendarme I advise you to stop making threats," Donovan said. "As I recall, you threatened to kill Bennett last night, and with the very same murder weapon we're discussing this morning."

Mosko gave Donovan a sharp look but refrained from addressing that point. Instead, he said to Yeager, "You just went to sleep leaving your boat unlocked and full of people?"

"What were they going to do, steal it? This ship barely moves under its own power, and you pretty much got to be fuckin' Magellan to maneuver it."

"You weren't afraid of being . . . I don't know, mugged?"

"By Caren Piermatty? She's welcome to jump me anytime. Anytime but today, that is." Yeager squeezed his eyes shut and said, "My head is killing me."

Donovan leaned into the bridge intercom—or what remained of it—and said, "Doctor McCoy, report to the bridge."

Yeager smiled despite the obvious pain. Then he said, "Didn't Caren try to jump *you* last night?"

Taking monumental interest, Mosko said, "What's this? What's this?"

"I had my bodyguard with me," Donovan said.

"Mrs. D guards him from other womens' bodies," Mosko explained.

"Go on," Donovan said to Yeager.

"I left my guests, and went to my cabin to put my head down for a minute. Just for a minute, you see . . ."

"And goodnight noises everywhere," Donovan said.

"This morning I got up and made coffee," Yeager continued, stretching his arm up to the top of the telegraph and plucking a mug of black coffee from atop it. Then he brought the mug to his lips, sipped, and rolled his eyes. "I found this great old tin percolator at a junk shop near the Fifty-ninth Street Bridge and keep it on a hot plate in my cabin."

"I would *love* to get my hands on an old tin percolator," Donovan said.

"If I go to jail you can have mine. Look, I started the fire under the pot and went below to make sure everything was okay down in the theater space. I have problems with the wiring down there."

"So you said," Donovan replied.

"Sometimes it sparks for no reason. I make a point of checking every morning to make sure no weird sparks are jumping around. This may be an old ship that once was sunk, but it *is* a ship and there is the smell of diesel oil around down below, and I'm phobic about the whole thing going blammo on me."

"Checking daily seems like a sensible precaution," Donovan said.

"Were there any problems?" Mosko asked.

"Not one. The band unplugged everything."

"Including your cerebral cortex," Donovan said. "I'll bet it was largely the noise that put you in this pain."

"I guess that's not out of the question," Yeager allowed.

"That's when you found the body," Mosko said.

"Yeah. But not right away. I went down the back way and came out in the aft part of the old engine room, behind where the stage is now."

"There's another way down to the theater space?" Mosko asked.

"There are three," Donovan said.

Yeager nodded. "Port, starboard, and aft. Last night I had everyone coming and going by the starboard gangway."

"Why?" Mosko asked.

"It's better located. It leads right down to the dance floor. The other ways are dark and not as well restored."

"Not as well restored?" Mosko asked, poking a finger at a bit of barnacle shell on the wall. "Whaddya got, petrified sea horses runnin' a Preakness down there?"

"It's the synergy between the soft ultrasophistication of my guests and the pirate-shipwreck motif of *Sevastopol Trader* that provides the appeal as a party boat," Yeager said.

"I guess that's better than having a party for pirates at Le Cirque," Mosko said.

"Not that it hasn't been done," Donovan replied.

Slipping momentarily into a thought of ships and piracy, Donovan grasped the wheel and said, "All hands on deck! Prepare to repel boarders!"

"Don't turn the wheel when the ship is at dock," Yeager scolded.

"I wasn't turning it," Donovan replied, releasing the wheel anyway. He continued, "Tell me how you found the body."

"Quite dead."

"And how the hell did Rob Ingram get on your ship?"

Yeager took a swallow of morning harbor air, blew it out, and said, "I can't tell you how he *got* here . . ."

"Can't or won't?" Donovan asked.

"Can't. No idea. Certainly not via the front door. The bouncer told me that you and Marcy were the only ones to get on board who weren't on the guest list. But as for when his spirit *left* . . . I finished checking backstage and was taking the shortcut across the dance floor . . .'cause the coffee would be done by then, and I had to get me a dose, you know? And since I *was* in the hold of a ship the light ain't exactly high noon in Havana."

"It's dark down there."

"Pitch black. And the backstage light is a forty-watt bulb hanging from the end of an extension cord, so it doesn't illuminate much. But walking across the stage more or less by memory I can see a glimmer of daylight coming down from the starboard gangway. So I was headed for it, picking my way across the dance floor when, boom! Body!"

"How'd you know that's what it was?"

"This is a party boat," Yeager said. "I've tripped over drunks before. Which is what I thought I had done again."

"How did you learn otherwise?" Donovan asked.

"I reached down and touched it and it felt cold. I went and put the main lights on and that's when I could see what happened."

"What did you do then?" Mosko asked.

"Barfed in a fire bucket. Want to see it?"

"I'll pass," Mosko replied.

"I went to my cabin and called for help. And here you are."

"And right behind us, a political and media extravaganza," Donovan said.

Yeager asked what he meant, and the captain explained. Yeager snapped, "Bennett's not coming aboard my ship!"

"Can you stop him?" Mosko asked.

Donovan said, "*We* can. This is Dennis's ship and my crime scene."

"I guess I'm not gonna work for the FBI," Mosko lamented.

Donovan said, "We don't have much time and I need to know more. You found the body in the middle of the dance floor, right?"

Yeager nodded. "Just below the catwalk you and I were on last night when I showed you the mincing knife."

"Used to mince whales," Mosko added.

"But used last night to mince Rob Ingram," Donovan replied.

"Yeah," Yeager said. "Did you see the knife?"

"Not since you showed it to me. Did you move it like you said you were going to?"

"Yeah. Just before I went to bed I put it backstage, along with some other equipment I got back there."

"Where backstage?" Donovan asked.

"In my utility room . . . top shelf of the utility shelves . . . I just stuck it there."

"Was it you or the first cops on the scene who found the knife?" Donovan asked.

Yeager tapped himself on the chest with his coffee mug.

"Where was the knife?" Donovan asked.

"Tossed to one side. It landed next to the stage. I must have stepped right over it when I got to the floor."

"Did you touch it?" Mosko asked.

"Are you kidding? After all the movies I've seen?"

"Of course, you touched it last night when you showed it to me," Donovan said.

Yeager nodded again.

"So did Marcy and I," Donovan said.

Mosko rolled his eyes. "Tell me that the Donovan family fingerprints aren't on the murder weapon," he said to his boss.

"No can do. Hey, the guy shows off his newly collected antique. What are we supposed to do, tell him, 'Sorry, I can't touch that 'cause it might be used to kill someone'?"

"That would have been nice," Mosko replied. "Well, Bonaci can filter out the prints left by you and the missus. No real harm done. It just looks bad when the report hits the deputy commissioner's desk."

He returned his attention to Yeager, asking, "Why'd you keep the knife in that overhead compartment above the cat-walk?"

"Do you live in a house with a big basement, Sergeant?" Mosko said that he did.

"It was where I happened to be walking when it occurred to me to hide the knife before last night's guests arrived," Yeager said.

"Why'd you want to hide it? This place is full of antiques. You have showcases full of tchotchkes."

"The knife is a valuable antique. Most of the rest of my collection is . . . let's face it . . . tin-pot percolators picked up at junk shops."

"Who knew where you kept it?" Mosko asked.

"Bill, Marcy, and me."

"Plus the forty or fifty people who might have been watching when you showed off your new acquisition last night," Donovan said.

"Oh," Yeager replied. "I guess that wasn't very good planning on my part."

Donovan said, "I think I know a way to get a handle on who on the dance floor might have been watching us. Did anyone see you move the knife backstage?"

Yeager offered a forlorn look.

"Right," Donovan said, "you were four sheets to the wind."

Mosko grunted and made some notes, and then grunted louder when his cell phone rang. He answered, "Yeah?"

"This is probably bad news," Donovan said to Yeager, who had bad news of his own, staring as he was at the desolate, dry bottom of his coffee mug. The look of woe on his face was enough to invoke pity in a boulder.

When Mosko got off the phone, Donovan asked, "Where are they?"

"On West Street near West Houston. They're stuck in traffic."

Donovan brightened. "What happened?"

"A tractor trailor jackknifed," Mosko reported.

"How did we arrange that?"

"We didn't. It just jackknifed."

"God smiles on the innocent and coffeeless," Donovan then said.

Then he slipped from the pilot's chair and touched Yeager on the shoulder as that man struggled bravely to rise and face the trek back to his cabin for more coffee. "Turning the helm back over to you," Donovan said.

"Unh, yeah . . . swell. Am I free to move about my ship?"

"Don't go off it," Donovan said as he led Mosko out of the wheelhouse and aft toward the starboard gangway that led down into the bowels of the ship.

Donovan found the dance floor on which the night before he watched the video crews taping the band setting up and the revelers dancing to the recorded disco tunes. Now, however, all that resonated on the iron floor was the irregular thumping of detectives' shoes.

The body—and once again Donovan found himself reflecting on the significance of the word "remains"—lay face up precisely in the middle of the dance floor. It was uncovered, the arms spread out as if Ingram's last act on earth was making a snow angel in the party debris. Beyond the corpse, maybe twenty feet away, several forensics technicians pored over the knife. The old meat slicer gave the appearance of having been tossed aside, and somewhat peremptorily, as it doubtless was when its usefulness as an implement of whale dissection ended a century earlier. It rested against the edge of the stage, next to which Howard Bonaci stood, overseeing his crew as they finished their work.

Donovan recognized the sights and sounds of crime-scene completion—notepads shutting, briefcases closing, cameras and chemicals being shut back in their carriers, and cell phones beeping as reports and commands were sent to various offices downtown.

"Hey, Cap," Bonaci called as he began to stroll over.

Donovan's crime scene guru was unlike the many detectives who took each new case as a hideous wrong to be avenged and the few who reacted with a tired professional athlete's "time to get out on the field" sigh of compliance. (The latter didn't last long in Special Investigations, the atmosphere of which mirrored Donovan's law that said "Good people should live forever and appropriate revenge should be taken when evil intervenes.") Bonaci treated each new corpse as a Christmas present, the fancy wrapping of which cried out to be torn away.

"Are you done with the body?" Donovan asked.

"We were about to roll him over, but other than that we are done. If you want to do the honors, have a ball."

Donovan and Moskowitz walked up to the corpse and bent over it. Ingram's eyes were open and wide. In death he stared straight up, as if in search . . . of what, Donovan wondered. The last time he spoke with the man, Ingram was in search of excitement and money.

"Time of death was between four and five this morning," Bonaci said. "The deceased was stabbed once, a straight thrust to the heart, up from under the rib cage."

Donovan picked up the front of the man's shirt and lifted it away from the bloody torso.

Bonaci continued, saying, "I would guess he was killed by a right-handed person who was facing him."

"And who stabbed Ingram while his shirt was open," Donovan added.

"Yeah, you noticed that? The shirt is intact."

"Apart from the three quarts of blood on it," Mosko said.

"But no stab through the shirt," Donovan said. "Good thing, too, cause this was a custom shirt. Must have cost a few hundred bucks."

"Worn without a T-shirt," Bonaci added. "I never could understand guys who wear dress shirts . . . formal shirts, too . . . without T-shirts."

Mosko pointed at Donovan.

"You, too?" Bonaci asked.

"You got to see the captain in the gym sometime. He ain't in bad shape for an old guy."

"An old guy who turns cranky when the subject of your annual raises come up," Donovan grumbled.

"As I was saying, the captain don't need T-shirts to hold his gut in," Mosko said quickly.

"T-shirts make me itch," Donovan said. "And if I sweat up my good shirt, I put on another one. Bobby Kennedy did that . . . up to three shirts a day."

"Why couldn't you pick a better idol?" Bonaci asked.

"As if you're old enough to know who he is."

"Hey, you're not the only one who reads."

"I didn't know that *Sports Illustrated* ran articles about politics," Donovan said. "Anyway, Bobby Kennedy wasn't my idol. Just another guy who tried to do some good in this world and got himself killed for the effort."

"Like Ingram, you're suggesting?" Mosko said.

Donovan snickered. "Not exactly."

"You thought Ingram was a bad guy," Mosko said.

"Yeah, but he didn't deserve to be killed for it. He should have gotten what he deserved—defeat in the polls for his boss and quick retirement to a job that better fits his temperament, like running a school board in Oklahoma and banning books on evolution. Where's Ingram's bow tie? I don't see it."

They looked around.

"It ain't anywhere in this room," Bonaci said.

"Let's look under," Donovan replied. Mosko and he stuck their fingers under Ingram's shoulders and lower back and lifted him up onto his right side. Under the middle of the back was Ingram's distinctive bow tie—navy-blue with red-and-white trim.

"Found it," Donovan said, and Bonaci waved a technician to come over with surgical gloves and an evidence bag.

After the tie had been scooped into the bag and he got the chance to inspect it up close, Donovan let the body fall back down. He stood, stretched, and said, "I want the tie, the shirt, the cummerbund . . . if you look closely, you'll see that it was shoved down and the shirt pulled out of it a little . . . and this guy's neck and face gone over really close for perfume, body lotion, lipstick . . ."

Bonaci squatted and pointed out one smudge to the left of the dead man's lips.

Donovan continued, ". . . blush, lip liner, yadda, yadda, yadda."

"He was on the prowl last night," Mosko said.

"Yeah, and I think I know what he found," Donovan said. "In fact, I'm pretty sure he was about to consummate the quest . . ."

"Right here, in the middle of the dance floor?" Mosko exclaimed.

Donovan gave him a withering look, and the sergeant tossed up his hands and said, "Okay, I got it, we're not in Canarsie anymore."

". . . when he wound up getting minced instead," Donovan said.

"Are you looking for any special kind of yadda, yadda, yadda on this guy?" Bonaci asked.

"Yeah. Cascini."

"Which is what?"

"The brand of perfume that was launched last night. That's what the party was for."

"I don't suppose you have a bottle we can compare against."

"As a matter of fact, I do," Donovan said. "Send someone to my place to pick it up."

"Your very own bottle of perfume?" Bonaci said with a slight smile.

"Yeah, mine. My personal bottle. You got a problem with that?"

"Nope, not me," Bonaci replied.

"Me, either," Mosko said.

"And while you're at my place, go into the hamper and get the formal shirt I wore last night," Donovan said.

"I sense a drama unfolding," Mosko said.

"Is this one of those shirts with the frilly stuff on the front?" Bonaci asked.

"Exactly. One of those."

"And you wore it with the perfume?"

Donovan scowled at the man, and said, "No, the perfume was a sample that we got on the way out the door or, I should say, down the gangplank."

"Whaddya want the shirt for?" Bonaci asked.

"Because I wiped some lipstick off my mouth onto the right-hand shirt cuff, that's why," Donovan replied.

"Who from?"

"Do you really need to know this now?" Donovan asked.

"Yes," Bonaci and Mosko said, more or less in unison.

"Caren Piermatty," Donovan replied, looking away so they couldn't see him smile.

"You were kissed by Caren Piermatty!" Bonaci said.

"Oh man, why didn't you tell me?" Mosko replied.

Looking back, Donovan said, "Because it was just a little hello, nice-to-meet-you kiss and because I don't want to be one of those guys who stands around talking about women."

"What did Mrs. D think about this?" Mosko asked.

"The kiss she didn't mind. But dancing with Caren was out of the question."

"She asked you to dance?" Bonaci asked.

"It was like the kiss, meaningless, a kind of flattery that I've seen before from celebrity types. Can we move on?"

"Can I go with you the next time you hang out with celebrities?" Mosko asked.

"Especially chick celebrities," Bonaci added.

"I wouldn't call Caren Piermatty a *chick*," Donovan said.

"I saw her on the cover of *Sports Illustrated*," Bonaci replied.

"No doubt you did. I bet you got her swimsuit cover taped up in the back of your van."

"No, but that's not a bad idea. Hey, Cap, do you think that Caren *killed* Ingram?"

"I just want you to check and see if that's her lipstick on his cheek," Donovan said.

"They were both here," Mosko added.

"If we believe Yeager, Caren was here when he went to sleep around three," Donovan said. "So was Veronica Cascini. There may have been others, and at some point Ingram shows up on the prowl. We need to talk to everyone who was here. We need to interview folks on the *Trinidad Princess*, including whatever crew members were on duty last night and, unfortunately, we need to talk to the pols."

"The pols?" Bonaci asked.

"The politicians, including Bennett."

"Your opportunity currently is stuck in traffic," Mosko said.

"I don't think that conversation will take place today," Donovan said. "*Mainly* we need to find out who was on this ship between three and seven in the morning. And I'd like to know where the fuck that rope ladder is."

"Rope ladder?" Bonaci asked.

"Did you see one?"

"Nope."

"Well, when you do make sure it's gone over."

Mosko added, "Yeah, and there's a stretch of rail topside that needs to be checked."

"Take me to it," Bonaci said.

"And get some guys up on the catwalk and give a com-

plete going-over to the overhead fire ax compartment,"
Donovan said. He pointed it out to Bonaci.

"What was in there?"

"The murder weapon."

6. A CAN OF TUNA, A BOTTLE OF CENTRUM SILVER VITAMINS, A BOX OF LOW-FAT WHEAT THINS, AND A TUBE OF FIXODENT.

"Why'd Yeager keep it *there*?" Bonaci asked.

"He told me that was where he happened to be when
it occurred to him to hide the knife," Donovan said.

"Do you believe him?"

Donovan nodded. "It's exactly the dopey sort of place a
guy who has a hundred and thirty-three feet of nooks and
crannies would choose."

"What's a hundred and thirty-three feet?" Mosko asked.

"The length of this ship. I can see Dennis ambling along
the catwalk when the light bulb goes on over his head that
he ought to hide the only valuable antique he has and thinking, 'I'll stash it here.' Another thing is, that's hardly the
hiding place you would pick if you want ready access to a
murder weapon."

"We'll check it out," Bonaci said.

"See what fingerprints you can get off that fire hose
box," Donovan said.

"Will any of them belong to a Donovan?"

Donovan shook his head. "Also check the utility room
backstage, where Dennis moved the knife to before he
sacked out. Look for prints on a utility shelf, top shelf."

Then Donovan changed the subject and said, "Dennis can't have killed Ingram. For one thing, he was too drunk last night to have made . . . how many stab wounds did you say there were?"

"One and one only," Bonaci replied.

"Coming up under the rib cage from below, you said?"

Bonaci nodded.

"Sounds like there was a certain amount of deliberation," Donovan said.

"You mean planning and control."

"That's what I mean."

"Yeah, I'd say so."

"Dennis was not in control last night," Donovan said. "I can't see him picking up anything more deadly than a Pepto-Bismol and wielding it effectively. And if he *was* somehow in control, he would have really cleaned the knife well afterward, especially since I knew about it. Furthermore, that knife is eighteen inches long."

"So?" Mosko asked.

"You're talking a lot of . . . what do you call it, torque? Sideways pressure on the handle. You take a knife with a very long blade and you stick it straight into a living body and you find it ain't exactly the consistency of a Jell-O mold. There's muscle and ligament to be gotten through. In last night's murder, somebody stuck somebody basically with a bayonet, but without the rifle attached to provide leverage. It had to have taken a strong man."

"Or woman," Mosko said, taking notes.

"I salute your conversion to feminism," Donovan said. Then he added, "Dennis is shorter than Ingram. The knife was designed to slice, not stab. I'm telling you, there's a lot of things wrong with the notion of Dennis killing Ingram."

"I get hives each time you start calling the prime suspect by his first name," Mosko said.

"I've known the man a long time," Donovan said.

"Yeah, and you like Manhattan eccentrics like poets who live in Central Park or guys who live in boats filled with garbage."

"So what?"

"Do you think that *Caren* is innocent?"

"Find out where she was at the time of the crime and I'll tell you," Donovan said.

Bonaci excused himself and went off. He grabbed a pair of technicians and took them up the gangway that led to the catwalk.

Donovan knelt to pick at the party debris. It included invitations, promotional flyers for Cascini, and faux-velvet liners from the perfume boxes as well as cigarette butts, gum and candy wrappers, and miscellaneous bits of paper.

"We need all this gone through," Donovan said.

"I'll make sure the guys do it," Mosko replied. "What are we looking for?"

"Whatever. This, that, and the other thing."

"Especially the other thing," Mosko replied.

Donovan picked up a bit of white paper that someone had scrunched into a ball the size of a marble. He unwrapped it, peered at it for a moment, then said, "Someone here shops at Rite Aid," he said.

"Someone in *this* crowd shops at a discount pharmacy? What did he buy?"

"This paper has been around a lot of water," Donovan said, sniffing it. "It's damp and hard to read. But one of our party guests went shopping yesterday and picked up a can of tuna, a bottle of Centrum Silver vitamins, a box of low-fat Wheat Thins, and a tube of Fixodent."

"Sounds like a shopping list for someone in your age bracket," Mosko said.

Donovan stood and patted his friend on his bald spot. "Next time we'll get whoever it was to pick up your Minoxidyl," he said.

"Hey, the stuff works. It's been six months since I lost one fuckin' follicle."

Donovan said, "I saw a guy last night, an old guy with white hair and a full beard. Wearing jeans that could have been wet such as he just came from the sea."

"Up a rope ladder?" Mosko asked.

"Just like that."

"What was Santa Claus doing?"

"Talking to Dennis," Donovan replied, adding, with a nod heavenward, "Up there, on the catwalk."

Mosko looked up to see that Bonaci and his crew had arrived on the catwalk and were treating the vicinity of the box in which Yeager kept the knife to the compete forensics treatment.

"Bag this," Donovan said, handing the paper to his aide.

Donovan watched Bonaci and his crew for a time, then stuck his hands in his pockets and wandered over to where the murder weapon lay where the metal floor met the stage, which was an iron platform that long ago supported some sort of equipment or other.

The knife had already been gone over. It sat in an evidence bag, awaiting the captain's personal scrutiny. He knelt beside it and peered through the plastic. The old whaling blade was caked thoroughly with blood that also caked the wooden handle.

"Maybe it's the plastic bag, but I can't see anything special on that grip," he said.

"You mean, like a hand gripping it?" Mosko replied. "Me, either. Bonaci tells me there's something unusual there, but he won't know what for sure until the pros downtown spend some time with it."

"Is there any reason for the murder weapon to be sitting here?" Donovan asked.

"Not now that you've seen it."

"Then get it outta here and on its way downtown. I want it at least down past Macy's by the time that traffic jam Pilcrow's stuck in breaks up. You know how much he likes to wave murder weapons around at press conferences."

Mosko nodded, then plucked his cell phone from its belt holder and pressed some buttons. Donovan stood back up and watched, a smile bubbling to the surface, as the phone on Bonaci's belt went off. Up on the catwalk, the crime scene chief brought his phone to his ear.

"You guys are forty feet apart," Donovan said, the smile sinking, replaced by a hint of amazement.

"He's up there and I'm down here," Mosko replied.

"So shout."

"It's impolite to raise one's voice," Mosko replied. After that, he told Bonaci what the captain wanted.

"Right away, Brian," Donovan could hear Bonaci say— and through the air, too, not over the cellular ether.

"Hang up the fucking phones and fight crime," Donovan then bellowed.

The other men around looked over and laughed. With a look of shock, Mosko said, "We're the cyber generation, Cap. We're wired."

"You're fired," Donovan said.

"I'm off," Mosko replied, quickly sticking the phone

back on his belt. Then he turned toward Bonaci and yelled, "Let's get the goddamn knife downtown."

It was Donovan's turn to smile.

Then he scrutinized the stage, looking at the spot where he remembered seeing Yeager help fix the electricity the night before. The area at the back of the stage, Donovan noted, was a bird's nest of extension cords. No wonder Yeager worried about sparks.

Then Donovan heard a familiar voice say, "Oh Jesus," and when he looked around he saw Yeager traversing the dance floor carrying his coffee mug, purposefully averting his eyes from the corpse. Two uniformed patrolmen followed him. One of them said, "This guy said he had to see you, Captain."

Donovan asked, "Are you okay?"

"Yeah. I'm good."

"No more nausea?"

"I'm barfed out, Bill."

Donovan pointed down at the evidence bag and said, "Your antique has a few more miles on it."

Yeager leaned forward, bending at the hip, sort of, to peer at the knife. Then he saw the blood and straightened up and breathed out loudly.

"Having a bloody history that includes whales *and* humans will add to its value," Donovan added.

"If the goddamn thing ever gets out of the evidence system," Mosko added.

A courier hustled the knife into a leather pouch and ran off with it. In his wake, a detective walked briskly across the paper-strewn floor and whispered something to Moskowitz, who drew Donovan aside and said, "*Nada* on the rope ladder."

"Can't find it anywhere?" Donovan asked.

Mosko shook his head.

"Where'd you look?"

"Upstairs. Downstairs."

"Everywhere below deck?" Donovan asked.

Mosko nodded. "And elsewhere *on* deck."

"I had a thought. What about the cabin roof?"

"What about it?"

"Did you look there?"

"Nope."

"Why not?"

"It's a *roof.* Who goes on the . . . oh, you mean . . ."

"I'll take it from here," Donovan replied. Returning to Yeager, he placed a comradely hand on the man's shoulder and said, "You tossed it on the roof, didn't you?"

"No, like I said, I tossed in a bucket," Yeager replied.

"Dammit, I don't mean your cookies. I mean the rope ladder. You tossed it up there so it would dry in the sun."

Yeager held his breath in for a moment and his thoughts as well. His expression betrayed the naughty but well-loved boy who was just caught with his hand in the cookie jar.

"The rope ladder," he said.

Donovan sensed that Yeager was probing to discover how much the captain knew.

"Yeah. What you would use should you get an irresistible hankering to dip your toes in our delightful Hudson River water."

"And risk getting bitten by one of the alligators that came out of the sewers," Mosko added.

"You saw the rope ladder," Yeager said flatly.

"No, I got the notion from watching an old pirate movie," Donovan replied. "Of course I saw the rope ladder . . . and the tiny harbor launch that it led down to."

"You saw the launch, too," Yeager replied, less flatly. Donovan detected an admission about to pounce.

"Both Marcy and I saw it. Tied up too tightly, too, as if the owner wasn't planning on staying long. Which is a shame, because I hear the vegan roast beef was outstanding."

Yeager smiled.

"The launch was gone this morning," Donovan said.

Yeager went over to the edge of the stage and sat. He watched quietly as forensics technicians stuffed slips of papers into evidence bags.

Donovan added, "That was how the white-bearded old guy I saw you talking to last night got here."

Yeager nodded. "Peter," he said, exhaling a little sigh.

"I saw you talking to *Peter* up there, on the catwalk, right about where you hid the knife."

Donovan tossed his head in the direction of Bonaci, who saw the motion and offered a fleeting wave. "We're finding prints," Bonaci said, this time shouting it.

Donovan gave his forensics chief the thumbs-up sign.

"One has nothing to do with the other," Yeager said. "Only you, Marcy, and me knew where the knife was hidden. Besides, Peter is a gentle man. He couldn't . . . wouldn't . . . hurt anyone."

"What's his last name?" Donovan asked.

"Lachaise."

"Spell it," Mosko said, and Yeager complied.

"French?" Donovan asked.

"I guess. French and American. I basically don't know."

"Who is he?"

"Is this necessary?" Yeager asked.

Donovan assured him that it was. "Especially since you told me that your guests, the caterers, the video crew, and

Marcy and me were the only ones on board besides you and the recently departed."

Yeager hung his head for a moment, looking between his knees. Then the forensics man who was plucking evidence from the floor stuck his hand down there to scoop a bit of foil-backed paper, and Yeager looked back up. He seemed deeply distressed.

Mosko said, "If you wanna barf again I'll send someone out to get a clean bucket."

"No," Yeager said. "I'm okay. Look, I'm sorry that I didn't tell you about Peter. I was afraid."

"Of what?" Donovan asked.

"Of you finding out the real reason I'm docked at this pier."

Mosko eyeballed the man, his gaze narrowing.

"I thought you got eighty-sixed everywhere else," Donovan said.

Yeager shook his head. "Not really. There are a couple hundred miles of waterfront in this town and I'm still okay in a few of them. The real reason I'm here is to spy on the *Trinidad Princess* and others of her ilk."

"Spy?" Mosko asked. "What for?"

"Toxic waste dumping," Donovan replied.

Yeager looked over, clearly surprised. "How'd you know?" he asked.

"You always talked about pollution of the seas as if it were a form of Armageddon. And environmental activists have gotten the goods on a couple of cruise liners recently, resulting in million of dollars in fines."

"But no one has gotten the goods on *that* tub," Yeager said, tossing his head in the direction of the cruise liner. "Stay with me sometime. Listen to the sounds at night. You can hear the pumps churning . . . pumping *something* out, and always at ebb tide."

"When the water is going out," Donovan translated for his assistant, who nodded appreciatively.

"So we test the water, Peter and I. The science lab equipment you see decorating some of the cabins and the old mess hall . . . it's not all for show. I can run a pretty good, basic tox screen here. And if I get a sample I suspect will prove my point that my evil neighbor is discharging toxic waste into the sea, Peter will take it and give it to a friendly, fully equipped lab."

"Chugging off in his old launch with the goods in a sack," Donovan said.

"That's about the size of it," Yeager replied. "Then, right to the Environmental Protection Agency. They levy the fines."

"There's nothing wrong and everything right with what you're doing," Donovan said.

"Why didn't you just tell the captain?" Mosko asked.

"I didn't want it to get out," Yeager replied. "I still hope to nab the bastards."

"I hope you do," Donovan said. "So what was your friend doing here last night?"

"He wanted to break out the testing gear and collect samples of the water. I told him, 'No way. I've got paying customers.' "

"You can't save the world if you can't pay the rent," Donovan said.

"Exactly."

"What did the guy say?" Mosko asked.

"He got pissed and left."

"So the gentle man has a temper," Donovan said.

"He thought that my guests were interfering with our

work. Do you remember the old saying, 'If you're not part of the solution, you're part of the problem?' "

"I've heard it," Donovan said, rolling his eyes. "But not much recently."

"He thought that the paying customers were frivolous," Yeager said.

"I've come to learn that there's a place for frivolity, too," Donovan said. "What time did he leave?"

"Around one, I think."

"How do you know he left?" Mosko asked.

"He said he was going to," Yeager replied.

Frowning, Donovan stared him down until Yeager said, "Wait, I had to pull up the rope ladder. I did that right after 1 . . ."

"Got my coffee?" Donovan suggested.

Yeager nodded sheepishly.

"We need to talk to this Peter," Mosko said. "Where's he hang up his hair shirt?"

"I don't know," Yeager replied. "He says he lives on a boat around upriver."

"And you believed him?" Donovan asked.

"Not the upriver part. We both know what's there."

Donovan nodded. "A handful of commercial piers, the city's garbage pier, the Trump construction in the west Sixties, and then nothing until the Seventy-Ninth Street Boat Basin. He'd never make it that far with the tide going out. And it's hard to hide at the boat basin. For one thing, I can see every inch of it from my living room window. How long have you known this guy?"

"We just met a few months ago. He came on board when I was docked at South Street Seaport and asked if I could help him get the goods on harbor polluters. I said, 'Sure, I'll help if I can.' The *Sevastopol Trader* is pretty good cover. No one suspects that anything more serious than the occasional celebrity bash goes on here. So when the chance came to dock next to the *Trinidad Princess*, I took it."

"Did you see him leave last night?" Donovan asked.

"Unh, no. But he was mad and I assumed he left. Did I do something wrong?"

"Not if he didn't kill Rob Ingram," Donovan replied.

"I don't think he's capable of that," Yeager said.

"We'll let you know if you're wrong," Mosko told the man.

"Who do *you* think did it?"

Donovan stretched and said, "Oh, I don't know. I'll fumble around and find out a bit about this guy . . ."

"Or girl," Mosko said.

". . . a little bit about that one, and eventually a likely candidate will emerge for the role of murder suspect."

"You said before not to leave the ship," Yeager said. "Does that mean I'm a suspect?"

"It mainly means that you pissed me off when you didn't tell me the part about Peter and the rope ladder," Donovan said.

"You piss off the captain when you lie to him," Mosko said. "It switches on his gene for pursuit."

"In the old days it only pissed him off when there wasn't enough ice for his drink," Yeager said.

"I've learned to channel my anger more effectively," Donovan replied.

Mosko's cell phone rang. He listened for a moment, then said, "All hands on deck! Prepare to repel boarders."

"Pilcrow is here," Donovan said.

"Parking his limo next to Bonaci's van. We better get up there, boss."

"Who's Pilcrow?" Yeager asked.

"The NYPD's Clarence Thomas clone," Donovan replied. "Bennett is with him."

"That Nazi Bennett is *not* coming aboard my ship," Yeager spat. He straightened himself, puffed out his chest—without being aware of it, Donovan felt—and bolted down the last of his coffee before taking a step in the direction of the gangway.

Donovan held the man back. "Go to your cabin or stay in the wheelhouse. Let me handle it."

"He's *not* coming on my ship," Yeager said again, quite angrily this time, betraying a temper that Donovan hadn't seen.

"I said I'll handle it. If you need something to keep busy with, take Brian up and show him where you tossed the rope ladder. But *don't touch it* again!"

Yeager nodded, a bit reluctant at losing the chance to stand on the gangplank and personally bar the presidential candidate from his ship, Donovan thought.

7. "IGNORING THE POSSIBILITY HE WAS ABDUCTED BY ALIENS AND BROUGHT HERE AGAINST HIS WILL..."

Donovan left the two men and went up on deck. As he walked down the gangplank to the pier he saw the entourage approaching. If storm clouds could take human form that was what they would look like. Pilcrow and Bennett walked pointedly up the dock, accompanied by Valerie Bennett. She wore a dark suit and a hat from which a black veil descended like a Hudson morning fog bank. The men were likewise somber and even the flock of young attendants, some of whom Donovan recognized as those he had seen in festive mode the night before, had lost their glee-club sheen. The only glint of excitement about the pier came from the press corps, which clicked cameras and waved notepads frantically behind blue police barricades. Feeling a bit like Gary Cooper waiting for the train to pull into town bearing the bad guys in *High Noon*, Donovan stepped onto the pier and stood, hands on hips, ready.

As usual when forced to deal with his high-profile and sometimes maddening captain, Pilcrow's countenance appeared a mix of anger and dread.

Donovan said, "Good morning, Paul. Good to see you again, Senator. I'm sorry it has to be under such circumstances. You must be Mrs. Bennett. May I extend my condolences for your loss."

If Bennett took particular note of Donovan's choice of words, the senator didn't show it. Mrs. Bennett, however, pulled aside the veil and said, "Thank you, Captain. Rob was very dear to both my husband and me."

The whites of her eyes were red; from crying, Donovan presumed. And the skin beneath them was puffy, not at all in keeping with the carefully if excessively made-up image displayed in the many photos Donovan had seen in newspapers and magazines.

Donovan said, "Rob told me that 'Ree' worked very closely with him and was indispensable to the campaign."

That time Bennett noticed. His famous Southern charm lingered on the precipice, then stepped back. He said, "I would be completely lost without my dear wife, who shares my grief at this terrible crime. I'm confident you'll be able to bring the murderer to justice expeditiously."

"I assured Senator Bennett that you are our best man," Pilcrow said.

"The deputy chief flatters me," Donovan replied.

"How did Rob get on board *this ship?*" Bennett asked, looking at the *Sevastopol Trader* as if it were a train wreck.

"I have no idea," Donovan said, telling no lie.

"What on earth could have attracted him to *this?*"

"There was a party on board with supermodels," Donovan said. "You could see it from the promenade deck of the *Trinidad Princess.* Did he say anything about coming down here?"

"Not to *me*, that's for sure. Boys?"

Bennett addressed that question to his retainers, who shook their heads nearly in unison.

Donovan asked, "Did Rob have, how do they say it in country songs, 'a wandering eye'?"

"Certainly not," Bennett replied. "He was a rock-solid family-values person."

Mrs. Bennett was looking away, so Donovan added, "Who was also single and attractive."

The comment got a reaction from her. But Bennett said, "Rob wouldn't do anything foolish that would jeopardize my candidacy, which is the thing he was living for. The man had a sparkling future. The sky was the limit, including the possibility of high elective office of his own. He would *not* risk that by skipping out on my big night to cavort with *supermodels.*"

Donovan said, "Ignoring the possibility he was abducted by aliens and brought here against his will . . ."

"Can we see the body?" Pilcrow interrupted.

"This is still an active crime scene with forensics on site," Donovan replied. "So I'll have to keep Senator and Mrs. Bennett off it. I hope you understand, Senator."

"I *was* a prosecutor," Bennett objected.

"Trust me that it's for the best," Donovan said.

Pilcrow smiled at the Bennetts, said, "Excuse us a minute," and took Donovan by the arm and led him across the pier. A seagull atop a post—Donovan wondered if it wasn't the same bird that eyed his bagel earlier in the hour—squawked and flapped away.

Pilcrow said, "I know that civilians shouldn't go onto crime scenes, but for God's sake, Bill, the man is going to be president of the United States."

Donovan withheld his skepticism. Instead, he said something sure to make the deputy chief see an even deeper shade of red: "Bennett is a suspect."

Pilcrow was startled, even though a decade of dealing with Donovan should have made him immune to surprise.

"Say what?"

"Do you know where the man was between four and five this morning?" Donovan asked.

"You know I don't."

"Then he's a suspect. He knew Ingram, and Ingram had a personal relationship with Mrs. Bennett."

"How on earth do you know *that*?"

"You saw how he reacted when I used the pet name Ingram called her."

"Oh, the 'Ree' thing? That's her pet name?"

"Did you ever see it in the newspaper that she had one?" Donovan asked.

Pilcrow shook his head.

"How did you know that's what he called her? Wait, I forgot . . . I was in Albany and the commissioner asked you to be at the fund-raiser last night, didn't he?"

"Bennett didn't mention meeting me?" Donovan said, his eyebrows curling.

"Not a word."

"The man was introduced to me by the deceased, shook my hand, demonstrated knowledge of both me and of my wife's father, asked me to give him tips on crime fighting, yet doesn't see fit to tell you we met?"

"He was upset," Pilcrow said.

"I would have grabbed you by the collar and said, 'Get that Irish cop I met last night to nab my friend's killer,' " Donovan said.

Pilcrow smiled faintly.

Donovan said, "It's a conspicuous absence."

"I don't think it's important," Pilcrow said. "Anyway, you've got this idea that Ingram and Mrs. Bennett had a thing going—just from the fact that Ingram called her by a nickname?"

"I feel that they did," Donovan replied.

"And on this flimsy . . . this *feeling* . . . you've got the nerve to rub it in the face of the presidential candidate?"

"I wanted him to know that I know," Donovan said. "And if there was nothing to it, if everyone in their lives from his secretary to her scullery maid, called her 'Ree' there would be no reason for him to react. He reacted."

"You be *very* careful on this one, Captain. And you be very careful about making sarcastic suggestions about how the deceased got down here," Pilcrow said, just before turning and walking away.

Donovan followed the man back to Bennett, at which time the seagull returned to its roost. Donovan listened as Pilcrow said, "Captain Donovan is correct. It's better that you don't go aboard that ship. I'll go take a look and report back."

"Thank you, Deputy Chief," Bennett said.

Donovan thought that the man's face registered disappointment as Pilcrow went up the gangplank alone. Donovan was sure that at least part of the reason was the clicking of the press corps' cameras. It would have looked better for Bennett, the one-time tough prosecutor, to appear to be investigating the murder of his own campaign manager.

Valerie Bennett had let her veil slip back down. Although he could see her face no longer, Donovan was of the opinion that she had closed down emotionally. She revealed herself to him, then dropped down into her version of a dead funk and was staring nowhere . . . or across the river toward Weehawken, from which was steaming a ferryboat full of commuters. Several dozen were at the port rail, gawking at the commotion on the pier.

Unlike his wife, Bennett appeared focused on these potential voters. Donovan watched as the man stood up straighter and puffed out his chest, then tugged at his lapels. With a commanding air, Bennett turned to Donovan and said, "Tell me, Captain, who are your suspects?"

"I'm afraid I can't tell you right now," Donovan replied. "As you said, you used to be a prosecutor. You know how it goes."

Bennett nodded, then crossed his arms and said, "Everyone is a suspect at this point."

"That's right. Everyone who was likely to have been with Ingram between four and five this morning."

"Would you like to get it out of the way and ask where I was?" Bennett asked.

"I was hoping you would offer the information," Donovan said.

"I was in bed, of course."

"Aboard the *Trinidad Princess*?" Donovan asked.

"Yes. We have the Empire deck blocked off. My staff and I took all the cabins."

"Including Rob?"

"That is correct. His cabin was not far from my own."

"You were sleeping with Mrs. Bennett, I presume," Donovan said.

"Well, to be honest, we often sleep in adjacent cabins while on the campaign trail."

Mrs. Bennett did not look at her husband, as Donovan thought she might. Her attention remained on the river.

Bennett added, "The reason for this, of course, is that I am frequently awakened by phone calls, and I prefer not to burden my wife."

"That's very considerate," Donovan replied. "I would do the same for my wife, except that she likes to be joined at the hip and also is a former police person and accustomed to late-night phone calls."

Bennett said, "My wife would kill me if the phone went off at four in the morning."

"Unfortunately, what you tell me means that, unless you got calls that we can identify as reaching you in your cabin, you have no alibi for the time of the murder. And neither does your wife."

"That's exactly what I'm saying, Captain. Between four and five there were no witnesses, no phone calls, not one thing but blissful sleep following the fund-raising success of the year. Let the Democratic candidate have Asia. Let the Republican candidate have the oil and gun lobbies . . ."

"You'll take Wall Street," Donovan said.

Bennett nodded. "And New Jersey, Massachusetts, and Connecticut. There's a lot of good, old American values in the good old Northeast. I'm sorry if that isn't to your liking."

Donovan shrugged. "I believe that good people should live forever and that suitable vengeance should be taken when crime prevents that from happening," he said. "How old-fashioned is *that*?"

"Rob Ingram was a good man," Bennett replied.

Mrs. Bennett looked over, the veil swishing faintly on the shoulders of her carefully tailored suit jacket.

"Isn't that true, Valerie?" Bennett asked.

"Very," she replied, her voice cracking.

"The captain is too polite to ask if you have an alibi for the hours between four and five this morning. He was hoping to get the information out of someone else."

"Looks like I succeeded," Donovan said.

She shook her head.

"I guess I'll have to rely on your faith in good, old American honesty," Bennett said. "We have no proof we were where we say we were."

"I believe you," Donovan said. "Who do you think might have killed Ingram?"

"I have no idea. He had no enemies other than political ones, and as you know there were a lot of them. But we politicians don't kill people in the physical sense. A lot of my conservative colleagues hated Bill Clinton, but none of us wanted him dead . . . just gone."

"Are you enjoying Senator Hillary?" Donovan asked.

Bennett groaned and shook his head; sadly, Donovan thought. At least that was no lie.

"Please don't remind me. It's been rough enough a day."

"Who will replace Ingram as your campaign manager?" Donovan asked, looking at the bevy of eager apprentices standing in a semicircle around him.

"I don't know yet," Bennett replied.

Pilcrow was coming back then, his feet clanging down along the steel deck, while Moskowitz endured a torrent of abuse.

"It looks like the deputy chief has made his inspection," Bennett said.

Speaking quickly before the torrent turned to him, Donovan said, "I'm going to need more of your time. A lot more of your time."

Bennett checked his watch, looked around at his retainers. "Today could be a problem."

"How long will you be in town?" Donovan asked.

"Two more days."

"Still on the *Trinidad Princess?*"

"That's the spot for me."

"She doesn't have to *sail?*" Donovan said. "I thought that these big barges were only profitable if they put into port, quickly filled up with passengers, and steamed off."

"Let's just say that the owners are friends of mine," Bennett said. "They are generously allowing me two more days of meetings and consultations, during which I'll be living aboard. I'll try to make time available for you. Call this number . . ."

He snapped his fingers at an aide, who quickly handed over a business card.

Donovan responded with a card of his own.

"In the meantime," Bennett said, "I'll tell my staff to give you complete cooperation as well as access to the Empire deck."

Donovan nodded in appreciation, his attention momentarily focused on one particular figure standing furtively at the edge of the press corps. And then Pilcrow stormed down the gangplank, footfalls resonating with a sound that resembled that made by dropping rocks into a galvanized iron bucket. Pilcrow was steaming, his eyes popping like they did whenever he lost his famous temper. If the deputy chief had any appreciation of the value of subtlety, he left it home that day. Startling even the well-in-control candidate and his wife, Pilcrow half growled, half yelled, "Who is that *maniac*?"

Nonplussed, Donovan said, "Brian can't help himself. He's from Brooklyn."

"I don't mean Sergeant Moskowitz. I mean the captain of this ship!"

Donovan's eyes rolled. "What did he do?"

"This *man* . . . this *friend* of yours, and I don't why I should be surprised, proudly informed me that last night he threatened to *kill* Senator Bennett. And not only that but would *do so* if the senator tried to go aboard his miserable old ship."

"Who is the deputy chief talking about?" Bennett asked.

Donovan sighed and said, "Dennis Yeager, who owns this ship. I was here last night, after your party. My wife is friends with the woman who hired out the *Sevastopol Trader.*"

"Why didn't you say so?" Pilcrow asked.

"Because a lot of times you get more if people don't know so much about you," Donovan said.

"Did you see the deceased?"

"Not aboard *Sevastopol Trader*. Marcy and I stayed an hour and were home by midnight."

"Do you take this man Yeager seriously?" Bennett asked.

"Nope. He is, as we say in New York, patently full of shit. My apologies, Mrs. Bennett."

"I've heard the expression," she replied, turning away from the river and back toward the people around her husband and her. She also pulled the veil aside again, and then took her husband's arm and held it in full and proud sight of the press cameras.

"I want this Yeager arrested," Pilcrow snapped.

"If we arrested everyone in this town who was full of shit the streets would be empty," Donovan replied.

"He threatened Senator Bennett and probably killed Rob Ingram," Pilcrow said. "I want to see him in jail. And as for you, Captain, I want a full report on how you came to be aboard this ship and what you were doing here. On my desk by the end of the day."

Bennett looked at Pilcrow and then at Donovan and made eye contact with the latter, during which Donovan detected a "shit happens" expression of sympathy.

"We had best be going," Bennett said to the deputy chief. "Would you escort us back through the press?"

"Certainly, Senator Bennett," Pilcrow said, leading the way back up the pier with the Bennetts and their crowd of attendants in tow. Mosko was standing at the head of the gangplank waving at Donovan, but the captain had other plans. Taking advantage of the cover offered him by the rapidly moving circus that was the party of politicians and the press corps attacking it with poked cameras and shouted questions, Donovan ducked down and blended into the crowd. As the press surrounded Bennett and party as they tried to get into their limousine, Donovan broke off and crept around behind Bonaci's crime-scene van.

He lingered there a moment until he was certain that he had escaped. Then he peeked around the van toward one of the concrete stanchions that held up the ramp leading to the debark deck of the *Trinidad Princess'* pier. The lens from an expensive video camera poked out from behind the gray concrete, but was focused on the *Sevastopol Trader* and not on the politicians.

Donovan crept around behind the stanchion, moving silently, as he did often enough in the middle of the night in much-less-hospitable surroundings during his years as a street detective. He came up behind his quarry and recognized the leather jacket, the hair, the lurking in-the-shadows attitude that he caught sight of on the cusp of the dance floor the night before.

Donovan reached around the man, grabbed him by the lapels, and spun him around and slammed his back against the concrete.

"Gotcha," Donovan snapped.

Michael Avignon was startled, shocked, caught completely unawares, but recovered quickly. He stammered, then said, "Hey! Oh, Donovan! What are you doing? You're not the warden and this isn't the penal colony."

"Which is where I thought I left you, you son of a bitch," Donovan snarled.

8. AN APPARITION, AN EVIL THING, A SPECTER LURKING IN THE WEEDS.

"I got paroled," the man said, struggling against Donovan's still-formidable grip to no avail.

"I nailed you on accessory to murder and harboring a fugitive and you got paroled after how long?"

"Seven years. What do want from me? I set up a system teaching video art to prisoners. The head of the state prison system gave me a fucking award."

"Up against the wall," Donovan said, spinning the man, huge camera and all, until his cheek was pressed against the concrete.

"Hey! The camera is worth a fortune! Lemme put it down!"

"Slowly," Donovan said, releasing his grip and moving the hand to his shoulder holster.

Avignon bent slowly at the knees and let out a slight cry

of pain as he set the gigantic, professional video camera on the pavement alongside the stanchion.

"My knees! I wrecked my knees while in the joint!"

"I truly hope it was scrubbing toilets," Donovan said, letting the man stand back up but then pushing his face against the wall once again and searching him for concealed weapons. Then while the photographer turned and brushed himself off, Donovan punched some numbers on his cell phone and said, "Get over here. Behind the first concrete pillar holding up the on-ramp to the *Trinidad Princess* pier." The captain was silent for a second or two, then said, "It wasn't a fish that I caught, but it smells like one."

"Why do you hate me so much? I did my time."

"You killed three people," Donovan replied.

"Oh, bullshit."

"Bullshit, nothing. Three men died at the hands of a serial killer while you followed him around with your fucking camera, shooting footage for a documentary that never will see the light of day and howling about your First Amendment rights."

"I didn't shoot him killing people," Avignon protested.

"But you knew who he was and you didn't tell me, all the while professing to be my good and true friend."

The incident in question happened a decade earlier, when Donovan was investigating a series of killings in and around the Cathedral of St. John the Divine up on Morningside Heights. Avignon was there as a journalist, a professional videographer given to artistic depictions of the city's grit and crime. Because they were old friends, and because Avignon appealed to the same instinct in Donovan that led him to like Dennis Yeager and others of the city's artists and eccentrics, the captain gave the man extraordinary access to crime scenes and inside information. Only much later did

Donovan find out that his professed friend was holding out on him, with murderous results.

Donovan said, "You even harbored him in your studio in SoHo, which I was thrilled to see was treated the way Rome treated Carthage . . . ground to dust and sown with salt to prevent anything from ever growing there again."

"It's *still* a parking lot," Avignon said, a bit sadly.

"It should be a pissoir," Donovan said.

Footsteps heralded the approach of Brian Moskowitz, who a decade earlier was serving his first stint as a detective on the staff of the West Side Major Crimes Unit, headed by then-Lieutenant William M. Donovan. Mosko turned the corner, saw who Donovan had nabbed, and said, "Look what the tide brought in."

"I remember you," Avignon said. His confidence was building back up with each moment that he didn't find himself with severe bodily injury hunched over the corpse of his wrecked video camera. Such was the reputation of the NYPD, including Donovan in his earlier years, when pissed off.

"I remember you, too, pal," Mosko said, his voice the Canarsie, Brooklyn, snarl that, coming from the mouth atop the heavily muscled torso, scared the daylights out of so many suspects.

"More to the point, I remember you last night," Donovan said. "You were shooting video aboard the *Sevastopol Trader*. You saw me on the catwalk and ducked back in the alley, into the shadows alongside the stage, didn't you?"

Avignon shrugged, and said, "What of it?"

"What were you doing there?"

"Working, of course."

"Filming another murderer?" Mosko asked.

"Shooting a rock video, for Christ's sake. Don't you guys watch MTV or VH1?"

"No," Donovan and Mosko said in unison.

"Well, that's what I was doing," Avignon said. "It's not against the law. I'm creating art."

"Yeah you are," Donovan said.

"I'm gainfully employed. My parole officer approves."

"We'll see how approving he is after I show him you were working in a place where drugs were being used," Donovan said.

"I didn't see any drugs."

"As my friend here pointed out, I wasn't looking that closely. I think I'll have the forensics guys currently working there take a better look," Donovan said.

"You were there, too!" Avignon howled in protest. "I have footage of you there."

"Are you trying to blackmail me?" Donovan asked.

To illustrate his boss's point, Mosko took out his handcuffs and jingled them in Avignon's face.

"No," the photographer said quickly.

"Empty your pockets," Donovan said, then stood watching as Avignon placed atop a barrel a wallet, keys, some slips of paper, and a New York City Transit MetroCard. Donovan poked through the stuff, then told the man to put it away.

"I was gathering evidence," Donovan said grandly. "Both Marcy and I were gathering evidence."

"How is Marcy?" Avignon asked, sounding a bit exhausted by the fright he had just been given.

"She's good."

"Tell her I send my best wishes."

"She'll be thrilled. I want every foot of tape you shot last night."

"I have some home and some in my new digital camera."

He reached down and patted it. The huge black device,

at least six times the size of a household videocassette recorder, bristled with protuberances of various kinds, one of them recognizable as being a microphone, another a light. The others might have been docking ports for spacecraft as far as the uninitiated could tell.

"How did you afford that thing?" Donovan asked. "When I put you in jail I did my best to leave you broke."

"I had a few bucks left after they took my SoHo building and my car," Avignon said.

"What part of town are you haunting now?" Mosko asked.

"Williamsburg."

"The Latino part, the African-American part, the Hasidic part, the Polish part, or the fashionable-artist part?" Donovan asked.

"Which do you think?" Avignon replied.

"What do you pay in rent?" Donovan asked.

"Two bedrooms, twelve hundred per. I got a deal."

"And you make the rent by shooting rock videos?" Mosko asked.

"Sure. No problem. I'm contracted to get . . . Hey, do I have to tell you how much money I'm making?"

"After my last experience with you, you got to tell me everything," Donovan said.

"Fifty grand on signing. A hundred on first acceptance. Another hundred after the final edit. I mean to make enough money to get *Crystal Black* finished."

That was Avignon's long-planned documentary on the decline and fall of Western civilization as typified by New York City as the year 2000 approached. It was his relentless pursuit of ghastly footage that caused him to harbor a fugitive from justice a decade earlier and, in so doing, set himself up for a stretch in the pen that, Donovan thought, sealed the fate of the project. Donovan said, "You're never going to finish that. The year 2000 is history. And if you do finish your tape, no one is going to show it. I'll give you a clue, asshole—I saw part of it ten years ago and you ain't going to Cannes to pick up the Palm d'Or. Best independent documentary at Sundance? Kiss my ass. As for an Oscar . . ."

"My advice to you is to stick to videos and keep your nose clean," Mosko said.

"What do you need the footage from last night for?" Avignon asked.

"I'm looking for a killer, something you should be innately familiar with," Donovan said.

"And you think I caught him on camera?"

"Did you get Santa Claus?" Donovan asked.

"The old guy with white hair?" Avignon said, further emboldened by having successfully fathomed who his old friend and current adversary was asking about. "Yeah. Of course. He was *so* out of place, of course I did. You know I zoom in on the out-of-place."

"And crowd shots. Did you get a lot of crowd shots?"

"I got everything," Avignon said proudly.

"I'll take it all," Donovan said.

"Sure," Avignon replied, now eager to please. "This is digital, so I can make you copies, no problem."

Donovan thought for a second, then said, "When you were setting up . . . when you were walking around, visiting the head, whatever, did you see anyone else besides the bearded guy who seemed out of place?"

"No, the crowd was exactly what I expected. The guests. The caterers. The band."

"No tremors in the Force, no suspicious movements in the shadows . . ."

"Sorry, Lieutenant . . . er, I mean, *Captain*, and congratulations about the promotion."

"Thanks. I'll take the tapes now. Right now," Donovan said.

"Hey, I'm still shooting," the photographer protested.

"What does footage of policemen crawling over *Sevastopol Trader* have to do with a rock video?" Donovan asked.

"Color. You know, exotic shit. All those musicians like to imply that they're more intelligent and relevant than they are. Madonna had Christian images. I'm cutting in city images."

"Including cops and murder?" Mosko said.

"Why not?"

"When did you go home last night?" Donovan asked.

"After the band did. Around two."

"Can you prove it?" Mosko asked.

Avignon thought for a moment, then said, "Somebody must have seen me leaving. Hey, there was Boris."

"Who's Boris?" Donovan asked.

"The kid I hired to run the other camera," Avignon said. "He's a college kid . . . Brooklyn College . . . an intern in the TV program. Good cameraman. We got here and left together. In fact, we were together the whole night. Other than toilet breaks, of course."

"Where did you go onboard other than the dance floor?" Donovan asked.

"Uhm, the stairs, the toilet, the food. That's it."

"Nowhere else?"

"I was busy," Avignon replied, shaking his head.

Mosko asked for the other cameraman's last name and phone number, and duly recorded the information in the margin of a takeout menu from an all-night Chinese restaurant, which he found beneath their feet.

"Get someone to talk to him," Donovan said.

"We took a cab downtown," Avignon said. "Picked it up right here on West Street, out in front of the *Intrepid*. I dropped Boris off in the East Village . . . he lives on First Street over near the Hell's Angels . . . and continued on across the bridge to Williamsburg. I got home about three."

"Do you get a receipt from the cab driver?" Donovan asked.

"No. Oh, yes, *yes*. I'm very careful about collecting tax receipts these days. But I have it at home."

"Then we can get the cab's medallion number off the receipt and trace the driver," Mosko said.

"You can give us the receipt when we go to your place to make copies of the tapes," Donovan said. "Which, by the way, will be supervised by a police videographer."

"Christ, you're getting touchy in your old age," Avignon said.

Donovan poked the man in the chest, something he personally hated but knew it would put the man back in his place. "Don't start acting like we're friends," Donovan snarled.

"We should just impound this asshole's entire apartment," Mosko said, reinforcing the message.

"And we will if he doesn't cooperate. But you're cooperating, aren't you?"

"Yeah, yeah," Avignon said quickly. "I'll do whatever you want. Fuck the First Amendment."

"Words to my ears under the current circumstances," Donovan said.

The setting was romantic, in that bit-of-this, bit-of-that way the Donovans liked: two candles plunked down into heirloom silver holders and set on the coffee table on either side of the cardboard box in which the captain brought home a salad pizza. Marcy poured Kaliber into a tall glass for him and brewed an herb tea for herself. It had been several hours since the baby fell asleep for the night; Mary the nanny was bustling around a room or two away, making cleaning-up noises. The evening was cool with a river breeze blowing in the windows. Even on the fifteenth floor it was inescapable that they lived on an island. The faint smell of salt water and the now-and-again sound of a tugboat whistle punctuated the night.

Donovan lay back on the old and comfy couch with his feet propped up on the coffee table, fiddling with the fancy new video camera he bought the week before to take pictures of the baby. He stripped the yellow sealing tape off a fresh cassette and slipped the latter into the camera. Then he aimed the camera at the monitor and watched Avignon's tape through his own camera until that made him dizzy. He put down his new toy and rested his head on Marcy's shoulder. She also laid back, but plunked her legs atop his. Clicking the pause button on the remote so that the screen showed a frozen image of the two of them on the catwalk, she said, "I don't see any murderers in Avignon's footage. Just the usual suspects."

"The fashion people," Donovan replied.

"Pretty much all of these people have faces I've seen at one or another of my mother's parties. Or in the tent during Fashion Week. There's a few I don't know . . . new lovers for the old faces, I guess . . . but none of them look dangerous."

Fashion Week was the celebration of the New York fashion industry's showings, many of which took place under huge tents erected in Bryant Park.

"There's also the band, Dennis, and the guy with the beard," Donovan said.

She nodded. "What's his name?"

"Lachaise."

"Named after the cemetery in Paris, no doubt," Marcy said.

"I've never been to Paris and could care less," Donovan replied. "I assumed he was born on a chaise longue and named after it."

"He doesn't sound very dangerous."

"That was a pretty good argument Dennis and him were having," Donovan said.

"I think it's amazing that Avignon is back in your life," Marcy said.

Donovan sucked his breath in preparation for an outburst, but his wife patted him on his free hand and said, "Calm down, honey."

"Don't wanna," Donovan said, imitating a child.

"You got even with him. You ruined him financially, took away everything he owned, and put him in jail for most of a decade."

"Hey, don't make me the heavy in this matter. Avignon was responsible for three deaths."

"You're angry because he betrayed you," Marcy said.

"He was responsible for three deaths."

"*And* because he betrayed you," she maintained.

"Maybe, but to a *very* small extent," Donovan replied.

"You got even," Marcy said. "You don't have to do it again."

"Yes, I do," Donovan said. "Like I told Brian, the man is an apparition, an evil thing, a specter lurking in the weeds. It's in his nature to do evil, and he'll do it again. Besides, how even did I get? *Those three men are dead.* But Avignon is *still alive*. He's back. He's out of jail and trotting around a gigantic professional video camera again . . . *two* of them, both very expensive, plus supporting equipment. He's hiring people to help him. *And* he's working on the same project that brought him to grief in the first place. He's prowling around the city looking for blood. He's looking for . . . what was the phrase he used ten years ago? 'Photogenic catastrophes'?"

"You're right," Marcy replied.

"You add up the *Trinidad Princess, Sevastopol Trader,* Caren Piermatty, and Rob Ingram's bloody corpse and what you got is a photogenic catastrophe," Donovan said.

"I wish your English wouldn't always deteriorate when you get angry," Marcy said.

Donovan smiled at his wife and caressed her cheek. Then he flipped a slice of salad pizza onto his plate and absent-mindedly picked at the lettuce.

"Avignon is up to something," he said after a moment of reflection.

"Meaning that his being on Dennis's boat wasn't a coincidence?" Marcy asked.

"If Michael Avignon just happened to turn up on a boat where a murder was committed, then I really *am* still in the running for director of the FBI," Donovan said.

"He says he left two hours before the murder," Marcy said.

"He did. Mosko was able to locate the cab driver who picked him up. The guy had a vivid recollection of picking up two men carrying professional video cameras."

"Which take up a lot of space."

Donovan nodded. "The passenger's seat and the middle of the back seat," Donovan said. "The cabbie turns out to be a techno-freak . . . American, no less, who actually speaks

English . . . he prodded them for the details of their gear the whole ride."

"If Avignon was hiding something he'd be eager to have an alibi and would have mentioned that," Marcy said.

"Or else the career path he's chosen is finally catching up with him and he's shedding brain cells like dandruff," Donovan said. "Anyway, the kid who shot tape for him confirms his story. The cabbie picked them up in front of the *Intrepid* a little after two. The guy recalls because he just stopped off at the Howard Johnson's on Fifty-seventh and downloaded a bunch of drunks he picked up at a bar on Eighth Avenue that closes at two."

"*Downloaded* a bunch of drunks?" she laughed.

"Yeah, my English is going down the *terlet* again, as Brian's old Brooklyn grandma would say. So the cabbie drops the kid off in the East Village and shoots down to Delancey Street and across the Williamsburg Bridge and takes Avignon home. The bum lives in a two-bedroom apartment on Bedford Avenue not far from the converted girdle factory . . . you know, the place that has a lot of hip shops, Internet cafés, etc.? He lives above the Starbucks."

"They have a *Starbucks* in Williamsburg?"

"They're everywhere. Can you imagine living above a place where they're grinding coffee beans day and night? You'd have to staple your eyelids shut to get some sleep."

Marcy's attention had strayed to the image on the screen. "How do I look in that dress?" she asked.

"Sensational," Donovan replied, reaching over and grabbing the remote from her long enough to click it off.

"Hey! I was watching that!"

"No, you weren't. You were trying to avoid getting sucked into this case."

She gave him a sweet smile, one tinged with a note

of "we had this discussion." Which is exactly what she told him.

"I *want* you involved," he insisted.

"I'm a mommy. I'm getting my law degree."

"You have a nanny and the semester is nearly over," Donovan said.

"I still have course work to do," she replied.

"You passed your finals," he replied.

"It's nine o'clock and I have a busy day tomorrow."

"Doing what?" Donovan asked.

She hesitated for a moment, giving Donovan the answer he needed. Still, she said, "I have to spend an hour in the library and Daniel has the appointment at Columbia Presbyterian."

"When?"

"Three," she replied. "I'll call and tell you what the doctor says. What's on your schedule?"

"Breakfast with Caren. Brunch with Veronica. Afternoon interviews with the Bennetts . . . separately, of course."

"I am getting *very* tolerant of your behavior when I let you go alone to meet Caren Piermatty," Marcy said. "You be sure to keep your hands to yourself."

Donovan frowned, and said, "I'll warn her off in case she gets ideas. The point is we both have time to do some poking around *Sevastopol Trader*. I want to be aboard at the same time the murder took place."

"Searching for a tremor in the Force again?" she asked.

"I want to feel the sights and sounds where it happened at the hour it happened," Donovan said. "There's something strange going on with Dennis."

"He's a strange guy."

"Hopping around from pier to pier like that."

"Well," Marcy said idly, "he spent a couple of years in foster homes when he was a kid."

"What happened?"

"His father ran out on the family. Some sort of emotional problem. And his mother became sick and died."

"That's rough," Donovan said. "In light of all that I guess he's done pretty good for himself. We'll see him in the morning. Hey, you have time to come with me. Let's go to bed now so we'll be fresh. I'll set the alarm for three."

"At three in the morning? We'll be fresh at three in the morning?"

"I'll buy you a Starbucks," Donovan said cheerily.

9. LOOKING FOR THE CANARY IN GEMEINSCHAFT.

The water was high, approaching high tide, and the *Sevastopol Trader* rode high in relation to its dock. The gangplank rose up precipitously, requiring one to hold onto the support chairs with both hands. Donovan stopped at the top and turned to extend a hand to Marcy, who was carrying her Starbucks and had but one hand available.

She stood alongside him on the deck and looked back on the uniformed officer who stood guard over the crime scene and then out across the river, where the lights shined feverishly in Weehawken despite the hour. Nothing ever closes in New York City, and the communities around it feel the need to keep up. While there was no river traffic at that moment, the lights glistened off the small ripply waves made by a light southwest wind and, overhead, a black helicopter of uncertain parentage chopped leisurely north. Most of the exterior lights were off on the *Trinidad Princess*, save for those that illuminated the superstructure—the fake smokestacks, false signal masts, and exaggerated bridge, built to suggest that the ship wasn't entirely computerized and totally reliant on satellite navigation but functioned like an actual seagoing vessel in which a bearded, trustworthy old salt of a captain paced from port to starboard casting the protective cloak of his decades of experience over the passengers relaxing below. Along the starboard side of the vessel, which faced the *Sevastopol Trader*, there were no lights. A gray pallor at the level of the promenade deck degraded into an inky blue-black at the waterline.

"A yacht could sail in there and no one would notice," Donovan said, peering down into the darkness in a vain attempt to see something.

"Last night we could see that little boat, what did you call it, a tender?" Marcy said.

"That was before midnight when the *Trinidad Princess* had most of her lights on and the party was still raging aboard *Sevastopol Trader*," Donovan said.

"How could Ingram find his way here in the dark?" Marcy asked.

"A good question. When we last talked to him, he left the impression that even with a seeing-eye dog he couldn't find Alpo in broad daylight."

"But he did it."

"We know he was a smart little drone," Donovan said. "For one thing, he managed to get the info out of us that a hot time could be had below, then he feigned being too much of a country boy to handle it and announced he would take mom's advice and go to Tavern on the Green."

"But he let slip he was thinking about slipping away from his party and coming to ours," Marcy said.

"That's something he couldn't have done while his party was in progress," Donovan said. "He was Bennett's right-hand man. I suppose he could have left easily enough after Bennett and the rest of the reactionary munchkins went to sleep. Which happened after two."

"That's when Bennett turned in," Marcy said. "Is it true for the rest of his aides? How many of them are there . . . minus Ingram, of course."

"Eight."

"You have some Conservative friends from the old days. They never turn down a party, no matter how wrong the politics may be."

"Yeah, those guys *do* like to belly up to the bar. However, Bennett's aides told Brian this afternoon that they hit the rack about the same time as Bennett. Seems he has a rule about staff funny business. Can't have an aide to the future president turn up drunk in Times Square or trying to put the make on someone who turns out to be a transgender hooker."

"Can they *prove* they didn't leave their cabins?" Marcy asked.

"We're working on that," Donovan replied.

"Okay, so let's say Ingram turned in at two. But at two-thirty or three, when everyone else on the . . . what deck was that they were sleeping on?"

"The Empire deck," Donovan replied.

"When everyone else on the Empire deck is asleep, Ingram slips out of his cabin and sneaks down the hall. Any security guards?"

"Bennett has turned down Secret Service protection thus

far. As for private security, that's one of the things we're trying to find out. At the moment it appears that there was one guard controlling access to the entire ship."

They were distracted then by a sound from below, that of water sloshing around. The sound rose up out of the darkness and got Donovan to point his Maglite at it. He could see nothing.

"What's that? A fish?" Marcy asked.

"Sounds like something being pumped out of the *Trinidad Princess*," Donovan replied.

"The toxic waste that Dennis told you about?"

Donovan tossed up his hands. "It could be bilge water," he said.

"You don't mean that thing *leaks*," Marcy said, looking up askance at the big ship.

"Water shows up in boats without there being obvious leaks. Trust me on this."

"There was only one guard for this whole ship last night?" Marcy asked.

Donovan nodded. "The only passengers were Bennett and company on the Empire deck. Now, there's a whole community of *Trinidad Princess* employees . . . waiters, cooks, boutique-sales persons, assorted 'entertainment specialists' . . ."

"Aerobics instructors," Marcy added.

"Dance teachers, lifeguards, party hostesses, maybe even an occasional sailor . . . upwards of five hundred in total, living more or less permanently on the crew deck, which is supposed to be closed off to passengers."

"But not impossible to get to," Marcy said.

"Not impossible," Donovan replied. "Probably easier for the crew to find passengers than the other way around. Anyway, the way it looks now, and discounting the possibility he leaped to the mast on the *Sevastopol Trader* and shinnied down in his tuxedo, Ingram must have left his cabin, sneaked down the hall, and gone out the one and only entrance somewhere after two but before five."

"Did the guard see him?" Marcy asked.

"He says no."

"What about the bouncer who was taking names on *Sevastopol Trader?*" Marcy asked.

"Went home at two."

"And who was here after two?"

"Caren Piermatty, Veronica Cascini, and a couple of others," Donovan said.

"Did your guys talk to them?" Marcy asked.

Donovan shook his head. "Caren and Veronica will only talk to me. My guys were only able to talk to the 'couple of others,' which includes the head caterer and a bartender. There *is* one more guy I need to track down, a model named Harley."

"From the Cascini Agency? Don't know him."

"How many male models does your mom use?" Donovan asked.

"Lots," Marcy replied. "You just don't look at fashion spreads. A lot of the girl models are posed draped around male models."

"I must change my reading habits," Donovan replied dryly.

"Yeah, get your head out of the *New York Times* for two minutes. There are other things in the world behind news and facts. This Harley could be a guy I saw at the party who looks like Brad Pitt," Marcy said.

"Who's . . . ?"

"You *know* who Brad Pitt is," Marcy snapped.

Donovan shook his head.

"You saw him in *Legends of the Fall*. We watched it to-gether."

"*You* watched it. I was reading," Donovan replied.

Marcy gave her husband a playful slap on the arm. "Did the caterer see Ingram?" she asked.

"He said no. He said no one was on the ship after two but Dennis, Veronica, Caren, and Harley. But I want to talk to this Harley myself," Donovan said.

She perked up, and said, "Oh, can I come along?"

"I thought you weren't interested in helping me," Donovan replied.

"If you can talk to Caren Piermatty, I can talk to Harley Greave," Marcy said. "Now that I think about it, Veronica said a new face named Harley Greave would be at the party."

"Interesting that you remember his last name," Donovan said.

"It suddenly came to me."

Donovan said, "I'm trying to figure out why these three people—Cascini, Piermatty, and Greave—stayed on when everyone else left."

Footfalls came across the foredeck, and Donovan and Marcy turned to catch sight of Yeager coming over, a bottle of champagne in his hand. "For the same reason we used to pull all-nighters here in the old days," the man said. "It's fun."

Yeager had upon him the indomitable look of the master of his own fate. He looked like a man well proud not only of having banned a possible future president of the United States from his ship but also of having properly insulted his minion. Yeager not only glowed, he sparkled in the faint light that fell upon the foredeck from the dock lights.

"Let me guess," Donovan said. "Your principal guests . . . the one who signed the check plus a couple of her closest friends . . . came up on the cabin roof with you and continued the boogie for another few hours."

"Yeah, in the same spot where you guys had a drink with me," Yeager said. "Where we all used to waste Sunday afternoons and the occasional Friday night in the glory days before a Puritan was elected mayor of New York and you developed this midlife obsession with health and knowledge."

"The two aren't related," Donovan said.

"Besides, I can't end a party much before dawn. So doing goes against the pleasures of the harbor, you know? Jeez, this is the *waterfront*, not the priory."

"And so you all sat there, got whacked, and watched the river flow from two to around three," Donovan said.

"You bet. Caren and Veronica came up and they dragged along this dope who looks like Brad Pitt and we sat there for an hour or two and did exactly what you said," Yeager said.

"An hour or *two*?" Donovan said.

"Unh . . . yeah."

"You told me this morning that you turned in at three," Donovan said.

"Upon reflection and after having had a snooze . . ."

"You refined your recollection," Marcy said.

"Exactly. Good to see you two again, by the way." Yeager reached out his left hand and, turned it around backward, and shook hers briefly. Donovan wasn't sure if the unusual handshake was an expression of informality or something more. "Have a taste," Yeager said, waggling the champagne bottle with his free hand.

Both Donovans frowned.

"At five in the morning?" Marcy asked.

"I'm simply clearing out the leftovers," Yeager explained. And to Donovan he said, "I appreciate that you're a better and healthier man as a result of going on the wagon, but I never thought you'd do the Hickey thing on me."

"The Hickey thing?" Marcy asked.

"He's talking about the reformed drunk who spoiled the party in *The Iceman Cometh*," Donovan said.

"Your favorite playwright being O'Neill," Marcy said.

"I sense a synergy between me and him," Donovan replied.

"You used to be more fun," Yeager said.

"Becoming a murder suspect tends to sour the relationship with the investigating officer," Donovan said.

"How did I become a suspect? Oh, by threatening Bennett's life."

"Twice," Marcy said.

"By *repeatedly* threatening Bennett's life, and in front of my boss, the deputy chief inspector," Donovan said.

"Sorry 'bout that," Yeager replied.

"Cool move."

"The man came aboard *my* ship and got heavy with me," Yeager said. "Remember the law of the sea? Remember the part about the captain of the ship having absolute power?"

"While at sea, and maybe during the Napoleonic Wars," Donovan said. "In New York harbor and in the twenty-first century, forget about it." He pronounced that *fahgeddabowdid*, as everyone expects New Yorkers to do.

"I still have my rights," Yeager insisted, a bit peevishly. He took a nip of champagne.

"So now I'm hearing that you really went to bed at four," Donovan said.

"Maybe fifteen or twenty minutes before then. I went to the wheelhouse and switched off the light. I never leave it on after I go to bed. I farted around in my cabin for a while."

"What did you do?"

"Oh, I don't know. Put away some magazines I had left on the floor. Hung up my clothes that were on the floor. And I lay in bed for a while being pissed off about the *Trinidad Princess*. It wasn't until after four that I fell asleep. You see, I don't wear a watch."

"What about when you have paying guests arriving at a particular hour?" Donovan asked.

"I check when they arrive. I don't care when they leave."

"How did you know it was four?" Marcy asked.

"Shift change on the behemoth," Yeager replied.

"Shift change?" Donovan asked.

"Yeah, a third of their worker ants get off at four. Now, with the behemoth being mostly shut down last night so the oppressors of the masses could assemble for their private party . . ."

Donovan smiled.

"There weren't that many worker ants going off duty," Marcy said.

"But there must have been a few dozen . . . bartenders, waiters, casino workers, kitchen help . . ." Donovan said.

"Many of them stay on board and go back to their cabins after shift change," Yeager said. "But many of 'em leave, you know, to do the town."

"Some of 'em wearing the same tuxedos they wore while working the private party," Donovan said.

"Explaining how Ingram got off the ship," Marcy added.

"Exactly," Donovan replied. "He went to his cabin at three . . . cooled his heels until four, maybe taking a nap . . .

then sneaked down the hall and slipped out with the shift workers."

"What would make him think the party was still going on at that hour?" Marcy asked.

"They were sitting on the cabin roof," Donovan said.

Yeager nodded.

"The sight of Caren Piermatty sitting out in the open in *that* dress at four in the morning . . ."

". . . would have been enough to get Ingram out the door and down to the freighter," Marcy added.

"Now, I just need to know if *she* noticed *him*," Donovan said.

"He wasn't particularly good looking," Marcy said.

"No, but he was powerful, and that can go a long way. A model with any brains knows that it will last five, maybe ten years. But an attorney general of the United States is going to be around for a while. This ain't no flash-in-the-pan sort of career. Even if your political career crashes and burns, you still can run off and become CEO someplace. So if you're young and beautiful, a guy who is a catch the size of Ingram can be pretty attractive."

Yeager said, "I'm only a bystander here, but do you think that Ingram and Caren would have anything to say to one another politically?"

"The activity we're discussing doesn't take place at the cerebral level," Donovan said. "But you bring something up—I need to know more about Rob Ingram and his habits. And I know who to ask."

"George McCann," Marcy said.

"Who's that?" Yeager asked. "The name is familiar."

"Democratic strategist," Donovan said. "We used to play stickball together when I was a kid."

"Is this the guy who was an adviser to Clinton?"

"Yeah. An old-line West Side Democrat. Used to run with the Westies before he got his calling."

"I'm not a native New Yorker," Yeager said, "So . . ."

"The Westies were Irish thugs from the fifties and sixties. Had the local mafia afraid of 'em for a while. Crazy fuckers, and ruthless. No particular code of honor, like the movies would have us believe the mafia has. You know that sometimes I joke about how the Irish punks in *West Side Story* were patterned after friends of mine."

"He tells that story over and over," Marcy said.

Yeager nodded.

"Well, there you have it," Donovan said. "George also hung out with them, at least until he got into college and politics. Now he's a top strategist for progressive politicians . . . kind of Rob Ingram in reverse, or *was* until that little problem came up with the Hooters waitress who had a mafia brother."

"So the Westies *did* finally hook up with the Mafia," Yeager said.

"In a manner of speaking," Donovan replied. "Anyway, the West Side waterfront and blocks north was Westies turf. George has an office in New York these days, now that Clinton is out of office. So I think I'll give him a call. If there's dirt to be dug on Ingram, George will have a truckful."

"You always knew the best people, honey," Marcy said.

Yeager smiled and said, "Come on . . . come on up on the roof and have a drink."

Donovan shook his head. Checking his watch, he said, "It's nearly five . . . about the time Ingram was killed . . . I want to go below where it happened."

"Like I told you," Yeager said, "It's dark down there."

"That's what I want to see."

With Donovan in the lead this time, they walked aft along the port rail, following the spot of light from the Maglite. While the hour of five was approaching, there was the barest hint in the dark gray sky that day was imminent. Normally in New York City, there is so much ambient light that few corners get truly black as night. But on the side of an unlit freighter sheltered against a giant cruise liner, Yeager and the two detectives might as well have been on the dark side of the moon. Yet Donovan found the port gangway without much trouble and led the way down. Halfway down the iron stairs and keeping a hand on her husband's shoulder for guidance, Marcy said "This is like entering the Tomb of Eternal Desperation. How come the port gangway is so dark and the starboard one so bright?"

"Guests come down the starboard gangway, which faces the dock," Yeager answered. "That's why I have it decorated with antiques."

"Your secondhand-store junk," Donovan said.

"One man's junk is another man's gallery exhibit," Yeager replied. "Did I mention that my collection is featured on the American Association of Found Art website?"

"It must have slipped your mind," Donovan said.

They went down two more steps, at which point the faint ambient light from the New York City skyline followed them no longer. They were in a realm beyond subterranean—inside an old iron cook-pot that had been "seasoned" . . . allowed to become lined with years of charcoal crust.

Donovan said, "I've been in lots of boats over the years and found most of 'em roughly symmetrical. The port side more or less matched the starboard. So give me the *real* reason that the starboard gangway is your thrift-shop version of a grand staircase and its counterpart on the port side is a coal mine. He tapped one hand along a wall to make a searching sort of sound, and said, "I'm looking for the canary in your gemeinschaft."

"I keep it dark so nobody can see in," Yeager sighed.

"Nobody who?" Marcy asked.

"Sforza," Yeager admitted. "Can we go all the way below? You're making me nervous cramming me up in the gangway here."

"Who or what is Sforza?" Donovan asked.

"Cal Sforza," Yeager replied, pausing to spell the name. "Chief engineer on the *Trinidad Princess*. The Darth Vader of the harbor."

"I'm not following something," Marcy said.

"I think Dennis is saying that the straw boss next door has taken umbrage to his spying," Donovan said.

"Exactly. Can we go below?"

Donovan let go of the wall and led the way down to the dance floor, saying, "Let me get this straight. You're spying on the *Trinidad Princess* in an attempt to catch her dumping toxic waste. But the *Trinidad Princess* is spying back. This Sforza . . . he's dangerous?"

"He's the size of an ox and nearly as intelligent," Yeager replied. "He knows that Lachaise and I are onto him, and he's threatened to kill us."

"When did this happen?" Marcy asked.

"The day before yesterday," Yeager replied.

"How? In person? On the phone?" she asked.

"He yelled at me. He came out on my dock and yelled at me. It was right around dawn, right after Lachaise and I had taken water samples. They ran their pump and discharged *something* into the water . . . toxins, I'm sure . . ."

"We heard a pump running before you came down to talk to us," Donovan said.

"That's the one. It goes on about this time, but only

when the tide is going out, as it is now. If the pumping was innocent . . . you know, discharging condensation from the engine room . . . there would be no reason to wait for ebb tide."

"So the night before the party—actually, the *morning* before the party—you and your bearded chum sampled the water and Darth Vader caught you," Donovan said. "He stormed out of his ship and around and onto your dock, and he shook his fist at you and threatened to kill you. Was it something like that?"

"It was exactly like that," Yeager replied. "He said that he was watching to see if we took any more water samples, and if we did he would kill us."

"Did he come on board?" Marcy asked.

Yeager shook his head. But they couldn't see him in the dark, and he said, "He was going to, but I didn't let him."

"How'd you keep him off?" she asked. "A man like that probably wouldn't observe the proprieties."

"I threatened him back," Yeager replied.

"With what?" she asked. "You're not exactly the toughest guy in the world."

Donovan said, "You threatened him with the whaling knife, didn't you?"

"How'd you know?" Yeager asked, apparently astonished.

"Oh, it just *had* to be, didn't it?"

"Yes," Marcy said.

"Besides, it's the only weapon on this ship, right?" Donovan said.

"Yeah, didn't I tell you that?"

"You told me," Donovan said.

"So Sforza saw the knife," Marcy said.

"That's a pretty formidable weapon," Donovan said. "Is there any chance he saw where you hid it?"

"No," Yeager replied.

"Did he come aboard at any point?"

Again Yeager replied in the negative.

"But you don't know for sure," Marcy said.

"You went to bed at four last night," Donovan reminded the man. "Sforza could have come aboard after that and you wouldn't have known."

"True," Yeager admitted.

"Unless Caren, Veronica, and Harley saw him while they were finishing the party up on the roof," Marcy said.

"*If* they were even still here, *if* they were paying the slightest attention to anyone other than themselves, and *if* Sforza even came aboard," Donovan said.

"Do you really think that he would come aboard to kill me," Yeager asked.

"No. A lot of guys threaten to kill a lot of other guys without actually doing it. There's a face-off of some kind, an exchange of promises of dire consequences, and then everyone goes back to their day jobs. What Sforza may have done is sneak aboard looking for the place where you hid the evidence."

"Where is that?" Marcy asked.

"In a storage room behind the old engine room," Yeager replied.

"Let's see," Donovan said.

They got to the bottom of the gangway to find the theater space softly illuminated—as if by a night light—well enough to get a general orientation. The dance floor was a slate-black sheet of iron beneath their feet; the catwalk soared overhead, appearing farther off in the faint light, which came from behind the stage.

"Refresh my memory," Donovan said. "That light is a . . . ?"

"Forty-watt bulb hung from the ceiling," Yeager replied.

"Wasn't it turned on the night of the party?" Donovan said.

Yeager nodded. "It's on a timer. Goes on every night at about sundown and snaps off at six in the morning. It's there in case I need to go below in the middle of the night to fix something. It also helps when Peter and I go below to get the sampling gear."

"So it would have been on at the time of the murder," Marcy said.

Again Yeager nodded.

Marcy walked to the center of the dance floor, turned to face the other two, and asked, "Can you tell it's me?"

"Always," Donovan said. "You light up the void."

"Come on, really? Can you see me well enough to tell it's me?"

"Yes," Yeager said.

He was fifteen feet away.

"You're standing on the body," Donovan said.

"Oh," Marcy replied, then jumped, a little girlishly, to one side. She looked down as Donovan shined his light at her feet to reveal the taped outline of Ingram's body.

"I'm keeping that," Yeager said.

"The chalk outline," Marcy said.

"The taped outline. I'm keeping it. I'm going to put a couple of layers of polyurethane on it. My guests will *love* to dance on the spot where Rob Ingram died."

Donovan frowned, and said, "This is another tidbit you no doubt will go out of your way to pass on to the press and Pilcrow."

"You bet! What publicity!"

"I can see that it's you," Donovan replied, flicking off

his light and adding, "Even in the light from behind the stage. This was no mistaken-identity murder. Ingram was the target, all right. The question is, who killed him and why?"

"Why not?" Yeager said.

"Stop that," Donovan snapped. He walked over to his wife, put his arms around her, and kissed her.

"Now, now," Yeager admonished.

"You're especially cute standing over the outline of the corpse," Donovan told Marcy.

"Soon to be covered with polyurethane," Yeager said.

"And added to the collection along with the Pixieware and the tin percolator," Donovan said.

Marcy nuzzled Donovan's chest with her cheek. "You feel good," she said.

Donovan said, "Okay, I'm Ingram and you're Caren. We just kissed. I have your lipstick and perfume all over me."

"Do we know that was Caren's cosmetics on Ingram?" Marcy asked.

"No, but I think it's likely. At any rate, Ingram kissed *someone* before he died, and somehow I don't think that Veronica is the one. She seemed a little cold to me."

"She's reserved," Marcy said. "Couldn't Ingram have kissed someone at his *own* party?"

"And come away smelling of Cascini, the perfume?"

"Didn't you just say we don't know what he smelled of?"

Donovan used the Maglite to check his watch, then said, "I expect to know by breakfast." Then he looked around, at the light coming from behind the stage, at the dark walls of the cavernous belly of the ship, and at the soaring catwalk.

"There's something world-class wrong here," he said.

"Honey?" Marcy said.

"This murder is a lot more complicated than it seems. I need to talk to Caren, Veronica, and the male model . . . what's his name again?"

"Harley," she replied.

"Yeah. Does anybody know anything about this guy? Has your mom used him in her magazine?"

Marcy replied, "I don't think so. I never heard of him before."

"There's something wrong about naming a male model after a motorcycle. Anyway, we'll do those interviews later today. But my gut feeling is that there was someone else aboard this ship at the time of the murder."

A bit nervously, Yeager asked, "Do you think it was Sforza?"

Donovan tossed up his hands. "I don't know. It could have been Lachaise."

"He left," Yeager insisted.

"You don't know he didn't come back, having decided to do the testing himself after the guests left and you passed out. That would have put him down here at about the time Ingram was clutching with whoever."

"Whomever," Marcy said.

"We'll find out once we find him. If he came back like I said, he would have gone to the back room looking for the testing gear."

"This is true," Yeager said.

"And Sforza could have come after him," Donovan added.

Marcy said, "I see what you mean about this case being more complicated."

Donovan said, "Which brings me to the next suspect— Michael Avignon."

Yeager looked at the captain. "The video guy?" Yeager asked.

Donovan nodded.

"I thought you established that he went home," Yeager said.

"Michael Avignon is a truly evil man," Donovan said. "He can't help himself. It's in his bone marrow. One day he'll move next to you and your lawn will die. I don't put anything past him."

"Did you know him before last night?" Marcy asked Yeager.

"Sort of. He was here twice before, doing videos. And . . . well, I guess this is pertinent, now that I think of it . . . ."

"Here it comes," Donovan muttered.

"He expressed an interest in the work Lachaise and I are doing," Yeager said.

"I'll bet he did. That's right up his alley—supermodels and toxic waste in the same shot. The mere notion has Avignon stamped all over it."

"He said he wanted to shoot us one night while we collected samples of toxic waste discharge from the *Trinidad Princess*," Yeager said.

"Last night?" Marcy asked.

Yeager shook his head. "We never set a date. And like I told you, I made Lachaise leave; we didn't take samples."

Donovan stuck his hands in his pockets and walked away from the others, toward the stage. Then he said, his back still to them, "I want to see the back room."

"It's not exactly ready to receive company," Yeager said.

"I just need to see the place you keep your sampling stuff."

"Your men looked at every inch of this ship."

"Sometimes I see things they don't," Donovan replied.

Donovan and Marcy followed as Yeager led them back across the floor to the bottom of the port gangway. An equally dark passage led a short distance aft to emerge behind the stage, where an open door let out the light from the forty-watt bulb, which seemed to burn more brightly up close.

Nonetheless, as Donovan took the lead, stepping toward the open door his knee banged into something metallic, which then went over in a clatter of metal on metal. "Dammit," Donovan said, rubbing his knee and looking down at the old barbershop ashtray stand he had knocked over. It was bronzed metal and about three feet tall, ornately cast with a fake lion's paw holding the bronzed ashtray.

"My old man's barber used to have one of these by each chair," Donovan said, bending to pick the skinny antique back up.

Peering inside the utility room, Donovan saw a grapevine of extension cords—some with price tags still dangling—cascading from two mostly unwrapped power conduits. The small and yellowing bulb was like something seen in a old gangster movie, suspended alongside flypaper in a tiny room, the papered walls of which were aging yellow-brown like badly kept parchment. It swung perceptibly with the shifting of the ship on the tide, imparting to its long and knifelike shadows a slight insecurity that could leave one faintly dizzy. Black electrical tape, applied liberally, like frosting to a child's homemade cupcake, held the bulb in place.

Yeager's scientific gear occupied a gray metal utility shelf—the sort sold at Sears for $10.98, build-it-yourself—shoved against one bulkhead. There were beakers, boxes of chemicals, labeled test tubes held upright in racks, and an electronic gizmo the size of a videocassette player. On the top shelf was miscellaneous stuff—a large screwdriver, a box of Mallomars, and a liter of springwater.

The electronic gizmo was plugged into one of the cascading extension cords.

"You remember you said you worried about the whole place going blammo?" Donovan asked.

Yeager said that he did.

"Worry about it," the captain said.

Yeager frowned and pointed at the gear. He said, "That's my testing stuff and samples. Nothing is missing. I checked an hour ago. I was thinking of getting some samples tonight. I figured if Sforza saw me and came over again you could shoot him."

"Always glad to be of service," Donovan replied.

"If Lachaise was so hot to take water samples during the party, how come he didn't show up tonight with the same expectation?" Marcy asked.

"An excellent question," Donovan said.

"I'll bet he was afraid," Yeager said.

"Of Sforza?" Donovan asked.

"Nah. He said he could handle him. I'll bet Lachaise was afraid of getting mixed up in a murder investigation."

"Imagine that," Donovan said.

Still standing in the doorway and preventing the others from entering, he scanned the rest of the room. Opposing the science stuff was a small refrigerator—the sort found in studio apartments as a space-saving measure or in finished basements to hold the beer—as well as a card table and a metal folding chair. A cheap lamp, also connected to the extension cords, sat atop it alongside a 1960s-vintage transistor radio and a copy of the *Daily News* the front page headline of which read:

TOP POL KILLED
AFTER POSH PARTY

"There's something familiar and comforting about *Daily News* headlines," Donovan said. "I can remember going back to when I was a kid, politicians were always 'pols,' parties were always 'posh,' champagne was always 'the bubbly,' and women involved in crimes were preferably 'bottle blondes' or 'leggy brunettes.' "

"Were we mentioned as having been at the posh party?" Marcy asked.

"I was," Yeager said proudly.

"Not you and me, not yet, at least," Donovan said, rolling his eyes and crossing himself.

"You've started doing that again," Marcy said. "Stop it."

Also on the table was a coffee mug, a small blue china plate adorned with white seagulls and an anchor, as well as several kernels of brown rice, and the crumpled-up wrapper from a Hostess Coffee Cake. Donovan pressed a fingertip against the kernels, squashing them.

Donovan said, "You don't smoke, do you?"

"Me? Never," Yeager replied.

"But this isn't a smoke-free freighter."

"I only allow smoking topside and in the guest areas, and then only when there's a party. Why do you ask?"

"This room smells of smoke," Donovan said. "You don't smoke. Neither does Avignon."

"I would never allow someone to smoke in this room. I have testing gear in here. And can you imagine smoking in the same room where you test for toxic chemicals?"

"I once went into a surgical supply store on Broadway . . . you know, to buy an Ace bandage one time when I cracked a rib . . . and the owner was smoking *and* drinking," Donovan said.

"Unbelievable," Yeager replied.

Marcy stuck her head around her husband, sniffed the air, and said that she agreed. "Someone has smoked in here. Or someone who smokes a lot has been in here."

"Out of the question," Yeager said.

"Does Lachaise smoke?" Donovan asked.

"An environmental activist? You got to be kidding."

"Sforza, I wonder?"

"How would I . . . no, wait . . . he was smoking when he came over here to threaten me," Yeager said.

"Over the past two days, who has been in this room other than you?"

"Just Peter. I don't let anyone else in here."

"When was Peter in here last?" Donovan asked.

"The day before the party," Yeager said, looking at what Donovan had been looking at. "He always brings his stinking Chinese food with him. I hate it."

Donovan nodded and knelt in the doorway and scrutinized the floor, which like the dance floor the night before was littered with paper. But this trash seemed more of the chronic variety—Post-it Notes, graphs, notes on yellow legal paper and, swept by passing feet under the card table, the brightly colored menu from a take out Chinese restaurant. The menu had closeup photographs of the house specials,

General Tso's Chicken, Happy Family, orange beef, sesame chicken, Moo Goo Gai Pan . . . the usual suspects. Donovan picked around the miscellaneous trash found nearest the door. He paused to ponder the folded cardboard, decorated with an advertisement for a divorce attorney, that once was a pack of matches. He looked at the writing on several of the crunched-up papers, recognizing the scrawl as Yeager's. Several sheets noted the flow of the tide . . . mean high water at Sandy Hook, the Battery, and the George Washington Bridge.

"Those are my tide and collection logs," Yeager said.

"You don't need to keep them?" Donovan asked.

"Not after Peter has input the data onto his laptop."

"He brings it here with him?"

"Not all the time," Yeager replied. "Not the night of the murder, if that's what's on your mind."

Donovan said that it wasn't. He turned over a few more slips of paper: a store receipt of indeterminate origin, a losing ticket issued at an Off-Track Betting parlor on Tenth Avenue, and a Milky Way wrapper.

"I guess the cleaning lady took the week off," Donovan said.

"I guess she did. I usually clean up every couple of weeks. The time is coming."

"What's in the fridge?" Donovan asked, standing and walking over to open the small door and peer inside.

"Chemicals," Yeager replied. "Reagents."

Donovan noted assorted bottles and boxes, all of a scientific nature, and a bottle of Sprite and a container of Chinese food.

"What exactly is the toxic waste you think that Sforza is dumping into the harbor?" Donovan asked.

"Perchloroethylene, also known as 'perc,'" Yeager replied. "Do you know what that is?"

"No."

"It's dry-cleaning fluid," Yeager said. "Very toxic. Causes effects ranging from dizziness and confusion to liver and kidney damage and cancer. Is there anything else I can show you?"

"Where did you stash the knife after you brought it in here?" Donovan asked.

Yeager pointed to a spot atop the utility shelf, where it neared the ceiling.

The box of Mallomars that Donovan saw there was gone. "Was anything else there?" he asked.

"Nope. Anything else you want to see?"

"Yeah. Show me how the sampling works."

"The technique is low-tech," Yeager said, reaching to the top storage shelf and picking up a length of quarter-inch nylon line that had a small, tubular, stainless steel bucket on one end. The line was coiled neatly, as a professional sailor would.

"This is all it takes?"

"For a basic, no-frills sample, yeah. We're not doing research that will ever be published in scientific journals. We just need enough evidence to take to the Environmental Protection Agency and ask them to do a criminal investigation."

"That's all you will do . . . ?"

"Actually, Peter will do it."

". . . ask the EPA to investigate?" Donovan asked.

"And the press release, of course," Yeager added.

"Of course," Donovan said.

"Lachaise will put out a press release announcing that

the *Trinidad Princess* and its parent company are polluting New York Harbor?" Marcy asked.

Yeager nodded, then added, "And they're polluting the Atlantic, the Caribbean, and dozens of ports of call in each."

"And there will be a public outcry, this being an election year," Donovan said, "and considering that the owners of the *Trinidad Princess* are close friends and, almost certainly, financial backers of Pete Bennett, his opponents . . ."

"Will have a field day?" Yeager replied.

"I'm still waiting for someone to tell me just what a 'field day' is," Donovan added.

"Millions of dollars are at stake here," Marcy said.

"If not the fate of empires," Donovan added. "Remember how Michael Dukakis got hammered for the pollution of Boston Harbor in 1988?"

Marcy touched her husband on the cheek, and said, "You're right, honey . . . this murder is a lot more complicated than it seemed at first."

"Am I off the hook yet?" Yeager asked.

"No," Donovan and Marcy said, together.

"I need to check out this Sforza guy," Donovan said, leading the way out of the room and back toward the port gangway. The light faded back to a glow and stopped almost entirely at the foot of the stairs, as they knew it would.

Yeager asked, "Are you done down here?"

Donovan answered in the affirmative. But when Yeager started up the gangway with Marcy following, Donovan suddenly said, "I left my flashlight in that back room. You guys go on up on deck and I'll catch up with you."

"Sure, honey," Marcy replied, a familiar, heard–it–before lilt in her voice.

As the sound of voices chatting amiably receded, Donovan went back to the storage room and reopened the fridge.

He pulled out the box of Chinese food and peered inside. He stuck a finger deep into the lump of noodles. He returned the box to the refrigerator and closed the door, then bent over beside the card table and plucked the Chinese menu from beneath.

The menu was of the sort that also served as an order form. On it the cashier had checked off Chicken Chow Fun and fried rice. Donovan put the menu in an evidence book, and looked around for the trash.

He found a five-gallon tin that once held fancy popcorn—three flavors, caramel, cheddar, and regular—but now was the garbage can. In it Donovan discovered the empty fried rice container, a plastic fork and spoon, some used packets of soy sauce, the white paper bag that the feast came in, and a thin strip of thin, yellow plastic. Donovan carefully folded the container flat and slipped it into the evidence bag along with the plastic spoon, two of the used soy sauce packets, and the plastic strip. Then he swept the used-up matchbox from the floor and added it to his booty.

Donovan then looked at the copy of the *Daily News*. Beneath the massive headline proclaiming the posh-party demise of Rob Ingram were smaller letters informing the would-be reader that the complete story would be found on pages four and five. Donovan opened the paper to those pages. Splashed over the photo of *Sevastopol Trader*—a different angle from that on page one—was a trace of soy sauce. *Hard to tear open those packets without getting it all over*, he thought. *Or without leaving fat thumbprints.*

The evidence bag fit easily into the loose-fitting khakis he made a point of wearing on jaunts when he might expect to covertly collect evidence. Then he plucked his Maglite from the spot atop the fridge where he left it earlier, and hurried to rejoin the others.

He found them back at the port rail, peering over it.

"The pump stopped," Marcy said.

"The behemoth has finished pissing in the Harbor for the time being," Yeager added.

"This is the spot they sample from," Marcy said.

"And so far you've found . . . ?"

"Direct and incontrovertible evidence that they're discharging perc," Yeager said proudly. "All we need is two or three more samples to show that the pollution went on for an entire week."

"Not inconsequently, the same week that Bennett and company were staying aboard the *Trinidad Princess*," Donovan said.

"A bonus," Yeager admitted, with a smile.

"This is all very compelling and maybe a motive for murder, but it's not the real reason you're moored here, is it?" Donovan said.

Yeager gave Donovan a quizzical look, then said, "This dock space was a godsend. But I'm not staying here forever. It's too military."

He hooked his thumb over his shoulder at the *Intrepid*.

A puttering in the river betrayed the arrival of another boat, an older one, one that was lazing along. The putt-putting rang a bell in Donovan's head. There was a time, long before, when he traced a killer to his watery lair by riding a creaky old barge that, by logic, wasn't seaworthy enough to traverse a wading pond. The advantage that that boat, named the *Harbor Queen*, had to Donovan on that occasion was its invisibility. It chugged along the waterfront—quite literally all of the waterfront, not just the twenty-one miles of it that surrounded Manhattan Island—stopping at designated and unvarying spots to sample the water. Her journey went on for decades and decades . . . Donovan recalled having seen an envelope bearing a three-cent stamp stuck in a crevice in the cabin . . . to complete the city's official water-quality record. Hers was the real water sampling, unlike the amateur efforts of Yeager and Lachaise. If at times she looked, and certainly sounded, more like the *African Queen* than a modern research vessel, her work offered a detailed accounting of the steady progress made by city officials in improving the waterways that surrounded and suffused the Big Apple. Having been aboard the *Harbor Queen* for a day as she made her invisible journey was one of Donovan's abiding memories of life on the waterfront.

"Do you know what that is?" Donovan asked, excited.

"No," Yeager replied.

"The *Harbor Queen!*"

"Who?"

"Come *on*. You got to know about this boat." With that, Donovan took off on a run across the foredeck of the *Sevastopol Trader* to the starboard rail. From there he got a better look at the old survey boat as it puttered along with the current and tide, bypassing the stern of the *Intrepid*.

"Duke!" Donovan yelled, as loudly as he could, even though he knew there was no chance of being heard.

When the others caught up with Donovan, Yeager said, "What's the *Harbor Queen?*"

"Oh, never mind," Donovan said. "It's just an old barge I once hitched a ride on. Not to worry about it."

Marcy smiled, turning away as she did so, so that Yeager couldn't see her.

The *Harbor Queen* slipped from sight, lost past the *Intrepid* and the wake of a Weehawken commuter ferry bringing into the city the dawn's first flock of commuters. Seagulls, stirring, rose from their perches on pilings to begin the long day's quest for killies, shiners, and random bits of garbage.

Early-bird tourists filled the deck of a Circle Line boat about to take off for its peculiar circumnavigation of Manhattan, peculiar because the weight of the passengers lined up along the port rail made the small, slender boats tilt permanently to the left. A shorebound onlooker was likely to see one pass by every half hour or so, looking intoxicated. And up on the waterfront, the first of the day's morning traffic crunches was taking shape. The two legal lanes and one illegal lane of traffic making simultaneous left-hand turns from southbound West Street onto West Forty-second Street to traverse theatre row and enter midtown were blocking the other two downtown lanes. The result was the familiar horn-blaring, finger-raising fuss just off the starboard bow of the *Intrepid*.

"I'm hungry," Marcy said, taking her husband by the arm and tugging him in the direction of the dock.

"Yeah, I guess you guys got a full day ahead of you," Yeager replied.

Donovan said, "Marcy has to go to the library and then take Daniel to a doctor's appointment. I'm going out to breakfast."

"With Caren Piermatty," Marcy said pointedly.

"Where?" Yeager asked.

"The Bridge Café," Donovan replied.

"Talk about posh!" Yeager said. "They have a breakfast menu?"

"They do for me," Donovan replied.

11. THREE COWS, A GOAT, AND A CORNER OF THE TURNIP PATCH.

The sun was about a quarter of the way up from the eastern horizon. The shadow of the Brooklyn Bridge's eastern tower quivered in the rushing tide, but reaching only half the way across the East River from the Brooklyn shoreline to the Manhattan skyline. Yet the crosshatched spiderweb of the bridge's cables shined brightly steel blue and new-machine gray in the daylight pouring off Long Island and onto Manhattan. These visual delights made the little plaza just north of the Brooklyn end of the bridge the proud owner of the best view of the New York financial district skyline.

The sight of that skyline as framed in the soaring arch of the spiderwebbed bridge was precious—and none the more so than to advertising and fashion photographers. That morning's photo shoot was set like a miniature movie set. It included a cream-colored Winnebago to serve as office and dressing room, a buffet table set up with fruits, cheeses, and multigrain crackers and breads as well as decaf and caf coffee urns. Half a dozen people moved lights and light-reflecting umbrellas around a winsome blonde who stood out in the plaza beneath the bridge wearing a Wonderbra and panties. Off on mooring posts a distance away, three young seagulls and a grizzled old homeless man watched hungrily—the food or the woman, Donovan couldn't be sure.

He parked his Taurus by the side of the road, just behind a red Ferrari, and stepped over the knee-high barricade that kept the plaza from becoming an impromptu parking lot.

Donovan showed his gold captain's badge to the photographer's assistant who intercepted him, saying "Bill Donovan, New York Police . . . Ms. Piermatty is expecting me."

The door of the Winnebago opened and she stepped out, barefoot, wrapped in an eggshell-blue terrycloth bathrobe. She said, "Hi!" in a voice loud enough to get the others in her party to look around, but only for a second, before resuming the shoot.

Donovan walked into her widespread arms and hugged her. He exchanged kisses . . . on the cheek, this time . . . and told her he was glad to see her.

She responded, "Yes, me, too. Glad to see you. Marcy let you come into my clutches alone. Either she really trusts you or she's a very silly girl. Horrible, horrible, what happened."

Donovan saw that she had been crying. The whites of her eyes were pink and veined. He touched her cheek below her left eye. She smiled bravely and said, "They digitize the red out. Hard to turn down work. You know, ten thousand a day. Besides, no one who buys the catalog will be looking at my eyes."

She gave another smile and made a gesture as if to flash her robe open and shut. Then she added, "That's right, bare as a button under here. They want me to put on a pegnoir and I'm resisting."

"Isn't a pegnoir a kind of duck?" Donovan asked.

"It might as well be. What girl wants to wear a *pegnoir*? So what if this one is transparent? A girl is better off butt naked."

Donovan agreed, but added, "It's easier for a girl to go without fancy duds when she looks like you. Which brings us to the subject of Rob Ingram, who appears to have been hot on your trail just before he died."

She looked down at the pavement, bobbed her head up and down, and said, "I'm so sorry about him. I truly am."

"Let's have coffee and talk," Donovan said.

"Okay. But do you mind if we do it here? It doesn't bother me to walk over to the Café in my robe, but the guys need me here."

Donovan said that it would be no problem. The two of them got cups of coffee and plates of fruit, cheese, and multigrain crackers, and walked away from the others to a spot where folding chairs were set up right on the river. They sat with their feet up on the barricade that separated the plaza from the shorefront pilings and held their plates in their laps. She munched grapes while he phoned the Bridge Café to cancel his reservation.

When he put the phone back in his pocket, she said, "It amazes me that the Bridge Café will make breakfast for you. I know for a fact that they don't open until noon."

"The owner owes me," Donovan replied.

"Did you save his life?"

"I saved his business. To these guys it's the same thing. There was a murder there fifteen or so years ago. I caught the killer."

"Did you put him in jail?" Caren asked.

"She's dead," Donovan replied. "We put her in the *ground*."

"*She*? A lady killer?"

"It's been known to happen. Twice in my experience, so far."

Piermatty seemed genuinely amazed. She said, "What happened? Did you shoot her? Take out your pistol and *shoot* her?"

Donovan shook his head. "Actually, *she* took out her

pistol and tried to shoot *me*. Marcy blew her in half with a shotgun. A pump-action Remington, if my memory serves me well."

Caren seemed momentarily stunned. She stared across the river at Pier 17, the main restaurant at the South Street Seaport complex, then said, "Marcy shot someone? That sweet, gorgeous wife of yours *killed* someone."

"There also were two others," Donovan added.

"I knew she used to be a police officer, but . . ."

"She still is," Donovan replied. "The department has a quasi-official reserve program. Damn good idea, too, in my opinion. You give up active duty . . . say to become a mommy . . . but retain certain powers and privileges. Not too many people know about this."

"Marcy has killed people," Caren said.

"With a shotgun," Donovan said.

Caren laughed suddenly, then clapped her hands and said, "Well, sugar, I sure won't be messin' with *your* wife any time soon. Or with you, for that matter."

"Let's talk about Rob Ingram," Donovan said.

"Veronica and I were partying on the cabin roof with Harley Greaves and . . . what's the name of the guy that owns the boat?"

"Dennis Yeager."

"Yeah, with him. It must have been four in the morning. No, Dennis left about an hour before and crashed. Then Rob shows up . . . just pokes his head above the ladder . . . you know, climbed up without us seeing him and says, 'Hi. I'm the next attorney general of the United States.' "

"Modesty is so becoming in a politician," Donovan said.

"Ain't it just?"

"Had you known him before?"

"Me, know politicians? Not likely. Their photo gets taken with me and their wives, backers . . ."

"Constituents," Donovan added.

"Them, too, freak out. But you know, I had *seen* the man before, on *Larry King Live*, so when he said, 'Can I join the party?' I thought, why not? Besides, he was kind of cute."

"In a predatory sort of way," Donovan said, watching her eyes carefully to gauge the reaction.

After a pause, Caren said, "He joined us for a drink. Then he wanted to dance . . . and so did I to be honest with you."

"You like to dance," Donovan said.

"I was a little starved for a good dance with a man, especially after *you* turned me down."

"Go ahead, make all of this my fault," Donovan said.

"I knew that there was this giant boom box down there, so I took him downstairs."

"Which way did you take when you went down there?" Donovan asked.

"What do you mean, which way?" she asked.

"What gangway . . . stairway . . . right or left?"

"Why, the one on the right . . . closest to the dock . . . the one we used all the night of the party," Caren replied. "Is there another one?"

"Yeah. To the port. Left."

She shrugged. "I went down the one I said. So we got there and couldn't find the boom box. There was only a little light, coming from backstage."

"But you found each other," Donovan said.

"He *was* cute," Caren insisted.

"You stood in the middle of the dance floor and began to get it on," Donovan said.

"How'd you know that?"

"Your lipstick and perfume were all over him," Donovan replied. "I just got the lab report a little while ago."

She stared at him, clearly thinking, then said, "Okay, the perfume was all over the place . . . Cascini, you know, why we were at the party . . . but how'd you know it was my lipstick?"

Donovan touched a fingertip to his lips. "You also kissed me," he said. "I wiped my lips on my cuff."

"Boy, I have to be *real* careful around you guys, don't I?" she said.

"All you really have to do is tell me the truth."

"The man was sexy, what can I say? He was sexy and *straight*. Let's face it, finding a hetero man in the modeling industry is like finding one among figure skaters. Most of the gorgeous guys I work with are gay."

"Why didn't you finish what you started with him?" Donovan asked.

"What makes you think we didn't?" she asked.

"You really want to ask that?"

She nodded.

"Autopsy," he replied.

"I shouldn't have asked." Again she stared across the river and lapsed into momentary silence. A vintage sailboat, the schooner *Pioneer,* was setting sail on the first of its daily two-hour excursions carrying tourists around the harbor.

Caren shook her head, expelled some air, and said, "I never made love . . . never *almost* made love . . . to someone who died."

"I see," Donovan replied.

"Have you?"

"No. It must be a weird feeling. Why didn't you complete the act?"

"We were interrupted," Caren said.

"By?"

"I don't know. There was this big noise coming from behind the stage."

"What kind of noise?"

"A crashing sound. Something like falling down."

"What happened then?" Donovan asked.

Caren kind of blushed, kind of giggled, and said, "I screamed."

Donovan smiled.

"I'm a *girl*," she laughed.

"I noticed. And my wife—the shotgun-wielding killer—noticed that I noticed. What happened then?"

"It was really dark down there, like I said, except for that faint light coming from behind the stage."

"I've seen it," Donovan said.

"Then all of a sudden the light went out and it was *so dark* down there," Caren continued.

"Was there a sound when the light went out?"

She nodded.

"Another crash?" he asked.

"More like a door closing."

"What did you do then?"

"Are you kidding? I screamed again. Rob said, 'You get out of here. I'll be along in a minute.' "

"So you split," Donovan said.

"Faster than you can imagine," Caren replied.

"How'd you find your way out?"

"Oh, I always know where the escape route is. You know what I mean?"

Donovan nodded. "Why are there so many Jewish violinists?"

"I don't know."

"Because it's hard to escape on two hours' notice carrying a piano," Donovan replied.

"I hear you."

"So Rob Ingram stayed below to slay the dragon. What did you do then?"

"I got up on deck and was about to go looking for Dennis when there was Veronica."

"Where?" Donovan asked.

"Up front. On the . . . what do you call it?"

"Bow. Foredeck."

"She was coming around from the left side of the boat," Caren said.

"From the port. Did she say what she was doing there?"

Caren shook her head. "I think she may have been using the bathroom."

"Next?"

"She made some joke about why Rob wasn't with me, like, you know, and I guess I shouldn't be telling you this . . ."

"Those are the stories I like best," Donovan said.

"She said, 'Where's your friend? Did you kill him?' "

Donovan smiled, and said, "Killed as in . . . ?"

"Yeah, that. I told Veronica, 'I didn't get the chance. There was a big noise and I ran the hell outta there.' "

"And Veronica said . . . ?"

"She said, 'And he stayed behind to kick the shit out of someone?' "

"What then?" Donovan asked.

"I laughed and said yeah, and she said, 'Let's go get a cab. Enough of this already.' And I said, 'What about Harley and Rob?' And she said, 'They found their way here, they can find their way home.' So we walked up to West Street and caught a cab."

"Where's your dress right now?"

"My dress! Oh, you liked it, didn't you."

"It's fabulous."

"It was made for me," she said proudly. "It's the only one like it in the world."

"I don't suppose there are that many six-one women who could pull off wearing that thing," Donovan said.

"I'm special. Anyway, the dress is home, in my closet. Why do you ask? Do you want to borrow it for Marcy to wear?"

"She would be swimming in it," he replied.

"Why do you want it?"

"I need to check it out," he said. "You know how it goes."

She thought for a moment, then a wicked smile came over her. "You're looking for *blood*," she said, appearing to feel even more special than usual. "I'm a *suspect*! That's really exciting."

"You didn't get it dry-cleaned, did you?"

"Can you get anything dry cleaned in twenty-four hours?" she asked. "Besides, this is the sort of dress you never clean. You wear it three or four times and then pitch it."

"Kind of an expensive way to live, isn't it?"

She smiled, and said, "I guess you don't know how much I make for one of these shoots."

"You said ten."

"It's ten."

"You're worth it. Rob Ingram thought so, anyway."

"And now I'm a suspect in his murder."

"You're a suspect along with everyone else on the ship that night," Donovan said.

"Including you and Marcy?"

"Of course. Detective Moskowitz is investigating

us. Want to meet him? If you like big, brawny guys . . ."

"Bring him *on*," she said.

"Unfortunately, he's married."

Caren shrugged, and said, "If you can't be with the one you love, love the one you're with. At least, that's what I think they said during my father's time."

It was Donovan's turn to stare across the East River looking faintly stricken. When he recovered, he said, "Let's rule you out as a murderess right now so we can get on with our lives. We don't want anyone calling the *Post* and complaining that you got special treatment because . . ."

"I'm gorgeous, talented . . ."

"And black," Donovan said.

"Okay, come get the dress. Or send someone. I'll be home after three or four this afternoon. The light will be from the west by then. Too tricky to shoot a black woman with the sun behind her. That's a fashion no-no. The shoot will end."

Donovan put a piece of cheese on a final multigrain cracker and bit the assemblage in half. He said, "Too bad about Ingram. He didn't deserve to die, even though he was something of a troglodyte concerning women's rights."

"People change," Caren replied sharply as Donovan watched her eyes.

They chatted for a while longer, until the photographer dismissed the blonde and called for Caren. "Pegnoir time," she said, petulantly, but getting to her feet nonetheless.

"My condolences," Donovan replied, then walked her to the Winnebago, chatting about nothing in particular.

He got back in his Taurus and drove back across the Brooklyn Bridge. He took the ramp onto the FDR Drive north and headed uptown.

Traffic was light at midmorning, and Donovan made the trip to the Upper East Side in under ten minutes. He took the Sixty-third Street off-ramp and circumnavigated local streets until he was able to double park in front of the townhouse on East Sixty-second Street.

The house was four stories high, with a tan brick facade, decorated on the ground level with white windowsills upon which sat red pottery flower boxes filled with marigolds that someone, it seemed, was paid well to maintain. Two blue spruces rose from gigantic stone pots to frame the entrance, which was through a varnished oak door four steps up from the scrubbed pavement. A discrete bronze plaque read THE CASCINI AGENCY.

Donovan rang the bell. Within a few seconds, the door was pulled open by a thin and waifish, but beautiful, girl of perhaps nineteen years whose head was surrounded by a halo of Shirley Temple curls. Donovan recognized her as the striking young model who was with Cascini and Piermatty at the party. He thought, *Rite of passage at the Cascini Agency—receptionist.* She said, "You must be Captain Donovan."

He replied, "It does seem to be a job requirement."

She gave him an at-a-loss-for-words look, then smiled politely and said, "Yes . . . come in. Veronica is expecting you."

She led him through a white-leather-upholstered couch-and-chairs reception area in which three more young women, each thinner and with bigger eyes and poutier lips than the last, sat filling out forms.

Donovan followed the receptionist down a hall that led past two offices before finding himself in an ultramodern kitchen, pure white with Formica counters and matching island, and stainless steel utensils suspended from a similar ceiling rack. Herb tea and flavored coffee were the scents that Donovan encountered, not Cascini perfume.

The girl led him to a cobblestoned backyard garden in which Veronica Cascini sat at a glass-and-stainless steel umbrella table accompanied by a phone and a laptop. She wore a white silk bouse over a brown skirt, and when she spotted him quickly said, "He's here. I'll call you back," into the phone and hung up.

"Hi," Donovan said.

"Hi, Marcy's husband," she replied. "So good to see you again so soon. I wish the circumstances were better."

Donovan nodded, saying, "Rob Ingram deserved only *career* death."

She stood long enough for them to exchange perfunctory hugs, then waved him into a chair and sat back down herself.

She sort of nodded, but not with a great deal of apparent conviction. Then she said, "The man crashed my party," and let her voice trail off.

Then Veronica looked up at Donovan, and maybe she detected a hint of surprise in his expression. For she quickly added, "Of course, that's no reason he should *die*."

"Oh, I don't know," Donovan said jauntily, "back in the Studio 54 days, party crashers were routinely executed on the corner of Seventh Avenue."

"You could never have been at Studio 54," Veronica said.

"Why not? Am I too young or too old?"

"Neither," she replied. "I would think too disinterested."

"Actually, I was interested enough to try it once. *Once*."

"How did you get in?"

"I walked right in," Donovan said. "It was all a matter of attitude. Those bouncers could smell fear a block off. But if you acted like you belonged, they opened the gates. Or, as Marcy would say, 'He or she who asks permission is doomed.' So, when did you first notice that the subsequently deceased had crashed your party?"

"That arrogant little man came up to where we were sitting and said, 'Hi, I'm the next attorney general of the United States.' What nerve!"

"What ignorance of the realities of American politics," Donovan added.

"You don't think that Pete Bennett will be president?" she asked.

"You know what I think. Global warming will increase. The polar ice caps will melt. And my fifteenth-floor apartment will become beachfront property before Bennett becomes president of the United States."

Veronica smiled, and that one seemed genuine. "I don't like Ingram," she said.

"That came through," Donovan replied.

"What was your question?"

"When did you first notice him?"

"Oh, it was when he introduced himself, just like I said. Of course, the introduction was more to *Caren* than to me."

"I suspected the man had no taste," Donovan said.

"You're sweet," Veronica said. "But you needn't say things like that. I'm accustomed to men looking right past me at Caren. If you think about it, Captain . . . Bill . . . what shall I call you?"

"It's not important to me," Donovan replied.

"William, then. I'm accustomed to going out to lunch with one or two of my girls and feeling . . ."

"Like the fly on the wall?"

"More like the wall," she replied. "Do you know what it's like to be treated like the invisible woman?"

"I have a feeling that you get your vengeance on payday," Donovan said.

Veronica smiled an especially broad smile, all the while bobbing her head up and down vehemently.

"And my career will *last*, too," she added. "Those girls will be washed up by the age of thirty, for the most part. You would be surprised how many models *can't* do the Lauren Hutton thing and make it go on forever."

Donovan said that he wouldn't be surprised at all.

She continued, saying, "For most of my girls, if they don't invest their money carefully they better have hooked themselves rich men by the time they hit thirty."

"How old is Caren?" Donovan asked.

"Twenty-nine," Veronica replied, but without a smile.

"And how is her portfolio these days?"

"Almost entirely in Italian rolling stock."

"Ferraris," Donovan translated.

"She has two. One for herself and one as a kind of dowry to give her future husband."

"There's something sweet and old-fashioned about that," Donovan said. "Kind of like the old country where the girl's dad would present the groom with three cows, a goat, and a corner of the turnip patch."

"I like Caren," Veronica continued. "She's a *big* part of my business. I hope she keeps her looks forever, for her sake and mine, because . . ."

"Her taste in men . . ."

"Sucks," Veronica replied.

The agency owner hesitated, as if a regret made a fleeting appearance, then added quickly, "Except that she was attracted to *you*, of course."

"That was idle bullshit, but it felt good at the time," Donovan said.

"But again, there you have the problem with her. She's attracted to men she can't have. *You're* married . . ."

"And a lot older . . ."

"That wouldn't stop her. But your wife is *in the room*."

"And a terrific shot," Donovan said. "A better shot than I am, the guys at the pistol range like to remind me. Tell me, is Caren really desperate to hook somebody?"

"Not desperate," Veronica replied. "Thinking ahead. That's the only thinking ahead that she does. In my experience, all beautiful women are acutely aware that it will end. For Caren, finding a rich husband is an easier concept to grasp than saving money or investing."

"I can't believe that she has trouble finding men," Donovan said.

"Are you kidding? She scares the pants off men."

"I'm not sure that's the image we're looking for."

"You know what I mean, a lot of guys take a look at her and are terrified that they won't be able to, you know . . ."

"Perform," Donovan said.

Veronica nodded, and said, "In every possible meaning of the word. My God, she's six-one and thirty-eight C. She's gorgeous. She's *black*."

"She's been on the cover of *Sports Illustrated*," Donovan added. "In a string bikini."

"Not even in *that*. It was *painted* on her so there wouldn't be lines. She actually did that shoot in the nude. Did you notice how tight the suit looked?"

Donovan said, "I don't read *Sports Illustrated* and haven't seen the shot. But I seem to have trouble finding anyone who believes me."

"I believe you," Veronica said. "You're an intellectual."

"I have a gorgeous wife," Donovan replied. "I don't need to look elsewhere."

"You also are unafraid of strong women."

"I seem to be fatally attracted to them," Donovan said, a bit of a sigh escaping on its own.

"You're Irish and, I'll bet, an only child," Veronica said.

Donovan replied, "Half Irish."

"Close enough. But most other men are *intimidated* by Caren Piermatty. Trust me on this. She frightens them."

"Do you think that Caren saw Ingram as a prospective husband?" Donovan asked.

"I call only tell you that she's always got her eyes open. What that says about who killed who, I can't tell you."

"Who do you think killed Ingram?" Donovan asked.

"I have no idea."

"Did you?"

"Of course not. The idea is laughable."

"I like a good laugh," Donovan replied. "Do you think Caren did?"

"Even more laughable. She had no reason to. If he came on to her and she didn't want it, all she had to do was turn tail and stalk out of the room in that haughty way she's so good at."

"And if he came after her?"

"She would slap his face and keep walking."

"Did she know him before the party?" Donovan asked.

"Only as someone to be avoided," Veronica replied, shaking her head. "I'm telling you, Caren Piermatty has no problem ditching men who don't please her. Look, William, I don't know who killed Ingram, but I'm not mourning."

"Tell me what happened after two in the morning."

"We went up on the cabin roof, where Dennis likes to hang out."

"How'd you get up from the theater space?" Donovan asked.

"The same way we went down. The starboard gangway. And the ladder, of course. That's quite a feat, getting up and down that ladder in the middle of the night after you've had a few drinks."

"On a ship the captain of which doesn't care for light that much," Donovan added.

"We went up there, Tink, Caren, Dennis, and I did, and that other man followed us."

Donovan's eyebrows curled slightly. "Other man?" he asked.

"What's he call himself? Healey? Haley? Harley. That's it. The guy who showed up in the tux."

"You mean you don't know him?" Donovan asked.

"I don't know the man from Adam," Veronica replied. "He's a friend of Tink."

"Who's Tink?"

"Tinkerbelle," she replied.

"Oh."

"You met her. My receptionist. Very bright future."

Donovan asked that the young woman be called for. Veronica did that, adding a request that she show up with cups of espresso, Donovan having agreed that such would be a nice thing to have while sitting in the garden. When Tinkerbelle showed up five minutes later, interrupting some idle talk about the whitewashed fence, decorated with ivy and ceramic flower pots, that surrounded the tiny back yard, carrying gold-leafed cups of black liquid that steamed even in the late-spring morning's warmth, Donovan paid more attention to her. Her waifish body was dropped, like a wick into a candle, into an antique white, wide-weave dress that while floor length was transparent enough to reveal lavender bra and panties. Wondering if they were painted on her as the swimsuit was on Caren Piermatty, he asked, "How do you know Harley Greave?"

"I met him at the Starbucks on the corner of Third," she replied.

"How long ago?"

"Two weeks."

"Have you been going out with him?" Donovan asked.

"No," she replied, adding a giggle and helping herself to the third seat at the table. "He was just a guy I talked to at the coffee shop."

"How did he get to the party?"

"I invited him," the young woman replied. "Did I do something wrong?"

"Of course not," Veronica assured her.

"Anyone is entitled to go to a party," Donovan said agreeably. "But how did you know he was a model?"

"I asked him, and he said he was."

"Who spoke first?" Donovan asked.

"Why, he did. I was excited. He's gorgeous."

"But you haven't worked with him, either of you," Donovan said.

Both women shook their heads.

"So he got invited to the party because he's gorgeous," Donovan said.

"To be honest, William," Veronica replied, "that's how people get to know people in this business. If you look right, you've got a foot in the door. This is the same way you got into Studio 54. You acted like you belonged. Maybe later someone will ask you to prove yourself in some tangible way."

"But he wasn't asked," Donovan said.

"There's been no time," Veronica said. "Tink asked him to the party . . . she has my blanket approval to do that when she meets a hot prospect . . . so we could get a look at him. See how he looks. See how he moves. Maybe later we'll actually interview him."

"How did he do in the looks and moving department?" Donovan asked.

"Looks ten, moves zero," Veronica replied.

"He was kind of a doofus," Tink added.

"He was clumsy," Donovan said.

"Not clumsy. Just awkward. He kind of limped, you know. Which can be sexy. But he had *nothing* to say. And *fell asleep.*"

"That's a no-no," Donovan said.

"It's fine if you're super famous. Then you can do anything. Fall asleep. Throw up. Lose your clothes on the dance floor. Have liaisons with strangers."

"But not *kill* strangers."

"Major-league frowned upon," Veronica replied. "As I was saying, if you are a nobody and fall asleep at your first fashionable New York party, you may as well get on the bus back to Podunk. If he had comported himself well, like an experienced model, he would be invited to the next party or in for espresso, and we would find out if there was anything beneath the looks."

"Assuming you can find him," Donovan said.

Veronica asked what the captain meant.

"Did Harley leave a number? An address?"

"He gave me his phone number," Tinkerbelle said brightly.

"Would you get it for the captain?" Veronica asked.

"Sure."

To stop her from going *at that moment,* Donovan said, "I'll pick it up on the way out."

"Okay."

"When you had coffee with him, what did you talk about?" Donovan asked.

She thought for a moment, then said, "He asked if I was a model, and I told him yes, and I asked if he was a model, and he said yes. He said he was just in from Green Bay, Wisconsin, to try to get a major agency to rep him, and I said, 'You've got to meet Veronica.' "

"This is great," Donovan said. "This is like *A Star Is Born* or something. Gorgeous guy gets spotted by gorgeous girl and two weeks later is famous. Who's got the movie rights to this yarn?"

"It happens all the time," Veronica said.

"But Veronica is much too busy to give an actual *appointment* to an unknown who I found in the street, sort of, so I told him to get us his portfolio and come to the party," the girl said.

"Did he get you his portfolio?" Donovan asked.

The girl shook her head.

"He came to the party," Veronica added.

"Tell me," Donovan said, "I'm a young model who just hit town, looking for a big break, and by an amazing stroke of luck *just happen* to be in the Starbucks on the corner by the Cascini Agency and *just happen* to strike up a conversation with a model who works there."

"How could he have known I was a model?" Tinkerbelle asked.

Donovan said, "You ain't a supermarket cashier, kid. It don't take Sherlock Holmes to figure that out. So anyway, I get to New York and I'm invited to submit my portfolio to the owner of the world-famous Cascini Agency. How long does it take me to get it to you?"

"A minute and a half would be an eternity," Veronica said.

"And Harley has taken . . . what is it now? Two weeks?"

"I wondered about that," Veronica said.

"I wonder if there *is* a portfolio," Donovan replied.

"Why else would he be hanging around?" Veronica asked.

"There are a number of possibilities, one of which, of course, is to get close enough to Rob Ingram to kill him."

Both women's eyes widened, Bambi's caught in the headlights.

"But he passed out," Veronica said. "He had too much to drink and passed out."

"Do you know that for sure?"

"Well, I . . . well, no," Veronica said.

"You don't need a degree from the Actors Studio to fake falling asleep," Donovan said.

"On the roof he said two words, 'I'm tired,' and went to sleep. Before that . . . I didn't pay much attention to him. Tink, did you?"

The young woman shook her head. "I asked him to dance once, but he said he didn't dance. He was more interested in looking at the exhibits inside *Sevastopol Trader*. You know, in Dennis's old junk."

"He paid a lot of attention to that?"

"He was obsessed with the stuff Dennis has inside the ship. So I left him alone. Later on, he stayed when everyone else had gone, and then climbed up on the roof with Caren and Veronica and me and fell asleep."

"As I said, the young man made an impression, and it

was the wrong one. After that, no one paid him the slightest attention," Veronica said.

"Was he still 'sleeping' "—Donovan made quotation marks in the air with his fingers—"when you left for the night?"

Veronica nodded. "What happened was Caren went below with Ingram to dance, supposedly, leaving me up there with this sleeping guy I had, by then, decided I didn't want anything to do with. So I finished my drink, watched a boat go by . . ."

"What kind of boat?" Donovan asked.

"I don't know, a little boat. A little white boat was chugging along."

"Did this boat have any kind of cabin on it?"

"It had something with antennas or something sticking out of it. And someone inside had a light on. It was cute."

"Was the chugging especially loud?" Donovan asked.

"Yes. Like in *The African Queen*." She brightened at the thought.

"I know the boat. Go on."

Veronica said, "And then I left. I touched his arm and said, 'Hey, it's closing time . . . we're all leaving . . . nice to have met you,' but he didn't respond. So I went down the ladder."

"Where were you going? To find Caren?"

She shook her head. "Caren can take care of herself. *Boy*, can she, especially when she's got a man on the line. I was going to the bathroom and then home. So I went down to the . . . the head, I think it's called."

"Which one?" Donovan asked.

"Why, the one on the starboard side . . . nearest the dock."

"Why that one?"

"Ah . . . it's the only one I know of. Are there others?"

"Two more," Donovan replied.

She shrugged. "I'm not into ships."

"Did you go over to the port side? Near the cruise liner?"

"No. Why should I? It was dark over there. Of course, it was dark *everywhere*, but there were lights on the dock."

"What then?"

"I was heading for the gangway to the dock when I bumped into Caren."

"Where?"

"On the foredeck, near the gangway. She was upset because there was a noise downstairs that scared her."

"Six-one, C-cup notwithstanding," Donovan said.

"So Ingram sent her upstairs to safety while he investigated the noise."

"What then?" Donovan asked.

"We got a cab and went home. I dropped Caren off . . ."

"When would this be?"

"Four-fifteen. Four-thirty. In there someplace."

"And then you went home yourself," Donovan said.

"Of course."

"And 'home' is here?" he said, sweeping an arm up and around the back of her building.

She nodded, and said, "Top two floors."

"Did anyone see you?" he asked.

"No."

"What about the cab driver? Did you get a receipt? Maybe he can give you an alibi."

"No."

"Do you remember anything about him? Or her? An accent, maybe?"

"Sorry," Veronica replied. "He might have been Spanish. You know, Puerto Rican or something."

"Didn't he recognize Caren?" Donovan asked.

Veronica shook her head. "It was dark out."

"What about when you went into your house? Did anyone see you then?"

"No. No maid. No butler."

"No husband?"

"Not a man in sight anywhere, I'm sorry to say," she replied, a bit too jauntily, Donovan thought.

"I'll bet *you* scare men, too," he said.

"That's what my therapist says. Oh well, the price of success, and all that. A relationship is not high on my list of priorities right now."

"You're sure that Caren never mentioned Rob Ingram before?" Donovan asked.

Veronica laughed out loud. "Like I told you . . . Caren? Be seen in the daylight with a right-wing white troglodyte? I don't *think* so."

"But one could be fun for a early-morning tryst," Donovan said.

"I suppose those Bible Belt people aren't likely to carry a *disease*," Veronica replied.

"They also aren't likely to go around telling everyone who will listen that they had sex standing up with a black girl on a boat in New York Harbor," Donovan added. "Especially when they work for a conservative candidate for president."

"I'm sure that Caren never met him before the other night," Veronica insisted. "She probably didn't know who he was. She doesn't read or watch TV. She stands in front of a camera or parties."

"How did she react when he showed up?" Donovan said. "Tell me exactly what was said."

"As I told you, he said something about being the next attorney general, and at that point I looked away, because I recognized him and didn't want to breathe the same air. And Caren said, 'Hello, gorgeous,' which is kind of her line she uses on everyone in pants. That and, 'Who are you and what are you doing later?' And he said, 'Can I join you?' And Caren said something like, 'You're not getting away from me,' or, 'Do you think you're getting away from me?' I'm not sure because I was angry and not paying attention."

"Angry because . . ."

"I had *two* assholes on my hands. One asleep. The other a right-wing maniac who would ruin things for women were he to get into high office. Tink had gone home . . ."

"I'm sorry," the girl added quickly. "I was really tired."

"That's okay, honey. Anyway, I felt alone, so I wasn't paying attention to what Ingram and Caren said."

Donovan asked, "Instead of saying 'away from me,' could Caren have said 'away from Ree'?"

Veronica finished her espresso and put down the cup. "It's possible. Who's Ree?"

"Another woman in Ingram's life. What did Caren and Ingram talk about after that?"

"Actually, I don't know. I left them up there and went down to the deck, to check and see if *anyone else* I disapproved of was aboard."

"Find anyone?"

"Not a soul. Of course, I didn't go below. It's scary down there when you're alone. But I walked back . . . aft . . . to see who was on deck and grab a piece of vegan roast beef."

"How was it?" Donovan asked.

"Horrible. *Horrible!* I'll never let a caterer talk me into something again."

"What time was this, about?"

"Quarter to four? Four? I don't know."

Donovan sat and thought for a moment, and said, "You know, Tink—if I can call you that . . ."

"Sure," she said.

"If you *could* get me that phone number now."

"Be right back," she said, and dashed off, her hair bobbing around her head.

"Wonderful girl," Veronica said.

"What happened to the clothes you wore to the party?" Donovan asked.

"My clothes? Oh, you mean my suit. Dry cleaners. Why do you ask?"

"It would help me rule you out as a suspect."

"God, you're looking for *blood* on my clothes," she exclaimed. Then she shook her head, then laughed, a bit loud, Donovan thought. "You *would* find vegan roast beef sauce," she said.

"I hope the dry cleaning works on that," the captain replied, and then finished his espresso, being careful not to spill any on himself, an old tendency being to wear a fragment of his last meal at all times.

The girl came back, and handed him a Post-it Note on which she had written a phone number. Donovan thanked her, then used his cell phone to dial a number. Then he said, "Yeah . . . who did you expect? . . . No, *he's* dead. I'm pretty sure, anyway. At least, I went to the funeral . . . Take down this phone number . . . 555-4738. Tell me where it is. No, I want it *now*. I'll hold on."

Veronica smiled.

Donovan looked back at her for a moment, apologized for the interruption, and listened to background noise in Moskowitz's office for a moment. A ruckus was going on regarding betting on the National Basketball Association playoffs. Then Mosko came back on the line and Donovan listened for a moment, before saying, "Okay, get a warrant, suspicion of murder, and you can go over there later. See if you can find out his real name while you're at it. I'll see you in an hour in my office . . . Why an hour? . . . Because when I came uptown the FDR downtown was packed . . . okay, go look out the window . . . He's looking out the window," Donovan said to the two women.

A sparrow landed in one of the flowerpots and was looking down on the trio gathered beneath him. Seeing the bird, Veronica plucked a Lorna Doone from a crystal bowl, pulverized it between thumb and forefinger, and tossed the crumbs onto the cobblestones. The bird swooped down on them, and soon was followed by another.

Back on the phone, Donovan said, "The FDR is okay now? Okay, half an hour. Order Chinese for the three of us."

"You're a busy man," Veronica said, smiling fondly at her assistant, whose eyes were wide with astonishment.

"Like you said, the price of success. Look, Tink, your friend Harley, the one who came in flat broke from Green Bay, Wisconsin, to make it in modeling?"

"Yes?"

"He's staying at Manhattan Boardroom Suites."

"Oh, excuse *me*," Veronica laughed.

"What's Manhattan Boardroom Suites?" the young woman asked.

"Three hundred and change a day," Donovan replied.

"That's for the cheap rooms," Veronica added.

"So much for the broke boy from Wisconsin."

"Who *is* he, then?" Tink asked.

"Hard to be sure right now, but my inclination is toward hired-something . . . political spy is one possibility. Hit man is another."

"My God!" Tink exclaimed.

"Lucky you didn't date him, eh?"

"No kidding."

"And you think he killed Ingram?" Veronica said.

"Caren remains the last one known to have seen him alive," Donovan said. "But Harley Greave, and if that's his real name I'll be completely amazed, suddenly became a better suspect."

12. TORRID AFFAIR, HUSH-HUSH, DIDN'T WANT TO RUIN HIS CAREER.

When Donovan got to his office on the forty-second floor of One Police Plaza, the sun was bright up at the altitude below which traffic helicopters flew, and his associate had joined another man in looking out the window at the spectacular view of the East River, Brooklyn, Queens, and Long Island. The smell of Chinese food wafted from two immense white paper bags that sat atop Donovan's conference table.

Donovan joined them at the window, nudged the third fellow in the side with an elbow, and said, "If you look closely to the left there, off in the distance, you can see the southern tower of the Throg's Neck Bridge. How far is that from here? Must be fifteen miles. And off to the right"—he swept a finger over in that direction—"you have the control tower at Kennedy Airport. On days when wind is coming from the west, you get takeoffs coming in this direction before the planes bank left and head off across the harbor."

"We sit and watch them when we need to think," Mosko said.

"And down below, to the left there," Donovan continued, "you have Newtown Creek, a commercial waterway once so polluted that Mr. Clean would die if he stuck his toe in the water. But I'll be there, tomorrow at three in the morning. Want to join me?"

"Not this time, Billy me boy," George McCann said, pronouncing the latter word to rhyme with "buy."

"God help us, another Irishman is in the room," Donovan said, turning and shaking his childhood friend's hand. "How the hell are you, George?"

McCann was fiftyish, red-haired, round-faced, expensively dressed, and solidly built but not overweight, clearly someone who once lifted things for a living, no matter his current success.

"Fit and well, thank you. You're looking good. Fatherhood has come upon you, I hear."

"This is true," Donovan replied.

"A boy, still in diapers. Well, well . . . you never stop, do you?"

"My work on this planet is far from done," Donovan said grandly. "And you, you look like Paddy McGinty. Fell into a fortune, did you?"

"Well . . ."

"Look at this suit," Donovan said, fingering the lapel. "Custom made. How much did this cost you?"

"Ah, I don't know that," McCann said. "My financial manager signs the checks."

"Oh, your *financial manager.* We *have* come a long way since our stickball days, haven't we?"

"I hear that you're in the pink yourself."

Donovan shrugged. "I married for love. The fact that my bride has a couple of dollars is of no consequence to me."

"Bullshit," Moskowitz said, not quite under his breath.

Donovan smiled.

"And she's a Democrat, too. Well done!"

"Your financial manager wouldn't happen to keep rooms at Manhattan Boardroom Suites, would he?" Donovan asked.

"Your pal here, the honorable Detective Moskowitz, already asked me that," McCann said. "Bright lad. Has a dear old Irish mom, I'm glad to hear. Regarding Manhattan Boardroom Suites, nope, not me. I might put up someone at a good hotel, but it would be an old and respectable one, not a corporate Howard Johnson's. Whoever your quarry is this time, he's not mine."

"Let's eat," Mosko said, turning to open the bags.

A few minutes later, the trio was sitting around the maple conference table sharing from among a dozen paper containers. The smell of Chinese food, general before, had become more pointed—Moo Goo Gai Pan, Pork Lo Mein, beef with broccoli.

At the first sensible opportunity, Donovan asked, "So did my bright and aggressive colleague here ask you to come in, or did you just drop by on the way to see the bookie?"

Smiling, McCann said, "I came for the wake."

"The wake?"

"Of my late colleague, Rob Ingram."

"This is the wake?" Donovan asked. "Chinese food at police headquarters?"

"It's the only one I'll be invited to," McCann replied.

"True," Donovan said.

"Simply put, I read the papers, and saw your name mentioned in the same sentence with his, and thought I would toss my tuppence in."

"What do you know about Ingram?"

"What *don't* I? As someone said—and perhaps you could tell me who—'Keep your friends close . . . keep your enemies closer.' "

"Can't help you with that one," Donovan replied.

"With all the books you read in the years since you gave up the holy water?"

"Let's hear it. Whatever you have on Ingram that you think is important."

"You'll want to know if he had enemies other than me," McCann said. "There were at least a million, and that's just in politics. Now, politicians don't normally *kill*, actually *kill*, one another, just in the metaphoric sense."

"No matter what we heard about the Clintons and Vince Foster," Donovan said.

"Exactly," McCann replied.

"How *are* Bill and Hill these days?"

"In clover. As I was saying, *lots* of people count themselves . . . count*ed*, I should say, past tense . . . as Ingram's enemies. He caused a lot of trouble in his young life and was poised to cause more."

"Women trouble, for example?" Mosko asked.

"*Especially* women trouble. Now, let me tell you how I came to know these things . . ."

"You learned from the opposition," Donovan said.

"You betcha. That's my credo, kid. Wasn't that in the catechisms they beat into us at St. Dominic's?"

"Don't recall. I'm still a little numb from that."

"We learned from what the Republicans did to Clinton. After impeachment, I set up a fund to get the goods on any woman the top opposition candidates ever checked their Rolexes and gave the time of day to. The candidates *and* their noisy campaign managers. Which leads us to . . ."

"Caren Piermatty," Donovan said.

"You know that?" McCann said, a smile broadening. "I *knew* you'd know that. Nothing gets by you. You've seen the man in action, Detective Moskowitz?"

"Over and over," Mosko replied.

"Guys are being evasive, without even touching 'em, he does a Donovan mind-meld on 'em. I wish I had your instincts, Willie."

"I wish I had your tailor," Donovan said.

McCann speared a dumpling and bit it in half. He used the half still on the tip of his fork as a pointer, jabbing the air as he said, "Two years ago, Ingram was hot on the trail of his big-tent thing—trying to show they weren't a bunch of rich white bigots by running events that included all the folks they don't let into their country clubs. That included blacks, Latinos, Asians, everyone but the damn Dalai Lama, and only not him because he saw through their little minstrel show and refused to be bought."

"Plus you already had him signed," Donovan said.

"Don't be rude," McCann said. "Anyway, one of Ingram's schemes was a fund-raiser in St. Kitts with rappers, a black dance troupe from Chicago, and supermodels."

"That's where they met."

"That's the place . . . St. Kitts. You know the rest. Torrid affair, hush-hush, didn't want to ruin his career, which is what would happen if the news got out. Didn't want to ruin *her* career if it continued."

174

"How might it have done that?" Donovan asked.

"Mean streak," McCann said. "Bad temper, alcohol-fired."

"Ingram?" Mosko said.

Donovan gave his old friend a hard look. "Mean streak as in violent?" he asked.

McCann nodded. "He drinks too much, he loses it, and he's out of control. It's a very well-kept secret . . . cost me over a hundred grand in bribes to hotel maids and emergency room personnel to get the grisly details. I'm not sure if even Bennett knows as much as I do. Sure, Bennett knows about Ingram's fondness for scotch. God knows those boys put away a lot of Johnnie Walker, standing around their leather-lined, mahogany bars slandering the ethnic and unwashed. But it's doubtful Bennett knows about Ingram's temper tantrums. I mean, not even Bennett would choose a violent asshole to be attorney general of the United States . . . would he?"

Donovan suggested an answer by saying, "Hmmm."

"The medical examiner says that Ingram had enough booze in him to get arrested on any highway in America," Mosko added.

Donovan said, "I had a feeling that Ingram wasn't really a babe in the woods."

"He was more like the big, bad wolf," McCann said.

"Upon reflection, Ingram did seem a little disingenuous when he spotted Caren from the promenade deck of the *Trinidad Princess* and said, 'Wow, is that Caren Piermatty?' or words to that effect. It was like the guy had never picked up a copy of the *Sports Illustrated* swimsuit issue."

Mosko looked away to hide a smile.

McCann said, "I never understood why some gorgeous women go for these violent, wife-beater types."

Donovan tossed his hands up.

"What's the evidence he beat up on women?" Mosko asked.

"One hundred grand worth of depositions ready to be leaked to the press the instant Bennett and Ingram became a threat to civilized politicians," McCann said. "I have one glaring item. Two and a half years ago he beat up and raped a young campaign worker in Virginia."

"Beat up and *raped*?" Donovan said.

McCann nodded. "A sweet country girl with a sweetheart and everything. The EMTs took her to the hospital in an ambulance, where she told ER personnel that Ingram raped her and beat her up. Then all of a sudden she's surrounded by lawyers and the story becomes 'I fell down the stairs.' "

"She was bought off," Mosko said.

"You bet. She was bought off so well no one outside her family knew, not even her boyfriend. I understand she was really bent out of shape. She dropped out of college. Spent some time in a 'rest facility.' Yadda, yadda, yadda."

"What's her name?" Donovan asked.

"Dawn Huckins. But if you manage to track her down— and the last I have on her she was back living with her parents behind the family gas station in West Virginia and in seclusion—she won't talk."

"The money talks," Donovan said.

"And let me say that, six months later, *Caren* 'disappeared' for a couple of weeks just toward the end of the time she was hooked up with Ingram," McCann continued. "She showed up at an emergency room . . . the same one, as fate would have it . . . a couple of blocks away from Georgetown, where Ingram lives. Said she was mugged."

"A black girl mugged in Georgetown? Oh sure. Happens all the time," Donovan said.

"She lost a month's work at ten thousand a day," McCann said. "The ER workers said she looked like she fell down the stairs."

"I'll bet that Veronica Cascini lost ten percent of that lost income," Mosko added.

Donovan shook his head. "Marcy tells me that the Cascini Agency gets twenty percent. So if Caren doesn't work for, say, twenty days, Caren loses two hundred grand and Veronica loses forty grand."

"Cascini loses a lot more than twenty percent if she loses Caren permanently," Mosko said. "I checked this morning the way you told me, and our financial analyst confirms what Marcy heard from her mom—the Cascini Agency is in bad shape money-wise. Whether the launch of Cascini perfume will help the bottom line is a question mark. They didn't get much up-front money for it, and our analyst says that the perfume market is glutted. Sales of Cascini will depend on the agency continuing to be associated with beauty. But Caren is their only big star."

"I hear a motive for murder evolving from Ingram's threat to Caren Piermatty and the Cascini Agency," Donovan then said.

"I thought you might," McCann replied.

"Veronica may have wanted to kill Ingram to prevent his spoiling her big star," Donovan said. "Call her up and ask the name of her dry cleaners, and see if maybe they haven't . . . no, on second thought canvas all dry cleaners within ten blocks of her house. Maybe the suit hasn't been done yet. I mean, if I want something done in two days I have to yell and scream. Maybe it's the same with her."

McCann said, "I have another bit of information for you. I offer it up in case it means something."

Donovan said he wanted to hear it.

"The reason . . . the *real* reason . . . that Compassionate Conservatives held their fund-raiser aboard the *Trinidad Princess* . . ."

"I like it already," Donovan said.

"Is that Ingram owned a piece of the ship," McCann said, looking proud of himself.

Donovan slammed his fist down on the conference table, and shouted, "Yes!" A dumpling flew onto the floor and rolled out the door. A passing detective stooped to retrieve it, then stuck his arm in the door to Donovan's office and handed it back to the captain.

"Eating fast food again, Cap?" the man said.

"Sorry," Donovan replied, taking the errant morsel and tossing it into the Chinese food bag that had been designated to hold garbage.

"I *knew* there was something else going on beyond supermodels and sex," Donovan said. "You know how your pal, Carville, kept saying, 'It's the economy, stupid,' during the '92 campaign? Well, I keep telling the guys and gals in this office that, in New York City, 'It's real estate.' Even on the waterfront, it all comes down to what patch of turf you own, how much it's worth, and who wants to take it away from you."

Mosko added, "What the captain is saying is that sex wasn't the only reason that Ingram went to the party."

Donovan nodded. "The other reason may have been to spy on the spies. We didn't tell you, but the guy who owns the freighter is hooked up to an environmentalist who's out to prove the *Trinidad Princess* is dumping toxic waste into New York Harbor."

"Oh," McCann replied, his smile of understanding widening. *"Oh!"*

"This murder may have been about what a guy will go through to protect his real estate," Donovan said.

"We have to find Peter Lachaise," Mosko said.

"Who's that?" McCann asked. "Can I know?"

"The aforementioned environmentalist."

"There's been no sight of him yet, boss," Mosko said. "And we canvassed all the piers on the Hudson waterfront—both sides, Manhattan and Jersey. Did you know that kids are jet-skiing in the harbor now? Scary?"

"Got to try it," Donovan said. "I sure do want to run my jet ski into the QE2. Anyway, regarding Lachaise, I managed to get Duke on the phone. He finally got one—a phone, that is. Forty years after they replaced local operators with dials he managed to learn how to use the thing. I'm meeting him at four tomorrow morning at Newtown Creek. Are you sure you won't come along?"

"Oh, absolutely," Mosko said. "And yeah, I know the drill—stop at the shop on Coney Island Avenue and get you an everything bagel with butter."

"Well, go to sleep early, cause I want you to be sharp. And to give you something to think about as you lay in your Canarsie bed looking out the window at the aboveground pool, at three or four this afternoon you're going to Caren Piermatty's apartment to pick up the dress she wore the night of the murder."

Mosko's eyes grew larger than the dumplings. "Will she be there?" he asked.

"Waiting just for you," Donovan said.

"You're bullshitting me."

"Not me. And while you're there, tell her we know she had an affair with Ingram two years ago and why did she lie to us? Did he beat up on her? If so, why did she go below with him after the party? And what did Veronica think of his reappearing in her life?"

"These questions are designed to get her to like me, right?"

"That's it. Like I keep telling you, you're a bright lad. Have fun this afternoon. Hey, and if she's still in a good mood after you talk to her, ask her to show you the bathing suit she wore on the cover of *Sports Illustrated*."

"She still has it?"

"It will be with her always," Donovan said.

McCann put down his fork and pushed away his plate. He picked up a paper napkin and pressed it against his lips several times. He said, "I'm enjoying this, gentlemen, but I have to run. I have a client meeting."

Donovan held up a hand, and said, "I have a question for you. Do you know who 'Ree' is?"

"Sure. Valerie Bennett. That's the big man's pet name for her."

"How many people call her that?" Donovan asked.

"Just Bennett. How many people do you think called Princess Di 'Squidgy'?"

"Quite a few, after the . . ." Mosko said, chewing hard on a fortune cookie.

"That will do," Donovan snapped.

"Sure, boss."

McCann smiled. "Rough crowd you keep down here. Detective Moskowitz, your Irish mom must come from an IRA family. So who besides Pete calls her 'Ree'?"

"Ingram."

"*Really?* Interesting! So you think they had a relationship?"

"It ain't out of the question," Donovan said.

"I'm sure he wasn't beating *her* up," McCann said. "She is one tough cookie. And also kind of an old-style Southern belle bigot."

"In other words, if I were having a relationship with her and also cheating with a black woman . . ."

"You should be sure to lock the door before going to bed every night," McCann said.

"I have to look into this more," Donovan said.

"You'll keep me posted on what you find, of course."

"You didn't ask that question and I didn't respond," Donovan said.

"And I didn't hear squat," Mosko added, finishing his fortune cookie and tossing the cellophane wrapper into the garbage bag.

Donovan pushed away from the table, stood, and used one hand to flick some rice from his shirt and lap into his palm. Then he emptied that palm into the garbage and straightened his clothes. "But we will get together for a drink before too long," Donovan said.

"Name the time and place," McCann said.

"I'll call you . . . Hey, before you go, think back forty years."

"Jesus, Mary, and Joseph, I had pledged to forget."

"We were kids. We used to go into the tunnel that runs along the river, under Riverside Park."

"The abandoned railroad tunnel," McCann said.

"Yeah, to hang out with the Mole People," Donovan said.

He was referring to the subterranean homeless who lived as squatters in the old railroad tunnel, in the nooks and storage areas alongside the track while the trains were still operating, then all over the place once the freight line was abandoned.

"The matter rings a dim and distant bell," McCann said.

"There was one of 'em . . . we called him 'Chop Suey' . . . after a while, just 'Chops.' "

"Unh . . ."

"You remember," Donovan insisted. "He was about thirty at the time. Had run out and left a wife and kid in Boca Raton. Lost it mentally, which I guess can happen when you live in a town named 'Rat's Mouth.' Was schizophrenic . . . had these paranoid fantasies about the Nazis storming ashore and killing everyone on the waterfront."

McCann smiled. "Okay, got 'im. Had a beard and wore glasses. Thin guy. You always liked life's weirdos."

"Including present company," Donovan said.

"Thank you, sir," McCann said.

Mosko gave his boss the finger.

"Later on, fast-forward ahead thirty years, the train line is active again and the Mole People are being run out. So Chops lives on a subway grate, like the rest of the homeless, but has picked up this habit of buying or conning someone out of a container of Chinese food and then sneaking aboard one of the boats moored at the Seventy-ninth Street Boat Basin when the owner was away."

"I was on my way to the West Wing by then," McCann said.

"Right, and Marcy and I spent a summer at the Boat Basin. Anyway, he'd break into someone's boat, sit there, read a copy of the *Daily News*, eat his dinner, have a few smokes, and maybe stay overnight. But then the Nazis would be about to storm ashore and he'd split back to the subway grate, there to huddle in the cold of night and resume his vigil, keeping watch over the harbor for signs of the Nazis. So he could sound the warning, you know?"

"So what?" McCann said.

"I think he's still at it," Donovan replied.

Mosko's eyes turned piercing, more so than usual. "You saw him? On *Sevastopol Trader*? Is that what we're dealing with here?"

"No, but I only missed him by a few hours, I'm sure of it. Here." Donovan got the evidence bags collected earlier that day and gave them to Moskowitz, who held them up to the light and pondered the array of mostly Chinese-restaurant detritus.

"This is from the boat?"

"From the back room, the direction from which Caren heard a sound that frightened her. A door closing, something falling over, or something."

"Chops?" McCann asked. "A murderer?"

"Let him join the party," Donovan said. "He *is* crazy, and certifiably so, which gives him an edge over those other suspects who simply *might* be crazy."

"Who are they, for the sake of argument?" McCann asked.

"Dennis Yeager. Peter Lachaise. Caren Piermatty. Veronica Cascini. Harley Greave. Valerie Bennett, just maybe. And Cal Sforza."

"Who?"

"The Darth Vader of the harbor. And Chops, if those are his prints on the soy sauce packet. Also persons unknown."

"Not Bennett?"

"Nah," Donovan said.

"Pity. Okay, Willie . . . I'm off. Detective Moskowitz, it's been a pleasure."

"Likewise," Mosko replied.

13. "DID YOU EVER HEAR OF A WOMAN STABBING SOMEONE JUST ONCE?"

The two old friends exchanged idle commentary on the way to the elevator. When Donovan got back to his office, Mosko had cleaned up the bags and replaced them atop the conference table with his laptop. Next to it was the evidence the captain had collected while Marcy kept Yeager busy.

Donovan said, "I want forensics to concentrate on the soy sauce packet and the strip of yellow tape. Get me prints off both of them."

"Prints belonging to this guy Chops?" Mosko said.

"I believe that his will be on the soy sauce. He was printed years ago after being nailed coming out of someone's boat. So his prints are on record and I'll bet will match up. But somebody else's will be on the yellow tape."

"Whose?"

"I don't want to say yet."

"You're the boss," Mosko said, tapping a note onto his laptop.

"There's something very strange going on," Donovan said. "Do me a favor and try to track down Dennis Yeager's birth certificate."

"Why?"

"It must be on file. You can't get permission to keep your boat at city-owned piers for extended periods without giving details of your entire history, including proof of nationality."

"You're not going to tell me why you want it," Mosko said.

"I don't *know* why I want it," Donovan replied. "And go to the Chinese restaurant whose name is on the menu and see who bought Chow Fun around three or four in the morning the night of the murder."

"They probably sell a lot of it," Mosko replied.

"To homeless men at three in the morning?"

"You got a point," Mosko said. Then he looked over at the captain, and added, "Are you ready for a briefing on what we found so far?"

Donovan sipped his coffee and said, "No. How come Bennett postponed my appointment with them?"

"He cited the press of business. But the two of them can meet you at four-thirty—the man himself for five minutes and the wife for longer. He has to attend a dinner."

"It's actually better that way," Donovan said. "Bennett won't be any help, and mainly will get in the way. But I wonder why he's letting me see Mrs. B alone. Maybe he didn't really notice when I called her 'Ree' back on the dock."

"Maybe she has something to say," Mosko replied.

"A politician's wife? Well, if she's as strong as George says, maybe. Where am I meeting them?"

"At the Water Club. They made reservations."

Donovan brightened. "Across the East River from Newtown Creek. Appropriate. Maybe I'll just stay all night, sitting on the deck and watching the river flow."

"Worse things could happen to a guy," Mosko agreed.

"Okay," Donovan replied, "give me the briefing. It's been a day and a half. What did we find at the crime scene?"

"You want the latest on time of death?"

"We can start there."

"Okay, we have a revised estimate."

"Closer to five," Donovan said.

Mosko nodded appreciatively. "Between four and four-thirty," he said.

"And the stab wound?"

"Like we said—one straight thrust under the rib cage."

"As if the murderer was aiming at the heart," Donovan said.

"Yeah, just like he was aiming. And his aim was pretty good, too. I got to get this guy down to the arcade at Coney Island."

"I haven't been to Coney Island in a long time," Donovan said, looking across his office and out the window. A 757 out of JFK was taking off on a pattern that took it over the Coney Island Houses, visible as gray cubes where the southwest corner of Brooklyn met the sea.

"Did you ever hear of a woman stabbing someone just once?" Mosko said.

"No. Good point. Does Howard still think it was a right-handed perp?"

"Yeah, and that is no longer just your intuition. We got a good, strong left-handed bruise on the deceased's right shoulder."

To illustrate, Mosko reached across Donovan's chest and grabbed the captain's right shoulder and squeezed it. Donovan looked down and over at the hand until it was removed.

"Describe the bruise," Donovan said.

Mosko put his hand back and squeezed a little tighter, leaving slight impressions of his fingertips on the back of the captain's shoulder and pressing his thumb and the butt of his left hand against the front. Then he pulled the hand back.

Donovan said, "The killer held Ingram's shoulder with his left hand and stabbed him with the right."

"It looks that way," Mosko said.

"Is there anything you can infer from the position of the bruises about the height of the killer?" Donovan asked.

"Sorry, no."

"About the size of the hand?"

"Only that it didn't belong to a midget," Mosko replied.

"And all of our suspects are average height or above," Donovan said. "Was there anything on Ingram's hands . . . under his fingernails . . . especially on the right hand, which presumably he was using to grab at the killer or otherwise defend himself?"

Mosko smiled and replied, "Just perfume."

"Cascini?"

"The same. That's all there was on his hands, boss, save for traces of scotch. Especially on his index finger."

Mosko held up his right index finger. Donovan imitated him, then turned his finger downward and used it in a stirring-the-drink motion, using his left hand as a glass.

Mosko said, "Oh, you *would* be able to figure that one out."

"See if there's a corresponding patch of dried scotch on his right pants leg," Donovan said idly, moving his finger down that way and wiping it.

When his associate began to type that into his laptop, Donovan said, "I was kidding."

"Oh. It's hard to tell sometimes. So look, if Ingram tried to fend off the killer or grab at him . . ."

"Or her," Donovan reminded him.

"Or her . . . we're all feminists these days . . . then he wasn't very good at it."

"Stop the presses," Donovan said.

"As for your theory that the murderer needed super-human strength to control the torque on the murder weapon . . ."

"So 'torque' is the right word?" Donovan asked.

"Yeah. How about a little less concern with the words and a little more concern with the deeds?"

"Get on with it," Donovan growled.

"Howard says that a guy . . . or girl . . . with normal strength could control that weapon well enough to stick it in someone and pull it out. Remember now that Caren Pier-matty *does* rock climbing, so she ought to be pretty decent at grabbing onto stuff."

"Okay, and she had her arms around him, and maybe she stabbed him . . ."

"And all he got on him was some perfume when he was getting it on with her. Now, a guy mixes it up with a babe, you expect he might acquire some hairs or something, but . . ."

"Caren has a buzz cut. A nice one, too. Was there anything else on Ingram that suggests her?"

"Yeah, like you suspected, the lipstick was hers," Mosko said. "She kissed you around eleven, she kissed Ingram around four. If you had given her a cold, she could have given it to Ingram. Was what you gave her a sloppy kiss? Cause if it was, jeez, we might even find some of your spit on the victim."

"You're a strange man," Donovan said.

"I is who I is," Mosko said.

"But, hey, we got enough. Ingram had her lipstick and perfume on him. Some of her blush, too. I didn't know that black women wore blush. You learn something new every day. But he didn't scrape any skin off anybody. Now, if this guy was a white-trash wife-beater, or whoever-beater, like your friend George says . . ."

"You'd expect a little burst of temper, or rage, or something violent enough to do some damage to the attacker," Donovan said.

"But there's no sign of anything like that," Mosko replied.

"Which tells me that it happened quickly, before he could react," Donovan said. "Killer comes up in the dark. Left hand to shoulder. Right hand to plunge the knife in. One shot straight to heart. Hand comes out, tosses knife to one side. Ingram falls. Perp runs off."

"Ingram knew his murderer."

Donovan agreed. "He wouldn't have let just anyone walk up to him in a dark ship's hold."

"It *was* dark."

"But light enough to tell the difference between a six-foot, one-inch woman and a male stranger," Donovan said. "Here's how it may have happened. Ingram and Caren were together and getting hot. They could see each other well enough by the light coming from the utility room backstage, which was also good enough for Caren to have looked for the boom box. Then there's a noise—a third person came down the port gangway and knocked over the ashtray stand, just like I did."

"What's an ashtray stand?" Mosko asked.

"A pedestal thing barbers used to keep next to their chairs for guys who smoked. This is one of the growing number of items that occurred before your time. Anyway, the third person is heading for the utility room to get the knife, among other things. He or she closed the door. The light goes out in the dance area. Caren screams. Ingram sends her up on deck. Whoever closed the utility room door comes out and stabs Ingram, who is standing there doing what . . . ?"

"Not searching for the intruder, like he told Caren, that's for sure," Mosko said.

"I see that. It's almost like . . ."

"The real reason Ingram was on *Sevastopol Trader* was to meet someone other than her," Mosko said.

"Yeah. She was mainly the excuse Ingram was there in case he got caught," Donovan said. "If Bennett finds out about the after-hours escapade, or the press gets wind of it, chasing Caren Piermatty is something that everyone can understand, if not approve of. Who *wouldn't* want to get closer to her?"

"You didn't."

"Marcy is prettier," Donovan said.

"This is true," Mosko said.

"And also a more manageable size. I'm long past the point in life where I think that love has to be an Olympic event. I tell you, though, that one of the great gifts from Bill Clinton wasn't eight years of unprecedented peace and prosperity—it's that a married man who has an eye for women is no longer the hideous beast previous American pols made it seem."

"People understand a guy chasing a skirt," Mosko said.

"And *wait* till you see the skirt. The dress, that is," Donovan said.

"So what happens is Ingram sends Caren topside . . ."

"And stands there waiting for the guy he was expecting to meet."

"The guy spying on the spies," Mosko said.

"Maybe," Donovan nodded, adding, "now that we

know that Ingram had a big financial stake in the continued success of the *Trinidad Princess*."

"Who comes out from the backstage area carrying the knife by his side. Why *that* knife?"

"It was available. It was associated with Dennis, providing gullible cops . . ."

"Such as the deputy chief. . ." Mosko said.

"With a ready suspect. It was big enough to kill quickly with."

"So who did it?" Mosko asked.

Donovan shrugged. "Any of our suspects with the possible exception of the Bennetts," he said.

"Including Caren?" Mosko asked.

"Especially Caren," Donovan replied. "She's the only one we know of with a personal motive for vengeance. He put her in the hospital two years ago."

"Did I hear you say 'the only one we know of'?" Mosko asked.

"We still have a lot more to learn," Donovan said. "What else do we know from the crime scene?"

"As for fingerprint evidence," Mosko said, "let's start with the murder weapon." He pored over a couple of screens on his laptop.

"Are my prints on the knife?" Donovan asked.

"Nope," Mosko replied.

"Really?"

"You seem disappointed. Where did you touch it?"

"I grabbed the handle," Donovan replied.

"Well, there's the problem. The perp wrapped the handle in something. A rag. Or else he wore a glove. And not just any glove, a thick workman's glove. Remember how Bonaci mentioned something usual?"

Donovan remembered.

"The killer had fabric between his hand and the dagger. So the only prints are a couple of smudges on the handle . . . all of them Yeager's."

"Wait until Pilcrow hears that," Donovan grumbled. "He'll be around screaming 'Pick him up, pick him up.' "

"Now, about that fabric, I said it was rough? Well, it was rough enough to get things to stick to it. We found a couple of fibers."

"I have a feeling that these fibers were *not* gossamer from a designer dress," Donovan said.

Mosko nodded. "They were hemp."

"Hemp as in rope," Donovan said.

"You got it. And rope that had been soaked in salt water."

"Okay, now we're getting someplace that makes more sense than having a supermodel or her agency-prez boss stabbing someone. Did Bonaci also go over that stretch of rail . . . *not* to jump into the water . . . looking for prints?"

Mosko nodded. "Two sets."

"Who?"

"Yeager and an unknown. Listen to this. Yeager left a couple of damned good palm prints exactly where you would expect them from someone grabbing the rail and looking down into the water."

"And the unknown left them where you would expect from someone grabbing the rail from below and looking up onto the ship," Donovan said.

"That's the size of it."

"The boarding party and his host . . . Lachaise and Yeager. There's nothing in the national database on Lachaise?"

"Not a thing," Mosko said.

"Query the French. If he's an environmental activist

with a fondness for fighting battles involving the sea, he might have run afoul of French authorities. They used to have a running battle with Greenpeace in the South Pacific . . . sank one of Greenpeace's ships, too."

"I'll do that," Mosko said, making a note.

"Get Dennis on the phone and ask about gloves or a rag. Specifically, did he keep anything like that in the utility room?"

"Where someone could grab it just before grabbing the knife," Mosko said. "Anyway, the fibers on the knife match fibers from the rope ladder. We also found similar fibers on that stretch of railing. We now have a direct link between that little boat and the murder weapon."

"Lachaise," Donovan said.

"You got it. We just have to find the son of a bitch. I mean it, Cap, if that boat . . . what did you call it, a tender?"

Donovan nodded. "As in the little boat that tends the bigger boats."

"If that tender is anywhere along the waterfront, we haven't been able to find it."

"We'll see what Duke says tomorrow morning," Donovan added. "Did Howard find any prints on the lid of the compartment where Dennis stuck the knife while talking to me?"

Mosko peered at the screen for a moment, tapping an index finger on the down arrow. Then he said, "Yeager's. Just Yeager's."

"What about the stuff I found on the dance floor? The receipt for the supplies that somebody bought at Rite Aid?"

Mosko said, "Yeah, the Fixodent, the Centrum Silver vitamins, et cetera. We got one partial thumbprint off that receipt. It matches . . ."

"The prints of unknown origin Bonaci found on the rail," Donovan said.

"How'd you know that?"

"Lachaise is the only one at the party old enough to be buying Fixodent. Other than Chops, of course, and the last I saw *him* teeth were not high on his list of priorities."

"Explaining the love of Chinese food," Mosko said. "You can gum it."

Donovan smiled at his colleague.

"The receipt was also wet with salt water," Mosko continued. "And it had flecks of lint on it, you know . . ."

"Like you get when you keep a piece of paper balled up in your back pocket, and your pants get wet a lot because you ride around in a little boat."

"Just like that," Mosko said.

Donovan said, "Okay, Lachaise pulls up in his little boat, climbs up the rope ladder, leaves his prints on the railing, passes through the party and leaves his drugstore receipt on the dance floor, argues with Dennis on the catwalk, and leaves around one—or says he does. But he could easily have stayed on, hidden someplace, since Dennis hasn't a real clue, other than his word, as to when he split, and I seem to be the only one who noticed the tender. Or Lachaise could have left and come back. In either case, we have to find him."

"And his motive for killing Ingram is . . . ?"

"Let's suppose that George isn't the only one who knows that Ingram is an owner of the *Trinidad Princess*," Donovan replied.

Mosko nodded and made a note. "Your pal Duke may have some insights on where to find Lachaise," Mosko said.

"I hope so."

"Too bad he can't impart yon insights at a sensible hour. Ah, no problem. *Fahgeddabowdid!* So, one other thing you ought to know about . . ."

"Tell me," Donovan said.

"Harley Greave," Mosko said.

"Did you get the warrant for Manhattan Boardroom Suites?"

Mosko reached down and into his leather shoulder bag, which was propped up against a chair leg. He got a paper and put it on the table in front of his boss. "Just signed a little while ago. According to the boys, Greave took out the room for three weeks and is still checked in."

"How's he paying for it?" Donovan asked.

"You'd think American Express card," Mosko replied.

"That's what I'd think."

"Not true. He paid cash. Very unusual. Want to run over there with us?"

The déjà vu was palpable. Donovan had been to enough Association of Police Chiefs conventions, had given plenty of guest lectures at out-of-town law schools, had endured too many meetings in too many New York City business hotels, not to have the Marriott mentality imprinted on his prefrontal lobe. Harley Greave's rooms at Manhattan Board-room Suites were mainstream biz travel. Patterned dark beige wallpaper suggested dusky pinstripes. Wood-framed prints depicted fly-casting gear, English setters, and Scotsmen in nineteenth-century golf togs. An immense mahogany cabinet held both TV and minibar. A king-sized bed was separated from the mural windows overlooking Times Square by a plush armchair and matching ottoman. A leather-bound desk held a personal fax machine and an Internet hookup.

In the other room was a similarly decorated living room and kitchenette.

A young "guest service manager" named David Lyall buzzed around nervously, clutching the warrant and betraying both a Southern Ohio accent and a lingering fear that he had just stepped into what his parents had warned him would inevitably follow a work assignment in the city that never sleeps—involvement in a homicide.

"Where is he?" Donovan asked Lyall, watching as one of Bonaci's forensics teams scrutinized every inch of the place.

"Mr. Greave has not checked out," Lyall said. "We are still registering charges for him."

"When was he last seen?" Donovan asked.

"Two nights ago."

"The night of the party," Mosko said.

"He dressed and went out for the evening," Lyall said. "He stopped at my desk and asked directions to the waterfront."

"Let me get this straight," Mosko said. "You personally saw him both check in *and* ask directions? What, are you on the desk all the time?"

"We're not on the desk at all, in the usual sense," Lyall replied. "Each of our guests has a personal service manager who handles all his needs. Within reason, of course."

"Did he say where *exactly* where he was going?" Donovan asked.

"No, only that it was a high-society event."

"Sounds like a party aboard *Sevastopol Trader* to me," Donovan commented. "What was he wearing?"

"A tuxedo from the place on the corner," Lyall said, disapproval tinting his words.

"What place on the corner?" Mosko asked.

"The formal-wear rental shop."

"How do you know that?"

Lyall gave Moskowitz a look that said *please!*

Mosko gave Lyall his look that said, *Hey, I'm from Brooklyn. You got a problem with that?*

Donovan said, "You're a very observant man, Mr. Lyall. Tell me what else you noticed about Greave."

Lyall half smiled, then said, "Well, he said he was just in town from his home town in Wisconsin . . ."

"But you don't think so."

"Captain, I'm from Cincinnati, which is across the river from Kentucky. If Mr. Greave is from Wisconsin, I'm from Mars."

"He had a Southern accent?"

"West Virginia. Pure mountain. Like that man said in *Silence of the Lambs*, 'One generation out of the coal mines.' "

"Interesting," Donovan said. "What else did he lie about?"

"I don't know if 'lie' is the right word," Lyall said. "But when you work in the corporate hotel business like I do, you get to meet a lot of people who are accustomed to flying on their American Express cards."

"And Greave wasn't."

"I doubt he even has one. First of all, he paid cash."

"Cash? How much?"

"He phoned in a reservation, showed up, and put down three thousand dollars to cover a week's stay," Lyall said.

Mosko made a whistling noise.

"When did he show up?" Donovan asked.

"Three days ago," the hotel man replied.

"A day before the murder," Mosko said.

"This is fascinating, Mr. Lyall," Donovan said. "I don't suppose you have a record of where he called from?"

"Sorry," the man replied, shaking his head.

"Was there anything about the money he put down?" Donovan asked.

"I don't know what you mean."

"New bills?" Mosko asked.

Lyall said, "I think so. He paid using thousands. Three thousand-dollar bills."

Donovan's eyes blazed. "How often do you see thousand-dollar bills?"

"Almost never. One client asked me to break one a year ago. But this is the first time since."

Hoping intensely, Donovan said, "Please tell me you hung onto them."

"As a matter of fact, I did," Lyall said.

"Yes!" Donovan exclaimed.

Apparently pleased that he had pleased the captain, Lyall said, "I can call my assistant, Katy, and ask her to get them for you."

"If you don't mind. But tell her that a detective will be down to pick them up, and not to touch them again, if she has at all."

Lyall went to a room telephone—they seemed to be everywhere, on the desk, next to the bed, on a table next to the easy chair, in the kitchenette, on the coffee table, and in the bathroom—and made the call. While he was away, Donovan told Moskowitz, "See if any prints beyond Greave's and Lyall's are on those bills."

"You think someone gave them to him, as in, like, payment to kill Ingram?"

"I'm positive that Greave was paid off, but not sure what for," the captain said. Then he looked at the forensics men scouring the room, and yelled, "Anything yet?"

Bonaci came over, holding a small evidence bag. "Some

hair from the tub drain. Light brown. Pretty short. That's it so far."

"Clothes?"

"A bunch in the dresser. Nothing in the closet. Want to see?"

Donovan nodded, and followed his forensics guru across the room. Bonaci pulled out the drawers in the dresser, one at a time, to reveal underwear, socks, jeans, a pair of sneakers, and several generic white T-shirts.

"A bunch of shit is wrong with this story," Mosko said.

"Yeah," Bonaci agreed. "A guy dressed for Motel 6 drops three-seventy, four-fifty a night at one of the most expensive hotels in New York City."

"Howard!" a detective called from across the room.

"Touch nothing!" Donovan said grandly, raising a finger in the air, imitating the Albert Finney portrayal of Hercule Poirot.

"Whatcha got?" Mosko said, leading the others over to the desk.

"A business card in the top drawer," the man replied.

"Whose?" Donovan asked.

Peering down into the open drawer as if inspecting the Star of Bhopal sapphire in its museum case, the man replied, "Some guy named George McCann."

14. "INGRAM WAS AN ASSHOLE. HE GOT
REHAB. AND *THAT* MAKES HIM A
RECOVERING ASSHOLE."

Donovan joined the man, shoulder to shoulder, and joined him in peering down. Then he said, "There's nothing else of obvious evidentiary value in this suite, right?"

Bonaci waved the small plastic bag that contained a few hairs. "Just this and the clothes, which are from Kmart so far as I can tell without looking up the name of the manufacturer."

"But here we have George McCann's business card, sitting smack in the middle of the top drawer of the desk."

"Kinda childish, isn't it?" Mosko said.

"Yeah, you don't have to be a horticulturist to smell a plant. And the address on that card? That's George's *old* office, the one he had three years ago before the scandal involving the Hooters waitress."

Donovan and the other detectives moved back so a technician could use a tweezers to pluck the card from the drawer and put it in a bag. Donovan said, "There will be one set of prints on that card . . . belonging to Greave. It will otherwise have been wiped clean."

"Who's George McCann?" Bonaci asked.

"The guy we had lunch with," Mosko replied.

"In the office? Isn't he the guy who worked in the Clinton White House and popped the waitress with the wise guy brother?"

"The same," Mosko replied.

"Maybe he *did* give Greave the card," the detective said.

"I'll agree with that if George's fingerprints are on the money," Donovan said. "But that won't be the case."

"If Pilcrow finds out that McCann's card was found here . . ." Mosko said.

"Yeah, I got it. Let's make sure the forensics reports don't circulate beyond the unit without my permission."

Another detective walked over, palms up, saying. "That's it. Nothing else in the place but BVDs and prints."

"It'll take a while to get a handle on who they belong to," Bonaci said.

Lyall reappeared, and said, "Katy has the thousand-dollar bills. She hasn't touched them since I gave them to her."

"We'll need her fingerprints," Donovan said. "And yours, too."

"Plus all the service personnel who have been in this room," Bonaci added.

Lyall gave the directions to his office, and a detective headed off toward the elevators.

Donovan asked, "Mr. Lyall, when did Greave reserve his suite?"

"A few weeks ago."

"How?"

"By phone."

"Personally, with you?"

"That's correct," Lyall replied.

"What was his manner like?" Donovan asked.

"You know, I've been in the hotel business for six years, and at Manhattan Boardroom Suites for almost two . . ."

"Greave was unusual?"

"Captain, nearly all the men and women who are guests here have expense accounts and corporate cards. Moreover, they're at ease with using them and they expect to be served."

"But not Greave."

Lyall shook his head. "I don't think he ever stayed at a hotel before. Certainly he never stayed at one of this caliber. He was, you know . . ."

"A blue-collar kind of guy," Donovan said.

"Exactly," Lyall replied. "He acted a little like he was amazed that people wanted to do things for him."

"Like a kid staying at a hotel for the first time," Mosko said.

"Did he make any phone calls?" Donovan asked.

"No. Not one."

"Not *one* phone call?" Donovan asked.

"He may have had a cell, but I doubt it," Lyall replied.

"Do you have the records for TV use? What did he watch, if anything?"

Lyall shuffled papers, then ran a finger down a page, and said, "No pay-per-view. He seems to have spent a lot of time in his suite . . . was never seen in the coffee shop, for example, and I never ran into him after he signed in. So if he watched regular television there would be no record."

Donovan said, "A guy is in a fabulous suite, all paid for, and . . . you do have a lot of pay channels, don't you?"

"There are at least thirty first-run feature films available at all times," Lyall said proudly.

"And he never watched one? What do they cost, ten bucks each?"

"Nine ninety-five."

"Greave is definitely not a man used to traveling on expense account," Donovan said.

"Did he take anything out of the minibar?" Mosko asked.

Again Lyall checked his records, then said, "Four cans of Budweiser. Five dollars each."

Mosko said, "The guy could have as much of the best sauce on earth for free, and he takes four cans of Bud."

Donovan sighed, a sigh that implied he was finished with Manhattan Boardroom Suites. He said, "Okay, we'll need the address that Greave gave you, although I'm sure that the closest he's been to Green Bay, Wisconsin, was watching Packers games on TV."

A handful of minutes later, Donovan and Mosko were riding the elevator to the bottom floor and walking across the deep-piled and brocaded lobby when the captain's cell phone rang. Donovan checked his watch. "This must be her," he said.

Mosko asked, "Marcy? With the report from the doc?"

Donovan nodded, answered the phone, and listened quietly for a few moments, somber, saying, finally, "That's all he had to say? He doesn't know?" Then after another pause, Donovan said, "We'll talk again tonight."

He switched off the phone and put it back in his pocket. Mosko looked over at his friend and read the expression. "Hey, I'm sorry," he said.

"The best pediatric neurologist in the world and he doesn't know why my son can't walk," Donovan said, back on the sidewalk by then, angling his eyes up the north face of the skyscraper across the street, talking to New York City as much as to his companion.

Mosko smiled, abruptly, and did one of those guy things, a whack on the back hard enough to knock over a lesser man. And he said, "Come on, boss, lots of kids don't walk until they're two or three. I'll give you a ride downtown."

Donovan expected to find the Bennetts in the main dining room of the Water Club, the elegant, two-tiered floating restaurant lined with yacht models and huge, crystal-clear windows overlooking the East River. Donovan expected that the Bennetts would have taken over the dining room, turning it into an aide-encrusted version of the other night's gala. Instead, to his surprise he found them alone on the roof deck, a space oddly analogous to Dennis Yeager's cabin top haunt, and a place from which the rapid currents and ever-changing eddies of the East River could be watched from comfortable chairs served by snappily dressed waiters (and no climbing of ladders was required). The Bennetts sat at a table a few discrete paces away from a pack of handlers, watching as a single-engined seaplane roared up the river, taking off en route, Donovan presumed, to Fire Island or the Hamptons.

He walked up to the couple and exchanged greetings, shaking both their hands and noting that whatever distress Valerie Bennett felt the morning after the murder had evaporated. The puffiness around her eyes was gone. The facade of a professional political wife had returned. Still, Donovan felt she looked softer, chastened, perhaps, as one can be following the death of someone with whom the relationship was complex.

As aides watched warily—failing in apparent attempts to appear disinterested—Bennett said, "Sit down, Captain, and take a load off your feet. The past few days must have been busy."

"They're all busy," Donovan replied, pulling back a chair and picking up the bottle of Kaliber that had been left there for him.

"I don't have more than a few minutes more to give you," Bennett said. "I have to run off. But I have given the matter of Rob Ingram's murder a great deal of thought and remain at a loss for anything that may be of use to you. So, I ask, do you have specific questions?"

"Did you know that Ingram was part owner of the *Trinidad Princess*?" Donovan asked.

"Yes. He got us a good deal on the price for our event."

"Were you aware that the *Trinidad Princess* was being watched by environmental activists who were hoping to catch her discharging toxic waste?"

"No, but I'm not surprised. Were they successful?"

"I don't think so," Donovan said. "Do the names Peter Lachaise, Cal Sforza, and Harley Greave mean anything to you?"

Bennett said, "Um . . . no."

"Which of them rang a bell?" Donovan asked.

"What was that last one?"

"Harley Greave."

"I guess not. It's an unusual name and, as you may have noticed, many politicians have unusual names. Is Mr. Greave a politician?"

Donovan smiled, and said, "Probably not. He's very young and may or may not be a model."

"I don't know any models," Bennett said.

"But Rob did," Donovan added.

Bennett slipped into a rather long silence, taking advantage of the disturbance caused by the arrival of a sleek black helicopter at the adjacent helipad. He watched as three men in crisp dark gray or black suits debarked and, donning sunglasses, walked swiftly to one of two gray Mercedes limousines that were parked with their engines running.

Shaken from his reverie, and looking suddenly and oddly mellow, Bennett said, "Captain, I understand that you like to say you're not the lifestyle police."

Donovan nodded.

"By that I take it you mean you don't pass moral judgment on people's private foibles."

"If they do no harm," Donovan said, growing increasingly intrigued by the drift of the conversation.

"Your position is what lots of my colleagues in the conservative movement would consider liberal."

"I've been called that, among other things," Donovan replied.

"I'll bet you have," Bennett replied. "I, however, sense that you really are profoundly old-fashioned, in the American frontier way."

"Anything goes as long as there are no bodies littering the corral," Donovan said.

Bennett smiled and, for the first time, so did Mrs. Bennett.

Lowering his voice conspiratorially, Bennett asked, "From that, may I assume that you also have no interest in *telling the press* about something private that you may have learned . . . speaking as one gentleman to another?"

Donovan thought for a moment, then nodded. "I'm from the pre-Watergate school," he said. "If I had been at those cabinet meetings that LBJ held while in the can, the press wouldn't have been tipped off by *me*."

The senator smiled again. "I had a good feeling about you. Maybe we *can* sit down one day and discuss how to improve law enforcement across this great land of ours once I'm elected."

"I would be honored," Donovan said.

"All that said, I'm going to run off to my appointment and leave you in the good hands of my beloved wife, who can speak for me on all matters. She has a story to confide."

"I think I know what it is, too," Donovan said.

Bennett's face registered surprise that changed rapidly to pleasure. "You're as good as your reputation, Captain. Tell George McCann that I said hello."

With that, the two men rose and exchanged handshakes. Then Bennett quietly accumulated an entourage that followed him off in the direction of the Mercedes limousines.

When Donovan sat back down, Valerie Bennett reached across the table and touched his hand.

"Were you in love with Rob Ingram?" Donovan asked.

"As a friend, as a very close friend, or maybe a younger brother, yes, I was," she replied, her eyes as soft as Donovan had seen outside his family.

"Were you ever lovers?"

She paused, but only briefly, before saying, "Very briefly and long ago. My husband knows about it and has forgiven me."

"I can tell that you were dear friends."

"We became that," she replied, nodding. Then, after another pause, Valerie added, "He got treatment. I should say, *I* got him into treatment, with my husband's help. There's a psychiatrist in Washington who's very good with domestic abuse . . . that is, with treating the abuser. Rob had been seeing him for two years. Ever since those terrible things happened."

"With Caren Piermatty," Donovan said.

"And with a girl named Dawn Huckins," Valerie replied.

"Did Rob ever hit *you?*"

"*Never,*" she said, sternly, in a way that suggested dire consequences if he had. "I was older than the others, and Rob didn't have the issues with me that an angry young man might have with young women."

"Where *did* the anger come from?" Donovan asked.

"Does anyone ever know?" she replied, shrugging.

"Who paid off the Huckins girl?" Donovan asked.

"It wasn't us, and we really don't know for sure that she *was* compensated," Mrs. Bennett replied.

Donovan gave her a skeptical look.

"Rob had his own money," she replied.

"And he gave her a few dollars."

"As I said, I don't know anything about that. But I imagine he wanted to atone. Atoning is part of the recovery process."

"And how was he going to *atone* to Caren?" Donovan asked.

Mrs. Bennett hesitated a beat, and her eyelashes fluttered. She said, measuring her words, "Rob wanted her to give him another chance."

"Did he think she'd go for it?"

Mrs. Bennett nodded . . . gravely, Donovan thought.

"And what did *you* think about that possibility?" he asked.

Her lashes fluttered again, and once again the words were spoken carefully. She said, "I wanted only the best for him, of course."

"But for him to show up, in the middle of a campaign in which you're counting on the support of the religious right, with a black supermodel on his arm . . ."

"My husband has many supporters in the African-American community," she said stiffly.

Donovan thought, *Who are just dying to vote for an old, white prosecutor from Alabama.* He said, "I'm sure that he does."

"You may want to believe that someone on the Bennett team killed Rob in a misguided attempt to prevent him from scuttling the campaign . . ."

"Is that a possibility?" Donovan asked.

"No," she replied firmly.

"Who in the campaign stands to benefit from his death?" Donovan asked.

"No one currently on staff," she replied, lifting her glass and using it to gesture at the table nearby, which remained well-staffed with aides despite a number having followed Bennett to the limousines. "For that matter, no one in the city. My husband has made it perfectly clear that if we didn't have Rob as campaign manager, we would have Nick Garrett, who currently and provably is in London working on a position paper about the U.S. and NATO. If you like, you can check our phone records. He called in the night of the fund-raiser to give us his best."

Donovan said that someone from his office would get the particulars and do just that.

"It's obvious that Rob left the floor where you were all staying just before he was killed," Donovan said. "But is there any way of telling if anyone else did?"

She smiled faintly. "My husband likes to think that he spares me by sleeping in another room sometimes, but in fact I hear everything. My suite is right by the exit. I heard no one leave. Except Rob, of course."

Donovan had been watching a particular eddy, one that swirled around itself for no clear reason about thirty feet out in the river. He whipped his head around.

"You heard him leave?" Donovan asked.

She nodded. "I didn't dream it. Of course, I knew . . . I *felt* he was going to."

"Why?"

"He took me aside at our gala and said, 'Someone just told me that Caren is at a party on a boat next door,' and I looked down and saw her."

"Did he say he was going to go down there?"

"No. But I knew."

Reflecting on the irony of being the "someone" who

tipped off Ingram, Donovan said, "So you heard him leave. When?"

"Four. I keep a travel clock by my bed."

"And you didn't try to stop him."

"Why? He needed to atone."

Donovan took a sip of Kaliber and looked back at the eddy. It was mostly gone, disappearing amidst the general turmoil of the East River.

"What was your first thought when you heard that Rob was killed?" Donovan asked.

Mrs. Bennett frowned, and said, "I thought . . ." She hesitated, and then a smile replaced the frown and she said, "I thought, 'She killed him.' "

As Donovan watched, Valerie Bennett stuck her index finger in her drink and stirred it, the ice slipping around her finger and the glass and making a sound that soon was drowned out by the arrival next door of a tourist helicopter.

The tide was hurtling south toward the sea and the smell of salt was in the morning air at the peculiar accident of geography known as Spuyten Duyvil. This is where the broad and steady Hudson grew a branch—the one-time creek, now shipping canal and psychologic border—that separates Manhattan from the Bronx. There a small but arrogant portion of the Hudson water turns east to become the Harlem River, which roars around the north side of Manhattan before plunging south past Yankee Stadium, feeding the East River and Long Island Sound.

Spuyten Duyvil was where it began, and that was where Donovan and Marcy stood in another four A.M. blackness, huddled against one another on a cold spring morning when the temperature lingered in the forties and their breath was a fine mist in the still air. Up high and not far away, an

Amtrak train rumbled languidly over an old iron bridge. Farther still, an IRT number 1 train was early in its slow crawl from 242nd Street, Van Cortlandt Park, down to South Ferry at the southern tip of Manhattan. The sound of traffic—large trucks bearing the day's produce to the city's markets, was likewise far-off. So too was a lone ambulance hauling a victim of the night . . . what emergency room personnel jauntily called "the knife and gun club" . . . to nearby Harlem Hospital. Donovan reflected on the irony of residents of inner-city blocks—the word "ghetto" having gone so far out of fashion as to become a museum piece—wishing treatment in suburban medical centers for their heart bypasses while savvy suburbanites clamor for airlift to innercity trauma centers when by reason of poor fortune they acquire shivs between the shoulders.

A faint splashing sound . . . more like a sprinkle, a spray of water upon water . . . heralded the arrival of a school of shiners plucking morning meals from the alga-encrusted dock. A car drove up, around a corner and out of sight, and its engine was shut off. A door opened and closed. Donovan and Marcy unwrapped from one another and watched as Mosko turned the corner and walked along the dock, bearing two bags.

"I'm starting to feel like a delivery boy," he grumbled. "Hi, Marcy."

He handed her one of the bags.

"Hi," she said back.

"I brought the usual."

"Cream cheese or butter on his?" she asked.

"In honor of your presence, cream cheese," Mosko replied. "Sorry about the doctor's report yesterday."

"Everything will be fine," she replied.

"I know that it will."

"How was traffic?" Donovan asked.

"There are four new potholes on the BQE," Mosko replied.

"Why'd you come that way?"

"I wanted to hit the Major Deegan and drive by Yankee Stadium. It's my way of reminding myself that there *is* a God."

"Did you cross yourself when you drove past?" Donovan asked.

"You bet. I crossed myself with a bialy. Hey, how come your pal Duke wanted to meet us here and not at Newtown Creek?"

"The tide is better this way."

Donovan checked his watch as red and green running lights preceded the sound of an old engine chugging desperately. Then a white searchlight swept the Harlem River from the Bronx to the Manhattan shores. In the darkness, which was much more profound at the northern tip of Manhattan than at the West Side piers, Donovan wasn't able to see the *Harbor Queen* until it was virtually atop them. Then he flashed his Maglite several times, and the chugging slowed down. Soon a deep and husky voice . . . decades of assault by tobacco, rum, diesel fuel, and the brown creosote that protected docks from decay but was no good for the lungs, having taken their toll . . . yelled, "Bill! That you?"

"No, it's Al Gore, here to inspect the water!" Donovan yelled back.

"The water's good, man," was the reply.

As the boat pulled closer and slowed to a stop, Donovan made out the face of his old friend, his face still tanned brown like an old catcher's mitt and with black eyes that narrowed in the beam from the captain's Maglite. The *Harbor Queen* squeezed up against the dock, the two old tires roped to the port side squeaking protest.

"Hop aboard," the man said, leaving the wheel and taking a few steps over to extend a hand to Marcy. "How you doing, my lady?"

"Good, thanks. Good to see you, Duke."

"It's been what, ten years . . . ?"

"Fifteen, more like."

"Since you lived aboard the *West Wind*. That was a good boat. Too bad about her."

"What happened?" Marcy asked.

"Went down in a storm off the Azores," Chapman replied. "Oh well, it happens. That's how I want to go. Lost at sea."

Joining them aboard the *Harbor Queen* and then beckoning Moskowitz to follow, Donovan said, "In your case you're gonna go down after being rammed by the Staten Island Ferry."

"This is possible," Chapman replied, going back to the wheel, spinning it to starboard, and inching the throttle forward to pull away from the dock.

"You're gonna make New York City history," Donovan said. "Say hello to Brian Moskowitz."

The two men shook hands, Chapman pausing, as did everyone who met the sergeant, to take in the size of him. Then Chapman turned back to the wheel, shaking his head and smiling, and Mosko saying, "It is what it is."

As the boat headed out of Spuyten Duyvil and into the ebbing Hudson tide and turned south, it picked up speed and soon seemed to be zooming along despite the slow chug-chugging of its engine. The lights of the George Washington Bridge loomed ahead, lace across the southern sky.

"The water is so much better now than when we were kids," Chapman said. "Thirty years ago there was so little dissolved oxygen in some places—Newtown Creek, for example, and also Kill Van Kill—that a plastic fish would die. That is the God's honest truth. Water in Newtown Creek was so bad that if you left your boat overnight you'd need a new paint job. It would take the paint right off, just leave it in gobs alongside the dock."

"It's better now," Donovan said, taking a sip of coffee as the three visitors stood near the wheel, taking in the rare view of Manhattan Island afforded by a trip in a small boat.

"They're catching lobster under the Verrazano-Narrows Bridge," Chapman said.

"And riding personal watercraft down near Battery Park City," Marcy said. "I saw a girl on a Sunfish there last year."

"Thirty years ago the water would have eaten the Sunfish," Chapman said.

"So, Bill, my friend," Chapman said. "I've given the matter of this missing harbor launch a lot of thought. For one thing, my dad used to have one just like it that he used to run around City Island in. For another, like you said, the places, to take that thing are limited. In a way, it's like the real old days . . . eighteenth . . . nineteenth—what was the century before last? This millennium thing we recently survived has got me confused."

"You're talking about the nineteenth century, I think," Donovan replied.

"Yeah, that one. The one with the Civil War in it. Anyway, in those days you were limited by the tide. If your boat only makes six knots and you got a six-knot tidal flow, you ain't goin' nowhere, and not even fast. So this tender you told me about has pretty much got to go downstream on the ebb tide and upstream on the flood tide, and for the past couple of days the flood tide has occurred during the daylight hours, for the most part."

"When the boat would be easily seen," Donovan said.

"Yeah. The guy went downstream from the *Trinidad Princess* pier. But he wouldn't have gone too far downstream, cause he wants to come back, you would think. He could have gone cross-river to Jersey, but the waterfront in Weehawken, Hoboken, and Jersey City is being developed real fast and I'm not sure where he could hide there. That leaves only a certain stretch of West Side waterfront to look at, and I came up with a few possible places where we could catch this bum. What is he, a murderer?"

"Possibly," Donovan said.

"At the very least he's a material witness," Mosko added.

"What I'm getting at, do I have to worry about this guy or can I rely on you to handle him?"

"My colleague here will rip his head off if he gets out of line," Donovan said. Then he thought for a moment, sipping coffee, and added, "Or else my wife will."

The sound of the city was gone. Out in the Hudson, Manhattan Island became a silent mural with moving parts—early commuters on the West Side Highway, jets on the LaGuardia Airport approach pattern that took them up the West Side, then to bank right over Harlem, and a lonely police helicopter headed south, over the West Side waterfront, mirroring the downstream movement of the *Harbor Queen*.

Chapman pulled the craft under the George Washington Bridge. As his passengers looked up in awe at the sliver of roadway, wires, and lights above them, Chapman pounded his fist twice on the top of the small doorway leading down to the cabin, from which a faint and yellow light reminded Donovan of the same on *Sevastopol Trader*.

"We're at the GWB, Sid," Chapman yelled.

A mostly bald man of forty years or so emerged carrying a clipboard. He wore a khaki windbreaker over a cheap white business shirt that was tucked into cotton pants that could have stood a pressing. The contrast was startling with Chapman, who looked the popular image of a tugboat captain—red flannel shirt tucked into extra-sturdy jeans held up by broad gray suspenders. He introduced the man as Sid Barman, Ph.D., the *Harbor Queen*'s water-quality expert.

The others watched as he walked to the stern of the boat, now idling and drifting sideways with the tide, and took water samples.

"He's testing for dissolved oxygen, fecal coliform, chlorophyll, plankton concentrations, light transparency, and nutrients like phosphorus," Chapman said. "Dissolved oxygen is the big indicator. It tells if the fish can breathe or not."

"Can they?" Mosko asked.

"Better and better. The environmental protection laws are working. Thirty years ago you had all these venal sons of bitches dumping waste into the harbor. Now we catch 'em and put 'em in jail."

"In jail?" Donovan asked.

"Well, maybe not. But we hit 'em with big fines."

"What would you think of someone who dumped perc into the harbor?" Donovan asked.

"I'd say I'd like to get my hands on the venal son of a bitch," Chapman replied. "Who is it?"

"Maybe the *Trinidad Princess*," Donovan said.

"That tub? Who says she's dumping waste?"

"Dennis Yeager and Peter Lachaise."

"Who are they?" Chapman asked.

Donovan gave Chapman a quick rundown on the cast of characters, after which the man replied, "I don't know

Lachaise, who you say is the one we're after today. I don't know Yeager by name, but naturally I've seen his ship around. Around here, around there. He's not the first skipper with an exotic-looking old boat to hop around from dock to dock, staying in any one place just long enough to wear out his welcome. I guess he's doing no harm, and if he's really out to nail the *Trinidad Princess* for dumping waste, he's doing some good. Good luck to him."

Donovan and the others watched as the technologist lowered instruments into the water, pulled them back up, peered at them, poured a sample of water into a test tube before putting it into a rack, and made notes. Then he packed up his gear and said, "Okay," as he disappeared back down below to his coffee, sticky bun, and copy of the *Daily News*.

"We got one more testing site," Chapman announced.

"Where's that?" Donovan asked.

"Off the North River Water Treatment Plant. After that, we're cool all the way down to Chelsea Pier. That'll give us plenty of time to check out something I noticed yesterday."

"Such as?" Mosko asked.

"You'll see."

Chapman throttled up and turned the bow of the *Harbor Queen* downtown. They chugged out from under the bridge, past the little red lighthouse of children's literature fame, that stood bravely below the Manhattan side of the bridge. Then the boat entered a prolonged stretch of river that took them along Washington Heights, West Harlem, and the Upper West Side, with the one stop Chapman made outside the pollution plant.

The Donovans and Moskowitz sat on the starboard gunwale, watched the city slip by, and ate breakfast. After finishing his bagel, Donovan turned to his colleague and said,

"The volume of the silence coming from you on the subject of Caren Piermatty is deafening."

"What can I say? I don't meet that many celebrities. She's the biggest star I've met since running into Andrew Dice Clay at the Jack LaLanne in Sheepshead Bay."

Marcy grimaced, then asked, "Did you get her autograph?"

Smiling, Mosko opened his jacket and lifted the bottom of a T-shirt that read CANARSIE SOFTBALL.

Emblazoned across the sergeant's bulging pectorals, written large in black Magic Marker, was Caren Piermatty's autograph.

Donovan smiled.

"What does your wife think of that?" Marcy asked.

"I haven't gotten around to showing her," Mosko replied, lowering the shirt. "I need to show the guys at work and at the gym first."

"Then your wife," Marcy replied. "Then the undertaker."

"Did she show you the bathing suit?" Donovan asked.

Mosko blushed, and said, "She was going to, but propriety and my concern for my career got in the way. Look, I got the dress and had a forensics courier pick it up and take it to the lab. There were no bloodstains. No nothing, except for some Cascini perfume, some random cosmetics, and a splash of scotch."

"From Ingram," Donovan said.

"Yeah."

"What did she say about her past with Ingram?" Donovan asked.

"When confronted, she owned up to it and confirmed what McCann said. She met Ingram two years ago. Had an affair with him. It turned nasty. He beat her up when she wouldn't do exactly what he wanted when he wanted. But in her account she gave almost as good as she got."

"Except that Ingram didn't wind up in the hospital," Donovan said.

"Actually, he did go to the ER, only a different one from her. She brained him with a frying pan . . . okay, it was a light, Teflon-coated frying pan; this ain't like the old days I keep hearing about when women hit their husbands with cast-iron cookware. She says he had to get seven stitches to close the wound, and that if we check we'll find press reports about how Ingram had to get stitches after 'falling down while jogging.' "

"Which explains why Caren didn't tell us she knew him before the night of the party," Donovan said.

"So doing would involve admitting not only that she had motive for murder, but that she has a history of bloodying him up," Marcy said.

Donovan filled Mosko in on his conversation with Valerie Bennett. "So Caren *could have* asked Ingram, 'How did you get away from Ree?' when he poked his head up on top of the ladder to the cabin roof," Donovan said.

Mosko said, "If Ingram went through asshole rehab, then . . ."

"What did you say?" Marcy laughed.

Mosko shrugged. "Ingram was an asshole. He got rehab. And *that* makes him a recovering asshole."

"And from your lifetime in Brooklyn, you can tell us with absolute certainty that there ain't no such thing," Donovan said.

"Some conditions are harder to cure than others," Mosko replied.

Donovan pondered for a moment while his wife was chuckling, and then said, "Despite the fact I like Caren Pier-matty—"

Marcy stopped chuckling.

"—because she's a friend of my wife," he said hurriedly, "her value as a suspect is on the increase."

"Now that you mention it, we finally tracked down the doorman who was on duty at Caren's building the time of the murder. A guy named John Walsdorf."

"Good name for someone in the accommodations in-dustry. And?" Donovan asked.

"And he doesn't remember her coming home at *all* that night."

"Really!"

"Now, this would have been hardly the first time the lady stayed out all night, and I think you know that. So he wasn't exactly *looking* for her. And, I got to be honest, the man left the door . . . locked, of course . . . for ten minutes to go to the bathroom. This would have been half past four or thereabouts. She could have let herself in then. I knew this before I went to see her, and so I put the ques-tion to her. And Caren said, 'There was no doorman on duty when I got home. Frank must have been taking a leak.' Frank is the doorman, you see."

"So we only have Veronica's word for it that Caren got home around four-thirty," Donovan said.

"We're looking for the cab driver, but I wouldn't hold my breath," Mosko said. "And since Caren said she didn't make any calls that night, checking phone records will do no good."

"Two women, both of whom had motive to kill Rob Ingram, are alibiing one another," Donovan said.

"That's about the size of it," Mosko said.

"We have a murder between four and four-thirty," Marcy said. "If we believe everyone's stories." She began counting on her fingers. "Dennis went to his cabin a little before four and fell asleep a little after. Veronica and Caren stayed until, what would you say, four-fifteen?"

"Or four-twenty," Donovan said. "That's allowing time for Ingram to slip out with the shift workers and go over to *Sevastopol Trader* and get killed. His charade of using the shift change as cover was a charade that turned out to be unnecessary. Valerie Bennett says she heard him leave."

Marcy continued, "Veronica and Caren left at four-fifteen, four-twenty, and are each other's alibis. Who else?"

"Harley Greave, sleeping alone on the cabin roof, or pretending to," Donovan said.

"Pretending to?" she asked.

"Veronica left him alone up there to go visit the vegan roast beef," Donovan said. "He could have slipped down below, killed Ingram, and run back up before she returned."

"Who *is* that guy?" Marcy asked.

Mosko said, "His prints . . . the ones we presume to be his, anyway . . . are all over that room at Manhattan Boardroom Suites *and* on George McCann's business card. But they aren't on file with any law enforcement agencies that we queried."

"And who was that?" Donovan asked.

"FBI and Interpol."

"Check southern states, specifically Virginia and West Virginia."

"They would have turned up in the FBI search request," Mosko objected.

"Sometimes you get more when you ask individual states," Donovan replied.

"Why Virginia and West Virginia? Because the hotel guy said he thought that Greave had a Southern accent?"

"Yeah, and because I have a feeling," Donovan said.

"Oh, you have a feeling?"

"That's right," the captain replied firmly.

"Well, we ran down a couple of phone calls Greave made from his room in Manhattan Boardroom Suites. One was made the morning after the murder to a pay phone at a gas station in Hemlaw, West Virginia. So hugs and kisses to your feeling. The other call was to a number in . . . get this . . . the *Trinidad Princess.*"

"Interesting. And we can't find out who aboard the *Trinidad Princess* took the call."

"Not a chance."

"Were there any prints on the money?"

"Other than the Manhattan Boardroom Suites employees and Greave, we got a couple of smudges and one partial . . . hey, are you ready for this?"

Donovan frowned, thought a second, then said, "There are a couple of weird possibilities I could think of, but . . . nah, no way. Tell me."

"Rob Ingram," Mosko said, accenting the remark with a Cheshire cat grin.

"That was one of the weird possibilities," Donovan said.

"Wait a minute," Marcy said. "Ingram *paid* the man who may have killed him?"

"Nobody said that Greave killed Ingram," Mosko replied. Then to Donovan, he said, "Who was the other weird possibility you were thinking of just then?"

"Cal Sforza, the *Trinidad Princess* chief engineer who the lawyers . . . Ingram's lawyers, for that matter . . . won't let us talk to."

"This is very strange," Marcy said. "Here's this gorgeous

young guy, who said he was a model and looked for all the world like that's what he was. Okay, so he's new in town and doesn't know how to play the game."

"The game," Mosko said.

"Yes, the game. You meet Veronica Cascini, you send her your portfolio. You get asked to a party she throws, you try to stay awake. You make interesting conversation."

"If you can't pull *that* off," Donovan said, "you stand around posing like James Dean or the young Brando."

"Right, you pretend you're too beautiful to worry about civility. You do *something*," Marcy said. "You don't lump around like a nerd and fall asleep. Now we find out that this guy, this . . ."

"Lumpen nerd," Donovan added.

"Was being paid by Ingram and made calls to the *Trinidad Princess*, possibly to Sforza. Who *was* he?"

"A spy," Donovan said.

"Sent by Ingram to find out what Dennis and Lachaise knew," Marcy replied.

"And possibly to steal or destroy the evidence," Donovan replied.

"So he *could have* faked being asleep and then run below," Mosko said.

"But why then kill Ingram, who was paying him?" Marcy asked.

Donovan said, "We have to find Greave. And also Lachaise."

"Who left the party when?" Marcy asked.

"Around one, if Dennis's story is correct."

"So he was long gone by the time of the murder," Mosko said.

"People have feet," Donovan said, adding a shrug.

"Meaning that he could walk back," Marcy replied.

"Or take a bus or a cab. Or take a subway."

"I think somebody would have noticed him, with the beard and all," Mosko replied. "Dennis didn't get back to his cabin until just before four, and he was sober enough to turn out the wheelhouse light. Dennis would have noticed Lachaise returning, and he didn't."

"We have to get our hands on Lachaise," Donovan said.

15. "HE DOESN'T EAT IN THE NORMAL SENSE, HE SUCKS BLOOD."

"We got a response from the French," Mosko said. "They know who Lachaise is."

"I presume not an undercover operative for the Surete," Donovan said.

Mosko shook his head. "They said he's a Yank who they never heard of before 1970, when he turned up in Paris with a guitar and a hippie girlfriend. The year after, he surfaced as a minor figure in the protests against French nuclear testing in the South Pacific. They said he was a follower then, never a leader, but then split off and became an environmental activist with Greenpeace. Then he left Greenpeace and the French kind of lost track of him."

"What's their general assessment of him?" Donovan asked.

"They don't regard him as any big deal," Mosko replied. "He's small potatoes."

"At least they heard of him," Marcy said. "Unlike Greave, who we can't even find."

"I'm working on a couple of things," Mosko replied.

"Is one of them the matter of the Chinese food?" Donovan asked.

"Yeah. There were prints on the soy sauce packet, and they belong to a homeless guy by the name of Charlie Hickey."

"I don't know the name," Donovan said.

"He's in the homeless shelter database," Mosko said.

"Which says?"

"Five foot eight, about seventy-eight years old, gray-and-brown hair but not much of it, been in the homeless system . . . I should say, in and out of it . . . for thirty years. And they had a notation I don't understand. They called him 'category ED.' Do you know what that means?"

"Emotionally disturbed," Donovan replied. "This guy could be Chops. Is he in the criminal files?"

"Yeah," Mosko replied proudly. "Arrested in 1978 for breaking into a boat at the Seventy-ninth Street Boat Basin. Arrested in 1982 for breaking into a boat at South Street Seaport. There were four other arrests for the same thing, all over the waterfront."

"That's him," Donovan said. "So Chops bought the Chinese food I found in the *Sevastopol Trader*'s storage room. Did the restaurant . . . ?"

"Remember selling it to him? The guys who went on the graveyard shift there at midnight remember that a man who resembled Hickey came in around four-thirty or five and bought Chicken Chow Fun. Paid for it with change, too."

"Which is why they remembered," Donovan said.

"They said he looked homeless," Mosko added.

"So Chops bought Chinese food right about the time of the murder, slipped aboard *Sevastopol Trader* when? Where's the restaurant?"

"Fifty-first and Tenth."

"A ten-minute walk for a homeless old man, shuffling along. He gets on board, Christ, it must have been right after the murder. Goes below, following the light from that little bulb."

"How's he get to the storage room without seeing the body?" Marcy asked.

"Who says he didn't notice? Maybe he thought the corpse was a casualty of the Nazis storming ashore and went back into that room to hide. Anyway, a guy like Chops, adept at sneaking aboard boats and hanging out, would have gone down the port gangway, which is hidden from sight. And you can get from the base of it to the storage room without going onto the dance floor."

"Do you think Dennis knew about him?" Marcy asked.

"I'm sure of it," Donovan said. "What puzzles me is why Dennis lied and told me that Lachaise was the Chinese-food lover."

"We've got to find Lachaise," Mosko said.

The *Harbor Queen* continued downstream paralleling Riverside Drive, past the Soldiers and Sailors Monument, which was across the street from the Donovan residence, and past the Seventy-ninth Street Boat Basin, where Donovan and Marcy met Yeager a decade earlier. Then they chugged past the new Trump tower emerging from the iron and oil of the old West Side railroad yards, and finally moved along past the stern of the *Trinidad Princess*.

Seen from the water, the cruise ship and *Sevastopol Trader* looked like ships in a painting—stark and two-dimensional and devoid of life. In particular, *Sevastopol Trader* was quiet as a graveyard . . . except for the wheelhouse light, which burned brightly despite the proximity to five A.M. Donovan watched that light, and thought of what Veronica Cascini told him of seeing the *Harbor Queen* chug by, until Chapman had steered the survey vessel under the stern of the *Intrepid* and beyond the Circle Line pier.

After a time and following passage alongside a decrepit stretch of waterfront, Chapman said, "I got my eyes on this old gravel loader over here."

He pointed at a dark and ominous-looking stretch of waterfront that, to the untrained eye, appeared to be no more than a collection of black and rotting poles sticking out of sullen water.

"In *there?*" Mosko asked.

"That's the place," Chapman replied.

"Isn't that where the *Hesperus* was wrecked?"

"Could be." With that, he turned toward those poles and pulled back on the throttle until the *Harbor Queen* was barely making headway and eased the boat through an opening that Donovan could only see at the last moment. Within seconds, the *Harbor Queen* had slid into a coal-black industrial cove made decades earlier when two adjacent piers crumbled, the outer end of one falling inward toward the other. The result was a kind of lagoon between two piers that were far too collapsed to walk on, unlike the many others along the waterfront that neighborhood folks had turned into sunbathing and picnicking spots.

On the shore at the base of this rickety and rotted hiding spot was a three-story iron lattice surrounding a gigantic hopper—a funnel that once held gravel prior to its dispense through a narrow opening designed to fit the backs of dump trucks. On the second-story level was an old operator's shack reachable by means of a treacherous iron ladder. The walls of the shack were made of corrugated iron, the parts of which not covered with graffiti having long since rusted through. Where a door once stood someone had hung a clean sheet, newly purchased, Donovan imagined, at one of the discount shops along Fourteenth Street. The design showed lilacs printed so vividly that Donovan could nearly smell them. The entire edifice, and its piers, was cut off from foot or motor traffic by a ten-foot chain-link fence topped with barbed wire.

"This is the old West Side gravel dock," Chapman said. "Up through the end of the second World War, barges would bring gravel downriver from upstate quarries and offload them here. The gravel was stored in the hopper until trucks backed in off the street and hauled it off. A lot of the gravel that came through here went into road construction throughout the five boroughs. A lot of it also went into pothole repair."

"More is needed on the BQE," Mosko said.

Chapman cut the engine and let the *Harbor Queen* glide through the surface muck and half-floating plastic bottles toward a spot, at the base of the hopper, where someone had covered a small boat with a brown tarpaulin. Donovan went forward, getting handholds and walking sideways along the six-inch-wide space between the cabin and the gunwale as Marcy said, "Be careful."

He stood on the bow holding the bowline in his hands and his Maglite in his teeth. When they were close enough, he shined the light on one end of the tarpaulin and then felt around it. At the bottom, between the fabric and the water, was a hull painted white on the sides and, on the bottom, painted with red lead paint to discourage barnacles.

"Is that it?" Chapman called.

"Considering that someone is trying to hide it, yes," Donovan replied.

He climbed up on the dock and tossed a couple of half-hitches around a mooring post to tie the *Harbor Queen* to the dock. Then he hurried back to the stern of the boat to catch a stern line tossed by Chapman. That, too, Donovan tied off.

"Let's go," he said as Mosko and Marcy clambered up onto the dock to join him.

Noise from the West Side heliport a short distance away masked the noise they were making. But then one of those choppers sounded closer and lower, moving parallel to the water, and then it suddenly appeared in the moonlight, hovering above the lagoon.

"Want some light?" Mosko asked.

"As much as I can get," Donovan replied.

"You got it." The sergeant spoke into his cell phone, and within two or three seconds a sun appeared in the sky and the area of the gravel loader was lit brighter than ten daylights. Simultaneously, an amplified voice boomed, "Police! Come out slowly with your hands up!"

The lilac-pattern sheet suddenly burst outward and a startled, panicky Lachaise tried to block the light with one hand while pulling on his pants with the other. Then he half slid, half fell down the ladder and looked around in desperation for somewhere to hide.

"Police officers! Hold it right there!" Donovan yelled, reaching for his Smith & Wesson.

Lachaise spun around, looking for a way out, but seeing only Brian Moskowitz's fifty-inch chest and hearing him bark, "Wise up!"

So Lachaise lowered his head and ran toward the woman who faced him. As Donovan took his hand off his pistol, he saw her take up a defensive posture—the "swan eating a frog," or maybe it was the "snake staring at a lotus blossom"—Donovan couldn't tell one form of martial art from another, especially the ones with colorful expressions. Then

Donovan heard two smacks, one from a hand and another from a foot, and Lachaise was laying on his back gasping for breath.

Donovan walked up to the man, bent over him, and said, "I see you've met my wife."

Bonaci's forensics van was parked outside the section of chain-link fence that Donovan had just ordered torn down. Half a dozen other official vehicles were parked around, some of them blue-and-white with flashing lights and crackling radios, the rest the large and nondescript four-door sedans favored by detectives. The helicopter and its artificial sun were long gone; light came from several portable lights set up by the forensics team that now pored over Lachaise's hideaway.

The man himself sat on the broad bumper at the back of an EMS van, while a paramedic gave a few final pats to a gauze pad taped to the side of his head. He moaned lightly as Donovan said, "Now that you're able to talk, tell me why you ran."

"I thought you were him," Lachaise said, betraying a very slight French accent.

"Who him?" Donovan asked. "Sforza?"

Lachaise looked at the captain with amazed eyes. "You know him?"

"No, but I plan to make his acquaintance. He's threatened you?"

"God, he's threatened me all over the hemisphere. In Kingston, Jamaica, he beat me up. I'm afraid for my life. In Jamaica he told me he would kill me if he ever caught me spying on the *Trinidad Princess* again."

"Then why did you do it?" Mosko asked. "Pardon me for being blunt, pal, but you ain't no Bruce Lee."

"Someone has to save the planet," Lachaise replied.

"Why you?" the sergeant asked.

"I'm atoning."

"There's a lot of that going around," Donovan said. "What for?"

"I wasted the first part of my life singing in a rock band," Lachaise said.

"Is there a twelve-step program for that?" Donovan asked.

"Just killing off the old you and starting over."

"Where were you when the old you died?" Donovan asked idly.

"Paris," Lachaise replied.

"That's a good place for it," Marcy added.

"And I decided to spend the rest of my life doing something worthwhile."

"I think I get it," Donovan said. "You're one of those guys who climbs a redwood tree and sits there for two years to prevent loggers from cutting it down."

"Why are you making fun of me?" Lachaise said, sitting up.

"I'm not making fun," Donovan said.

"Yes you are," Lachaise insisted.

"I'm just wondering about the efficacy level. Personally, I would bring a truckload of manure to the stockholders' meeting, and then . . ."

"William," Marcy said.

"Yeah, that's the sort of thing I would do, except that the company that owns the *Trinidad Princess* isn't publicly owned," Lachaise said.

"Rob Ingram is one of the owners," Mosko said.

"I *know* that," Lachaise said. "I thought that if I got evidence that his company was dumping toxic waste into the sea, and confronted him with it during the election campaign . . ."

"You could get him to stop," Donovan said.

"Do you know how *easy* it is to put perc into a holding tank and dispose of it safely in port?" Lachaise said. "Do you know how *cheap* and *arrogant* you have to be . . ."

"Sounds like Ingram to me," Donovan added.

". . . to dump it at sea? Or in New York Harbor? Ingram was almost begging to be stopped . . ."

"I detect some of that, too."

". . . coming into New York City, a renowned hotbed of activism, and unnecessarily dumping toxic waste into the water?" Lachaise concluded.

"Were you willing to kill him to stop him?" Mosko asked.

"Are you kidding? Who needed to? All I needed was to lay a copy of a lab report on the *New York Times*."

"And stay alive long enough to do so," Donovan said. "Okay, Mr. Lachaise, I have to ask this—where were you between four and five in the morning on the day that Ingram was killed?"

"I was here," Lachaise said. "I mean, up *there*." He pointed at his second-story hideaway, now crawling with technicians.

"Was anyone with you?"

"Oh yeah, I get a lot of dates. No, I was alone. No one to vouch for my alibi."

Lachaise stuck his hands out to be cuffed.

Donovan patted the man on the shoulder and said, "Not today, my friend. Tell me one thing, when were you last in that little utility room on *Sevastopol Trader*? The one where Dennis keeps his lab stuff?"

"Uhm, the day before the party. We were running a promising sample."

"And?"

"It didn't test out. We need another good one."

"And you *didn't* eat Chicken Chow Fun, right?"

"I wouldn't be caught dead eating animal flesh," Lachaise replied.

Donovan nodded, smiling faintly. Then his look turned serious again, and he said, "The need to take a water sample the night of the party is what you and Dennis were arguing about on the catwalk, isn't it?" Donovan said.

"Yeah. I was sure we could get the sample we needed to nail the *Trinidad Princess* that night. I was really pissed when he chased me off. I mean, we wasted a night just so he could ring the cash register."

"Where did you go after the argument?"

"I don't know," Lachaise said, patting his bandage. "I walked around, across the dance floor. I listened to the band for a while."

"Did you like them?"

"Yeah. They're better than *my* band was. Then I went topside, grabbed some food, and went home."

"Did you have *any* Chinese food, such as steamed vegetables?" Donovan asked. "The caterer put some out."

"Me, eat processed food? You must be joking. I'm a vegan."

"Did you have the vegan roast beef?" Marcy asked.

"Yes," Lachaise said excitedly. "It was *wonderful!*"

"Who in Dennis's life eats Chinese food?" Donovan asked.

"You do, honey," Marcy said.

"Other than me."

"No one. He hates it, too," Lachaise said. "Why do you ask?"

"Do you know Michael Avignon?" Donovan asked.

"I don't think so. Who is he? Does *he* eat Chinese?"

"A photographer. Videographer. And he doesn't eat in the normal sense; he sucks blood."

Marcy looked at her husband and offered a smile that said *You're a bad boy, but I love you.*

"Avignon was on *Sevastopol Trader* taping the rock band," Donovan continued. "He was making their video."

"I didn't notice him," Lachaise said. "But then, on nights when I took samples I didn't stick around afterwards. I got them, ran a quick test, and left. I didn't go there to socialize."

"Ever see anyone else there, beyond Dennis?"

Lachaise shook his head.

Donovan pondered for a moment, then said, "I need you to do something for me."

"What?"

"Test the water outside *Trinidad Princess*. Take samples. Tomorrow morning, at the usual time. When Sforza will expect it and be watching."

"He said he would *kill* us," Lachaise said.

"Oh, I wouldn't worry about it," Donovan said. "I'll be there. And so will my colleague here and my wife."

"She's your *wife?*" Lachaise looked at Marcy suspiciously, trying to match up the slender body with the pain it caused him.

"Absolutely, in many ways—at least one of which you can vouch for—my better half. Hey, we'll have a little party, during which Dennis and you can take water samples."

"You want to have a party," Lachaise said.

"Some of the best ones in the world happen aboard *Sevastopol Trader*," Donovan replied.

A familiar voice from high above caught Donovan's attention. Bonaci yelled, "Hey, Cap!" until he looked up.

"What?" Donovan yelled back.

"I'm not using the cell phone? Proud of me?"

"Yeah. If I were king I'd knight you. Whaddya got?"

"Nothing. Nothing of interest."

"Fine," Donovan replied.

"We found the tube of Fixodent he bought at Rite Aid," Bonaci added.

Lachaise turned to Donovan and said, sheepishly, "I didn't take such good care of myself in the old days."

"You be sure to take good care of yourself from here on," Donovan added.

Marcy snaked a hand around her husband's neck, pulled him slightly in her direction, and gave him a kiss on the cheek. She said, "If *all of you* think you can take care of yourselves from here on in, I'm going to take off."

"It'll be a hump, but we'll manage," Mosko replied, a muscle or two flexing, perhaps subconsciously, in response.

"Where are you going?" Donovan asked.

"Home to make breakfast for Daniel. Then we have an early appointment."

"Where?"

"The neurologist I mentioned at Mount Sinai."

"I thought he didn't have any appointments until October."

"Baksheesh," she replied, using the Arabic term for "bribe."

"With a doctor?"

"I promised cash up front. Considering the way that managed care pays, their eyes light up."

"Whatever gets you in the door," Donovan said.

He kissed her back and hugged her, then walked her to the squad car assigned to take her home.

When Donovan got back to the ambulance, Lachaise said, "Can I go now?"

The man stood and tried to brush off his pants. An assortment of dockside debris had adhered to the back of his pants and sweatshirt, left there when Marcy tossed him.

"Go where?" Donovan asked.

"Home."

"To *this*?" Mosko asked, nodding up in the direction of Lachaise's second-story squatter shack.

"This is home these days," Lachaise added.

"Why here?" Donovan asked.

"For the same reason as for my activism. My father was a Navy man—I love the sea."

"No hotel for you, eh?"

"At New York prices?"

"Sensible man. As soon as my men are done they'll put the fence back up and life will return to normal. See you tomorrow morning," Donovan said. "Someone will call on you with arrangements."

After spending a minute or two overseeing minutia of the on-site investigation, the two men got into the back of a patrol car. The uniformed policewoman that held the door for the captain scrambled behind the wheel and said, "Where to, sir?"

"One Police Plaza," Mosko replied.

But Donovan held up a hand and said, "No. We're going to Pier 83. Take us to the dock just upriver from the *Intrepid*."

"What for?" Mosko asked, pronouncing the words "whaffo?"

"I got a suspicion there's a regular kind of champagne breakfast thing going on aboard *Sevastopol Trader*."

Mosko asked what he was talking about.

Donovan declined to answer, but said, "If I'm wrong you can call me a jerk and tell all the guys and girls about it. Let's go."

"Do I have to buy bagels this morning?" Mosko asked, a bit irritated by the prospect.

"Not this time, my friend. If I'm right, we'll be having Chinese."

Mosko grimaced. "Chinese food is only good for breakfast when you're having it cold after spending an incredible night with a babe and sitting there with your fried rice and trying to remember her name. It's like cold pizza in that regard. Can we stop and get American food?"

"Whaddya have in mind?" Donovan asked.

"Bacon, egg, and cheese on a roll with coffee," Mosko replied.

"You're on," Donovan said. Then, addressing the driver, said, "Officer . . . what's your name?"

"Joan Maddocks, sir."

"Do you know a place?"

"I know a thousand," the young woman replied.

"I'm buying," Donovan replied.

She drove them to a nook with a grill on Twenty-sixth Street in the wholesale flower district, where they got breakfast and ate it while driving uptown in the dawn glow. While it may have been above the horizon off to the east, over flat-as-a-tabletop Long Island, the sun was no more than a suggestion on the West Side waterfront, sheltered by the Manhattan skyline. The first hints of the morning rush were driving down West Street at the customary fury. Donovan called it "the Manhattan Grand Prix." Liberated from the congested, double- and triple-parked side streets, drivers went like blazes along the roads that girdled the island. That is, of course, when they found them open.

"First take us to the corner of Fifty-first and Tenth," Donovan said. "I want to check something."

Officer Maddocks drove over to and up Tenth Avenue through the early-morning haze and calm. The streets remained deserted, save for cabs, garbage trucks, and the occasional wanderer. The trucks belonged to private trash haulers and were creeping along the mostly industrial and retail avenue, picking up the previous day's leavings and making enough of a racket to ensure that anyone living nearby would have a sleep experience akin to that of country folk who live along railroad rights-of-way.

Mosko took his laptop out of his shoulder bag and used the cellular modem to log onto the Special Investigations e-mail system. Soon he was perusing the night's messages while Donovan watched. The captain never ceased being amused by the sight of his immense, muscle-bound colleague pecking away at the tiny keyboard. Mosko perused the inbox expressionlessly, then smiled and said, "I think I'm beginning to understand the Chinese food thing."

"What came in?" Donovan asked.

"We turned up your pal Yeager's birth certificate. It was on file just like you said. He was born in Fort Lauderdale."

"What was his birth name?"

"Hickey. Dennis Hickey. I guess in light of all we know that makes him Chops's son."

Donovan nodded. "Dennis must have taken his stepfather's surname."

"Yeager."

"This explains all the dock-hopping Dennis has been doing. The *Sevastopol Trader* isn't being thrown off docks. Dennis is moving it to keep an eye on his emotionally disturbed old man, who is sleeping on subway grates and in cardboard boxes all around the waterfront, keeping watch for the moment the Nazis storm ashore."

"Why didn't Yeager just *tell us* this?" Mosko asked.

"Tell us that his crazy old man, who has a police record, by the way, may have been aboard at the time of the murder?"

"Oh," Mosko replied.

"Tell us that he may have *witnessed* the crime? Or that he may even *be* the killer?"

"Gotcha."

"If Chops isn't the killer," Donovan continued, "then it's our job to protect him from the killer."

Mosko's eyes narrowed and he began to get a hard look. "I have the feeling he already has a guardian angel," Mosko said. "Or maybe you wouldn't use the word 'angel.' "

"I got a bad feeling about what you're leading up to," Donovan said.

"Remember that yellow plastic strip you found in the storage room? We got prints off it."

"Avignon," Donovan said.

"That's it. A clean thumbprint. What *is* that yellow plastic?"

"The tear-off safety strip from a cassette of high-end videotape. I have some of it at home. Great color and resolution."

"We'll book you to do the commercial," Mosko said.

"It's very expensive, though."

"Ah, who cares? You got the money."

"You know what this means, don't you?" Donovan asked. "Avignon lied when he said he was never in that room. He told us that the night of the murder he took a cab home. That was true as far as it goes, but he didn't mention leaving the gigantic, impossible-to-hide video camera at his apartment, picking up the miniature one, and going back to the ship."

"How did he do that?" Mosko asked.

"Subway."

"It will be hard to prove that."

"I think I know a way," Donovan said. "Is that all that came in tonight?"

"So far," Mosko replied.

"Did you ever get a response on your query to the police in West Virginia?"

Mosko perused the inbox again, then said, "No."

"Did you try the local cops in Hemlaw, West Virginia? Where Greave made a call to the gas station?"

"We're still trying to get through," Mosko replied.

"Keep trying," Donovan said, looking out the window as the police car pulled to the curb in front of the Famous Wing Lee Takeout Chinese Restaurant, We Never Close, a tiny storefront with a flyspecked window decorated, of sorts, with a handful of color blowups of featured entrees—Moo Goo Gai Pan, Mu Shu Pork, General Tso's Chicken, and Happy Family. Close to a dozen old black Schwinn delivery bikes were chained to the steel posts supporting, among other things, signs detailing the stultifyingly complex and often contradictory parking restrictions on that side of the block.

"Anyone want anything?" Mosko asked as he opened the car door.

"Not a chance," Donovan said.

The patrolwoman shook her head.

Mosko ducked inside the restaurant. Donovan watched through the window as the sergeant carried on what seemed to be complex negotiations with the man in charge at that hour, a skinny fellow with a comb-over and an athletic undershirt worn with corduroy pants. Every so often, the man gestured wildly at the kitchen help, who were hidden from Donovan's sight. After five minutes or so, Mosko emerged carrying a gigantic portion of something or other. When he climbed back into the car, Donovan said, "You're hungry *again?*"

"This isn't for me," the sergeant answered. "This is for Chops. He was in here two hours ago. Wanted chop suey and counted out the change but fell short. So he had to settle for a couple of egg rolls."

"Sad," Donovan replied.

"So I bought him a quart. You'll know where to find him."

"I know where to find the three of them," Donovan said.

16. "FIFTY THOUSAND DOLLARS FOR A PROFESSIONAL CAMERA, AND HE THINKS IT'S A MISSILE LAUNCHER."

With Mosko trailing behind and scrutinizing the shadows for anything foolish enough to threaten, Donovan walked quietly across the foredeck of the *Sevastopol Trader*. He turned aft at the port rail and, quieter still, crept to the entrance of the passageway. He peered below and saw the glow from the bulb in the storage room. It was sufficient to let him descend the steps cautiously, feeling his way along the rough surface of the neither restored nor adorned wall.

Halfway down he heard voices; two men, at least two

men, were in the small room. They were talking in the tones that men use when completely at ease, comfortable in the kind of way one finds among a family having breakfast. A few steps lower and Donovan heard the words "Yanks" and "pennant," words that in New York City signaled comfort and tradition the way "mom" and "apple pie" were said to have done at some distant, Norman Rockwell–period of middle American history.

Mosko took out his Penzler 9mm automatic and held it by his side. But then Donovan raised a hand to suggest that it wouldn't be necessary.

The captain walked silently to the storage room door— this time doing so without knocking over the old ash tray stand. He peeked around the doorjamb to see inside. Hidden by the darkness and the preoccupation of those inside the room, Donovan watched as the wharf rat he recalled from years ago in the then-abandoned train tunnel under River-side Park sat at the card table, working on a *Daily News* crossword puzzle with his son Dennis. Or he was *looking at* it, for the elder seemed to be most engaged rocking back and forth in his chair and mumbling half-words or words that Donovan couldn't quite catch. In one corner, sitting on the floor to get the oblique perspective favored by directors of avant-garde documentaries, was Michael Avignon. He was taping the father and son, using a small video camera much like the one that Donovan got from his father-in-law for Christmas, the better to record Daniel's awaited first steps.

After watching for a moment, Donovan stepped into the room, clearing his throat and saying, "Hickey and son and their pet snake! Hiya, boys."

Dennis looked over, startled but, Donovan thought, a little pleased. But Chops had a very different reaction. Shrieking like the number 1 IRT entering the South Ferry

Station, he leaped to his feet, overturning the table and hurling himself backward to the safety of the far wall. He had a large screwdriver and held it like a dagger, up high and ominous, to protect himself, and in the corner of his eye Donovan saw the muzzle of Mosko's automatic. "That won't be necessary," Donovan said, moving into the room and holding up a hand.

"I come in peace for all mankind," he added. "However, that bit with the screwdriver won't look too good in court if we go that far."

Dennis spun around and went to his father and calmed him with a combination of hugs and words. The detectives who had just burst into their lives were friends, he said. As he did so, Donovan went over to where Avignon sat in the corner, still taping. Donovan grabbed the man by the shirtfront and pulled him to his feet while Mosko relieved him of his camera and set the table back up.

"Strike two, asshole," Donovan swore.

"Whaddya mean?" the man stammered, though Donovan felt sure he knew quite well.

"Three felonies and you're up the river forever. You're two-thirds of the way there."

"Me? I . . ."

"You're under arrest. You have the right to remain silent. You have the right to be represented by an attorney. If you so desire and can't afford one, an inept shyster will be provided on the public's dime."

Donovan turned the man around, pushed him against the wall, and searched him for weapons.

"What did I do?"

"Same as some of the things we got you on last time. Impeding a police investigation, lying to investigators . . ."

"Being a pain in the ass," Mosko added.

"Empty your pockets on the table," Donovan commanded.

Maybe Avignon got the message that things were getting serious. He complied quickly, dumping onto the card table the content of all pockets. Then Mosko grabbed Avignon's hands, pulled them behind him, and clicked on the cuffs.

"Hey!" Avignon protested.

"What's the matter?" Donovan said. "You think I'm just saying this?"

He went through the contents of the man's pockets. Not so different from last time, Avignon's pockets contained a wallet with $21, a few dollars' worth of nickels, dimes, and quarters, and a well-worn MetroCard.

"What do you want with my stuff?"

"Just this," Donovan replied, picking up the MetroCard by the edges and dropping it into a evidence bag.

"My card!"

"You won't be needing it. Brian, would you call for a patrol car to come pick up this jerk?"

"I . . ."

"Sit down and shut up," Donovan said, shoving him down into a chair. "I have some things to say before we haul you off."

Chops had calmed down. Dennis convinced the confused old man that the two detectives were not, as he feared, the vanguard of an invading force. In fact, the elder Hickey had begun to stare at Donovan, the genesis of a memory in his wary eyes.

"I've seen you," he said.

"Long ago but not so far away," Donovan replied.

"Where?"

"In the tunnel. I was a kid."

"You used to run with them Irish toughs."

"I *was* an Irish tough," Donovan said.

"He still is," Mosko added.

"Put down the screwdriver and I'll forget that you picked it up."

Chops did as he was told and, a moment later, sat back down . . . but on a chair placed well away from Avignon.

Dennis looked at Donovan and said, "You know he's my father?" The voice carried astonishment.

"We're detectives," Mosko said.

"This is what we do," Donovan added.

"You do it well."

"You know, people look at a cop and are amazed that he knows something. Okay, so I didn't go to Harvard. When I need to know something I look it up, ask someone, or figure it out on my own. To me this is no big deal. If I were an academic, I'd say that I'm constantly accumulating knowledge. But I have a problem sounding that full of shit."

"I apologize for insulting you," Dennis said.

"We work stuff out," Mosko added.

"Now apologize for lying to me," Donovan added.

"I'm sorry for that, too. Look, Bill, my father and I made up a few years ago. He still wants his lifestyle, and I respect that. I just try to be there for him and provide a safe haven."

"Safe is good."

"We like safe," Mosko added.

Donovan said, "When you docked at South Street, he was . . ."

"Living in Chinatown," Dennis replied.

"Doubtless where certain culinary habits I recall from decades ago were reinforced," Donovan said. "And when you docked at Chelsea Pier?"

"My dad was living behind the old meat warehouse at West Eighteenth," Dennis replied.

"What will he do if and when you get your permanent dock?"

"We're talking about that. He may come live with me. On the other hand, there are plenty of old hiding places along the Chelsea waterfront. Did you really know him before?"

Donovan nodded. "He used to be one of the Mole People."

"On the West Side."

"Where else?" Donovan replied, his tone being that if a historic fact about New York City tilted toward the eccentric, the West Side was likely involved. Donovan himself was a West Sider, of course.

"After I came up from Florida and was ready to deal with it, I tracked him down," Dennis said. "He's okay, really, gentle and harmless."

The old man grunted, in agreement or disagreement Donovan couldn't be sure.

"Those were some good reflexes with the screwdriver," Mosko said.

"He was just trying to protect himself."

"Such as from Rob Ingram, using the knife."

"No," Dennis insisted.

"Where were you between four and five Wednesday morning?" Donovan asked Hickey.

"What day was Wednesday?"

"Two nights before last. There was a big party on the *Trinidad Princess*."

Hickey grunted again and shrugged. "I watch people. I hide from people. I keep a lookout. I don't keep track of nights."

"Where was he?" Donovan asked his son.

"He was here when I woke up," Dennis replied.

"But you don't know when he showed up."

"Sorry, for his sake, I really don't. But he wouldn't hurt anyone."

"Like you said, you don't pay attention to when the door is locked—to the extent it's *possible* to lock up a ship, and it really *isn't* unless you can afford guards—after hours, despite the fact someone truly nasty such as Cal Sforza could come aboard. It's because of your father."

Dennis nodded.

"We figured that he got here right about the time of the murder, maybe a little before," Donovan said. "Do you know which gangway he used?"

"Port," Chops said proudly.

"He's good at seeing in the dark," Dennis said. "And I keep it dark because it makes him comfortable."

Donovan turned to Chops and asked, "Was the knife here when you got here?"

"My antique knife, Dad," Dennis explained. "I left it on the top shelf where I always leave stuff for you."

"In case Sforza showed up again," Donovan said.

"Yes," Dennis replied. "I wanted my dad to have something to defend himself with."

Donovan said, "That's also why you had the knife in that overhead compartment earlier in the day, where it would be easy to run and get from the deck."

Dennis smiled and nodded. "That's exactly why I had it there."

"And you took it down later to leave where your dad could use it."

"There weren't no knife then," Chops said. "Only this."

He picked up the screwdriver again, and held it until

Mosko glared at the man and pointed downward. The screwdriver went back on the table.

Donovan asked Chops, "Once you were in this room, did you hear anything?"

"Like what?" the man asked suspiciously.

"Like voices. I bet you hear pretty good, too."

"Yep. I heard."

"A man and a woman?" Donovan asked.

Chops nodded.

"Anyone else?"

"Don't know. Maybe there were two men. Or two women. Can't be sure."

"You didn't go see?" Mosko asked.

"What's the most dangerous word you hear when you live on the street?" Chops asked.

" 'Hello,' " Donovan replied.

"That's right!" Chops replied; gleefully, Donovan thought, at having been understood. "You don't want no one saying hello to you, 'cause they could want to hurt you or steal something from you."

"So you heard voices, maybe two people, maybe three," Donovan said.

Chops nodded.

"But there was another noise. A big one."

Chops smiled. "My trap went off!"

"The ashtray stand. You put it where someone pretty much has to knock it over to get to this room," Donovan said.

"He puts it there so the Nazis will knock it over when they storm ashore. And that will give him warning," Dennis said.

"*He* knocked it over," Dennis said, nodding at Avignon.

"He always does," Chops said.

"And that was the noise that Caren heard," Donovan said. He turned to Avignon, who remained seated but had begun to show interest in the conversation, and said, "What did *you* see or hear?"

"Only him," Avignon replied, tilting his head in the direction of the old man.

"When did you get here? The truth this time."

"Oh, is this gonna be one of those deals like I see on *Law & Order* where the cops say, 'If you cooperate with us it will go easier on you,' hoping you'll forget about calling your lawyer?"

"Do you want a lawyer or not?" Donovan snapped.

"Eventually. Hey, I really am innocent this time. All I did was shoot some footage about a homeless guy living in the shadow of incredible luxury. This is right up my alley and you know it."

"When did you get here?"

"I got onto the L train at quarter to four. It took ten minutes for the train to come. I made the connections pretty good. I got here at four-thirty, maybe a little before. I came down the port gangway after sticking my head over the side to see if the *Trinidad Princess* was discharging waste. When I got down here, this guy was here already, eating."

"You knocked over the ashtray stand," Donovan said.

"Yeah. Even though I knew it was there."

"What happened then?"

"He grabbed the big knife from off the shelf and waved it at me, yelling his head off, but then he saw it was me and threw the knife down."

"Down where?" Donovan asked.

"Down on the floor and then I kicked it out the door," Avignon said. "I hate weapons."

"Did you hear a woman scream?"

"God, no. Who could hear anything beyond *him* screaming? But he calmed right down once he saw it was me."

"When did you start taping him?" Donovan asked.

"Ten minutes or so later. I gave him time to calm down and me time to set up the shot." Avignon said, "That one, from the corner," nodding in the direction of the spot he was sitting in before. "The same shot I was making when you guys showed up tonight. I was trying to finish what I didn't finish the other night."

"Of just him?" Donovan asked.

"Yeah. Dennis was in his cabin, asleep."

"How do you know that?" Mosko asked.

"I don't. I assumed. Anyway, he wasn't here."

Dennis looked a bit uncomfortable. "I was asleep like I said," he added.

"Okay," Donovan replied.

"I was in this room the whole time . . . what, an hour and a half, I guess, two and a half hours?" Avignon said. "Until around seven, when Dennis came down and told us there was a body on the dance floor and to take off."

"You sat here for over two hours with a stiff fifty feet away," Donovan said.

"This is New York, man. This is why I love it. Ironies and contrasts."

"And you didn't go shoot footage of the body after Dennis told you about it?"

"No, no, *noooo!*" Avignon said vociferously, shaking his head. "I wasn't going anywhere near a body. Not with my record. Besides, when Dennis said 'body' he left out the murder part, so I assumed it was an OD left over from the party, and who cares? So I split. Got back on the downtown IRT and went home."

Donovan waggled the evidence bag at him and said, "We can check that. As you no doubt know, whenever you use a MetroCard you sign your name in cyberspace. We can find out exactly when you got on that L train and when you went home."

"Check away. I'm telling the truth."

"This time."

"This time," Avignon admitted.

Pointing at the camera, Donovan said, "Is that the equipment you used? Why'd you go home at all?"

"To ditch the big cameras, which freak him out. He thinks they're military equipment. Fifty thousand dollars on a professional camera, and he thinks it's a missile launcher. So this is the camera I used, and in it is the tape I used, too. Take it and look. But I tell you, Bill, I went back over it for anything that would be useful regarding the murder, and there's nothing on there. No background voices, no nothing. Only Dennis showing up to tell us to split."

"There's time coding on that tape?"

"Yeah, day, hour, and minute. Pretty neat, huh?"

"We'll take it and give it back if you're telling the truth," Donovan said.

"You're starting to like me again, aren't you?" Avignon said. "A little bit, anyway."

"Don't flatter yourself. Dennis, about this port and starboard gangway thing. The way I see it, the starboard gangway is for guests. It's well lit, and decorated, in a manner of speaking."

Dennis nodded.

"And the port gangway is the stealth one," Donovan continued. "It's kept dark because your dad is more comfortable that way, and also so you and Lachaise can slip up and down to collect samples without tipping off Sforza."

"That's exactly correct," Dennis said.

"Why would Veronica Cascini use the port gangway?" Donovan asked.

Dennis looked surprised, and smiled wryly. "Can't imagine," he said.

"It's dark and filthy, but Caren said that Veronica used it when she went to the head before going home."

Dennis shook his head. "If she used the port head, she's a gymnast."

"No seat?" Donovan asked.

"No seat. No *light*. Guys can deal with that, but a classy lady like Veronica? Trust me, she didn't use it."

"Interesting."

"She said she went down the port gangway?" Dennis asked.

Donovan nodded. "And at the party, I saw Caren going *up* it."

Dennis said, "Why would those two women . . . ? Oh, never mind, I live alone on a boat. What do I know about women?"

"The two of 'em had a motive to kill Ingram and neither has an alibi for the time of the murder," Mosko whispered in Donovan's ear.

The captain said, "Gotcha."

"I didn't tell you the truth 'cause I was afraid you'd regard my dad as a suspect," Dennis said.

"Regrettably, we still do," Donovan said.

Dennis walked over behind his father and put his hands on the old man's shoulders. "He couldn't kill anyone," Dennis said.

"I couldn't kill anyone," Chops replied, in a vaguely singsong way that Donovan remembered from years before.

"Come on, Bill," Avignon said, "You're the crime-fighting genius. Who killed Rob Ingram?"

Donovan was lost in thought and had missed the sarcasm, which was a good thing for Avignon. Then Donovan motioned for Mosko to remove the handcuffs.

"Am I unarrested?" Avignon asked, when the task was accomplished.

"Two questions," Donovan said. "Are you available early tomorrow morning and can you pretend you're a Greenpeace photographer?"

17. A SHRIEK OF FEMALE FURY AND A FLURRY OF LIMBS.

It wasn't easy to arrange, given Donovan's shaky history with the press, but somehow the late edition of the *Daily News* carried blazing headlines announcing that the NYPD was looking for a Brazilian model named Paco in the murder of Rob Ingram. The model, the "anonymous source within the police department" let slip, was suspected of having knifed Ingram to death after the politician flirted with the woman he had his eye on.

All day long and into the evening, public speculation centered around the futility of the NYPD's "request for help from the Brazilian security forces, following up on a tip that the fugitive had fled the United States immediately after the crime." A whiff of normalcy returned to the City that Never Sleeps. Another heinous crime had been committed and gotten away with, the presumption being that Brazil was beyond the reach of even the famous Captain Donovan. And so it came to pass that when the next early-evening blackness descended over the harbor, it did so over yet another celebrity party aboard that consummate party boat, *Sevastopol Trader.*

As parties go, it was modest. And, typical for New York City parties, it was indoors in a dark place filled with food and drink and music and the allure of the illicit. The party was designed to make those on the outside wish they were in, to remind them that the hip and the connected lived in a world they could only glimpse via the tabloids.

Marcy put out a spread from her restaurant and ordered a selection of teas, coffees, and wines from the best little shops on Broadway. Donovan brought down one of his jazz tapes and started it playing on Dennis's boom box. It was one in the morning, and there was the promise of half a dozen hours of music and conversation and fine dining. The agenda was spiced, of course, with the expected Manhattan contradictions: the fashionably decrepit setting, the whiff of recent death, and the promise of a daybreak breakfast of steaming hot coffee and donuts served by a liveried waiter who would pick it up from Twin Donuts on Ninety-second Street, Donovan's favorite fast-food emporium.

Chris Conner's smoky rendering of "Lush Life" filled the hold of the freighter as Caren Piermatty and Veronica Cascini appeared on the catwalk, Caren yelling, "Hi, all!" and waving with both hands as would a child. While Cascini dressed in her usual corporate mode, Caren wore supple leather pants that were skin tight at the thigh and widened on the way down to approximate chaps. A suede jacket flew open to reveal a top of sorts—Donovan imagined he saw two Pancho Villa–style bandoliers that more or less covered her breasts.

Mosko looked up at this vision and said, "Jesus, Mary, and Joseph."

"Time for you to autograph *her* pecs," Donovan said.

"Don't start trouble, William," Marcy said. "You *know* that she'll let him do it."

"I was just talking."

"Hi," Veronica called, in a much more subdued voice and with a wave that was more like a twitch of the fingertips.

Donovan couldn't be sure, but thought she might be wearing the same suit as the night of the murder.

The two women finished walking across the catwalk, moving from starboard to port, then disappeared down the port gangway and a few seconds later appeared on the dance floor.

Caren's hands went up in the air and she fluttered them around to suggest pinwheels. Another ear-to-ear smile appeared and she cried, "I'm hee*rre!*" and ran to Marcy and enfolded her in long and willowy arms.

"Hi, Caren," Marcy said, with a look that said, *This woman is exhausting, but kind of fun.*

"God, I'm getting to see you *twice* in one week! This is so cool."

"It sure is," Marcy nodded, while extricating herself from Caren's arms.

Caren looked over at Donovan, and said, "As for *him,* I'm not going anywhere near *him,* not after I heard about you and the shotgun."

"Shotgun?" Marcy asked her husband.

"The Jones woman," Donovan replied.

"Oh, *her,*" Marcy said, the tone suggesting that the shooting had been just another day at the office.

Her promise notwithstanding, Caren breezed over to

Donovan, gave him a kiss on the cheek, and then quickly fluttered off, saying, "Oh, you *are* cute, but I just found m'*man!*"

She ran to Mosko, gave him a big hug, and kissed him on the lips. Then she said, "Hi, big boy! What are you doing later?"

Blushing, Mosko replied, "Trying to decide which to go to first—court-martial or divorce court."

"We may as well give them something to talk about," Caren said, giving him another kiss before pulling back and saying, "What a week!"

"How are you holding up?" Donovan asked.

"Good. *Great!* The cycle has been completed. The tide has come in and gone out and come in again. Things have gone around entirely—three hundred and fifty degrees."

"Three hundred and sixty," Donovan said.

"What-fuckin'-ever!" Caren said, with a big sigh, fanning her face with one hand. Then she traipsed over to the chalk outline that marked where Ingram's body had fallen and which, true to his word, Dennis had polyurethaned. She stood astride an imagined or remembered body, looked down on it, and said, "You tried to kill me, honey, but you weren't good enough, and I tried to kill you, and I wasn't good enough, but guess what? Somebody was!"

With that she wheeled and went to the buffet table, atop which sat a Louis Philippe vase stuffed with red roses. She plucked a petal and brought it back to the center of the dance floor. She held it delicately between outstretched fingertips then, with a flourish, flicked it down onto the chalk outline. "Goodbye, Rob," she said.

Veronica was looking away, looking aghast. Marcy smiled and dragged on her husband's arm to get him to the food.

He complied, but not before giving Caren a smattering of applause

As Caren grabbed Mosko and dragged him to dance—to the sound of "Too Marvelous for Words"—Marcy said, "Either she's entirely innocent or the best liar I've met since that time you told me you hated me and never wanted to see me again."

"Are you asking me what I think?" Donovan stuck a fork into a bit of poulet Marengo and brought it to his lips.

"How's the chicken?" Marcy asked.

"I have no idea if she killed Ingram," Donovan replied. "It's possible. She could have stabbed him and run home."

"With blood all over her?"

"The mex said there was very little forward projection of blood." The mex was the medical examiner. "And given how little she was wearing in the way of clothes . . ."

"Who knocked over the ashtray stand, then?"

"Avignon, creeping into the storage room," Donovan said.

"And he heard her scream and didn't come out to investigate?" Marcy asked.

"He said he couldn't hear anything over Chops screaming that the Nazis were landing."

"Now you believe Avignon?"

Donovan shrugged and said, "In this case."

"You don't think he could have killed Ingram?"

"Avignon is a watcher, not an actor," Donovan said. "He's a voyeur of life's crimes, not one who commits them. What, you don't remember the whole philosophy he's built up over the reporter's role as voyeur?"

"I always thought that was ridiculous," Marcy said.

"Avignon is a watcher," Donovan said with finality.

Marcy was about to say something else, but Donovan held a hand to quiet her. Veronica Cascini had shaken off the shock of Caren's performance and gotten herself a glass of Chateau Clerc-Milon. She walked up to the Donovans, shaking her head.

Smiling, Donovan said, "I think we have a contender for this year's Tony Award for best performance in an Off-Broadway drama."

"For sure. As for me, I would simply have called my attorney. Is she suspected?"

"Everyone is suspect," Donovan said, continuing to sample the food. "Except my wife, who can do no harm. Well, except to bad guys and"—he frowned at a item impaled on the end of a toothpick—"the occasional gluten-free crab ball."

"That isn't my recipe," Marcy said quickly. "I was talked into that by Veronica's caterer, the same man who baked the vegan roast beef."

"Artur's cooking is *wonderful*," Veronica protested.

"I mean to arrest *somebody* tonight, and it may as well be him," Donovan said.

Veronica said, "What about me?"

"Did *you* cook the crab balls?"

"No, I mean . . ."

"Is that the suit you wore the other night?" Donovan asked, stabbing the air in her direction with another toothpick.

"Yes," she said, recovering and showing a bit of the bravado that Donovan felt sure she had in mind when picking her outfit for the evening. "The exact one. It came back from the dry cleaners this morning."

"So I heard," Donovan replied.

"I'll give it to you," she said, handing him her glass while

taking off the jacket. Her motions were smooth and practiced, as expected of someone accustomed to getting in and
out of fine clothes.

"Thanks," he replied, accepting the jacket and holding
it up, momentarily, to what passed for light.

"Surely you can tell if blood was dry-cleaned out."

"Yep," he replied, lowering the jacket.

"Honey, Veronica couldn't kill anyone," Marcy said.

"Anyone can kill someone," Donovan replied. "But she
probably didn't, at least not this time."

Veronica started to smile, then rethought what he said
and her suspicion grew.

"On the other hand, it would have been nice if you had
an alibi," Donovan continued.

"That's how it goes," Veronica said.

"This is perplexing to me. Two of the most beautiful
women in Manhattan manage to spend what I feel confident
is a *rare night alone* on the very night that they come under
suspicion of murder."

Veronica's look grew more suspicious.

Marcy said, "My husband thinks in three dimensions,
sometimes four."

Veronica offered a wan smile, and sort of laughed. "I'm
confused," she said.

"So am I," Marcy said. "But stick around . . . it will at
least be interesting, and isn't that why we live in New York
City?"

Donovan folded Veronica's jacket and handed it to a
detective who appeared out of, and quickly went back into,
the shadows. Marcy didn't know the man was there, and
looked momentarily surprised. Then she smiled.

Donovan said, "Caren could have wanted to kill In-
gram . . . and after what she just said, clearly *did* want to kill

him at one time . . . and had the chance to do so. No alibi. You could have wanted to kill him, too . . ."

"Why, for God's sake?" Veronica asked.

"To protect the franchise," Donovan replied.

"Oh, I could do just fine without Caren, if that's what you mean."

"That's not what I hear. You had reason to kill him, and had the chance to do so. In fact, I'm kind of charmed by the notion that the two of you did it together and then went home, studiously refusing to alibi one another so as to appear innocent."

"That's the fourth dimension coming in," Marcy said, getting a bottle of Kaliber and handing it to her husband.

"May I have my jacket back?" Veronica asked.

"When I'm done with it," Donovan replied.

Marcy reached out a hand and touched Veronica on the shoulder, then leaned into her and whispered, "Everything will be fine."

"Easy for *you* to say," Veronica said, retrieving her glass and sipping the wine.

She stared at the tableful of food for a silent moment, then sighed deeply and got herself a plate. She began picking at her meal, holding a fork by the very tip and using it to circle each plate while she thought.

There was a crashing sound, a metal-on-metal sound coming from behind stage, and Caren screamed "Yow!" and "Oh God!" And grabbed Mosko's shoulders. "That's it! That's it!" she yelled at Donovan, pointing in the direction of the sound, which was followed up by several oaths and then the approaching sound of feet.

When Dennis appeared, walking first across stage and then hopping to the dance floor, Donovan said, "That would be the invasion detector?"

"That's it. I hate that thing. Hi, everyone."

"It's funny," Donovan said. "You can know exactly where something is in your house that will fall over if you touch it. You make New Year's resolutions to stay away. And still you knock it over. I asked Dennis to kick the ash tray stand over, but not until later in the evening. Oh well . . . it worked."

Not exactly listening, Caren dragged Mosko over, hauling him by a handful of shirtfront that she had in a tight grip. She said, "That's the sound I heard that night."

"I figured. Okay, Caren, you passed the midterm. You didn't hear anything else?"

"Not me . . . I ran. I don't like strange noises in the night. At least not when Brian isn't here."

" 'Brian'?"

"We're on a first-name basis now," Mosko said sheepishly.

"I'm very happy for the both of you," Donovan replied.

Dennis got himself a bottle of Steamboat Ferry Inn Ale and said, "I set everything up like you said, Bill. We're ready to go."

"What are we 'going' with?" Veronica asked.

"There are two people who 'Brian' and I have proved unable to get a hold of," Donovan said. "I have a plan to smoke 'em out."

"Oh good! Adventure! Someone to blame this on other than me. Harley Greave and who else?"

"Cal Sforza."

Her brow wrinkled. "Who? I thought you were going to say the 'Brazilian model.' "

"Did you like that one?" Donovan asked.

"I'm just glad you gave us enough warning so we could go along with you in case a reporter called," Veronica said.

"Did one?"

"Yes, but I didn't return the call."

"Sforza is the chief engineer of the *Trinidad Princess* and, we just found out, has a well-earned reputation as a bully," Donovan said. "He's been arrested several times for assault, usually in wharfside bars . . . twice in New Orleans . . ."

"A good place for it," Marcy added.

"And once here in New York. In that case he beat up a hooker he had solicited and who, of course . . ."

"Turned out to be a guy," Mosko added.

"Sforza was represented by a very big lawyer whose law firm also represents the owners of the *Trinidad Princess* in various matters, including the successful attempt to keep us off the premises following our initial search of Ingram's suite."

"These people are like the Ramseys," Mosko said.

"Sforza was pleaded down and got off with four months in jail," Donovan said. "Now, he did his time, if you can call it that, in the same facility with Michael Avignon, which is either a key piece of the puzzle or a coincidence."

"But not an *amazing* coincidence," Mosko said.

"We have no idea if they met. Sforza spent his time in the gym . . . some guys prefer muscles to neurons." Donovan smiled at his friend.

"I prefer both," Caren said, giving Mosko a playful punch in the chest.

"And some guys prefer the library. Avignon spent all his time in there, running a program about video. So-*ooo*, we'll see how important it is that Sforza went to jail."

"Who's Michael Avignon?" Caren asked.

"Didn't you notice the man who was shooting a video the night of the murder?"

"Who pays attention to cameras? They're everywhere. I just have fun and let whatever else happen."

"That was Avignon," Donovan said.

"My husband put him in jail ten years ago," Marcy said. "What for?"

"Accessory to murder. Harboring a fugitive."

"Being a pain in the ass," Mosko called out.

Veronica held out her glass for a refill, and watched as the waiter obliged. "Accessory to murder. What's that mean? Holding the ammunition?"

"The point could be argued," Donovan said. "But in this case it meant refusing to tell me the name of the killer."

"Oh, and this man is just running around free? And coming to the party? How thrilling? Why didn't you invite O. J. Simpson, too?"

"He was unavailable," Donovan replied.

"He's out on the golf course searching for the real killers," Mosko said.

The boom box began playing "In the Wee Small Hours of the Morning," and as if on cue Dennis picked up a chicken leg and, using it as an exclamation mark, began to outline the evening's agenda. He said, "This is how it's working tonight. It's almost two in the morning." He checked his watch, angling it to catch the wavering rays of light from a candle, and said, "Ten to two. The tide has just begun going out."

Mosko said, "Hey, Cap, when you were here the night of the murder it was before midnight and the tide had just begun going out."

"It starts forty-five to fifty minutes later every night," Donovan said.

"Oh. I should know that, right?"

"No," Donovan said patiently. "There's no reason for a city kid to know about tides unless he's going fishing or planning to dump a body into the East River. When you reach that crossroads in your life you can look it up, which is what I did, in the *Daily News*. Just below the weather map."

Mosko nodded and grabbed himself a chicken leg.

Dennis said, "Like I was saying, the tide has just begun going out. That's about the time the *Trinidad Princess* begins dumping waste."

"What did Lachaise and you normally do when taking samples?" Donovan asked.

"We'd wait until the tide started out. Then Peter would pull up in the launch. As you figured, he could only get here on the incoming tide and for a little while after. He should be here any time now."

"What happens next?" Donovan asked.

"I put out the rope ladder for him. He climbs up . . . I help him . . . and then we go below to get the testing equipment."

"And the time that Sforza came over and threatened you was right after then?"

Dennis nodded.

"I guess he's watching you, pal," Mosko said.

"I think he hears when the tender pulls up," Dennis said. "Peter isn't all that adept and tends to bump into the hull of my ship. It makes a racket. Plus I think that Sforza has a henchman."

"Oh, I'm *sure* that he does," Donovan said.

Dennis gave Donovan a strange look. Mosko said, "Believe it," and bit into his chicken leg.

There was a noise from topside, a conjunction of voices, two people talking, neither intelligible to those at the party.

"Peter? He brought someone?" Dennis said.

"Don't think so," Donovan said, looking up as his old friend, George McCann, walked out onto the catwalk looking slightly lost, very amused, and shepherding a lady wearing a black coat and veil. His own garb also was black, and he stopped at the middle of the catwalk, in the same spot where the Donovans inspected the eventual murder weapon a few nights earlier. He looked down and called out, "Would this be the wake?"

"It would indeed, yes," Donovan called back, mimicking the brogue.

The woman beside McCann also looked down, and pushed the veil off her head, and smiled. It was Valerie Bennett, and she waggled her fingertips in much the same way as did Veronica on *her* entrance. The veil was the same one that Valerie wore the morning that Ingram's body was found.

"Isn't that . . . ?" Dennis said.

"The candidate's wife," Donovan replied. " 'Ree,' to her close friends."

"I told you that I will not let Bennett on my ship," Dennis said.

"It's his *wife*, for God's sake," Donovan said.

"Same as him."

"Let her stay. For one thing, this could get you off the hook for Ingram's murder."

Dennis sighed, and said, "In that case, let the lady stick around for a while."

"I thought you'd see it my way," Donovan said.

Looking up in astonishment, Caren said, "What the hell did he see in *that*?"

"Possibly his murderer," Veronica said.

Donovan looked over at her, then back at the folks on

the catwalk. He called out to McCann, saying, "Come down and pay your respects to the deceased."

"Would there be a bottle at the end of this long and winding road?"

"There would be indeed."

"In that case, we would be delighted to attend." With that, McCann stuck his arm out for Mrs. Bennett to grab. She obliged, and the two of them continued across the catwalk and down the port gangway, disappearing from view for but a handful of seconds.

The pair walked up and McCann said, exaggerating the brogue, "God bless all here."

Donovan replied, "Yeah, yeah. How are you, Mrs. Bennett?"

"I'm fine, thank you. I'm afraid I don't know anyone else here, although I have heard a great deal about Miss Piermatty."

Donovan made the introductions, which went well, with the possible exception of those with Caren. She stiffened, which seemed to add an inch to her considerable height, and muttered a strained, "Hi."

"I wish things had turned out differently for Rob," Mrs. Bennett said.

Caren smiled, a forced one that nonetheless turned wider and more relaxed as the shock of meeting her much-older rival subsided and was replaced by her accustomed public *joie de vivre*.

Caren said, "Oh, I think Rob is fine where he is, as happy as he can be, having gotten to the place he was going for years."

"Do you also care to flick a rose onto the Rob Ingram memorial chalk outline?" Donovan asked.

Mosko got a rose from the vase and handed it to her, at

which time she noticed the outline and gaped at it. Donovan couldn't tell from her expression what she thought of the idea. Then she shook her head and turned away.

Donovan said, "I wanted you to be here to help me figure out what happened the night of the murder. And I didn't think that you could justify getting away from the campaign to meet me."

"And so the captain prevailed on me to offer my old bleeding heart to you as company," McCann said. "We had a fine dinner and discussed the possibility of my mediating the negotiations for a series of debates between her husband and the competition, that poor, deranged man who only wants to protect Social Security and the poor."

"Behave," Mrs. Bennett said, but with a faint grin.

"In any event, it offered the excuse to attend this fine and estimable gathering. I'd offer further expressions of gratitude were my throat not so parched."

Donovan motioned for the waiter to retrieve the bottle of Jameson's kept behind the buffet table. Then the captain poured some on the rocks and gave the glass to his friend. McCann took a sip, emitted a sigh of satisfaction, and looked at Mrs. Bennett and said, "Something for you?"

"A glass of wine, please."

Donovan got her a glass of the Chateau Clerc-Milon. After thanking him and taking a taste, she said, "Very nice selection. What will we be doing tonight?"

"Talking, mainly."

"George is very good at that."

"Believe me, I know."

A short period of small talk ensued, mostly about how *Sevastopol Trader* came to be a party boat. Caren dragged Mosko back onto the dance floor, this time to slow dance along to "Stormy Weather."

Then there came a slight sound, a deep sound, rather like that made when a rubber mallet strikes the side of a ship. Only it wasn't a mallet, but Lachaise's small boat coming alongside the freighter.

"That's Peter," Dennis said. He headed for the port gangway.

Donovan told the others to stay behind, with the exception of Mosko.

"Hey," Caren protested.

"Be right back, babe," he replied.

" 'Babe,' " she said, and went to the buffet table to take consolation in food.

18. "SOMETIMES I'M SO GODDAMN DENSE. OR MAYBE IT'S JUST BEEN *SO LONG!*"

The two detectives kept a few paces behind Dennis as he grabbed the rope ladder and rushed up the gangway. They didn't go out on deck, instead loitering in the dark inside the door and watching. Donovan heard the tender's clanky old engine sputter into silence.

Dennis secured the rope ladder and tossed the other end over the side. Donovan heard Lachaise say, "Shit," and several other oaths and then came the sound of fumbling around.

"This guy ain't no Captain Ahab," Mosko stage-whispered.

"You got that right," Donovan agreed.

Nonetheless, the small boat *was* finally tied up to the bigger one and Lachaise *did* manage to climb the rope ladder in the dark and, with a hand and encouragement from Dennis, clambered over the rail and onto the deck.

A great deal of clattering, banging, and cussing accompanied the feat, however, enough to wake the dead and certainly more than enough to get the attention of the bad-tempered chief engineer of the cruise liner docked just upriver. And Donovan noticed an unexpected accoutrement, one sure to enhance the value of the scene as a lure. He had expected Michael Avignon to arrive earlier, and perhaps the man did. For he had slipped silently aboard the *Sevastopol Trader* and was taping the two men. Emblazoned across the back of his classic photographer's vest were the words RAINBOW WARRIOR, stenciled in large block letters. That was the name of the legendary Greenpeace environmental crusade ship that French operatives had sunk in the South Pacific some years earlier.

"Your pal is here," Mosko said.

"And improvising brilliantly, I got to admit."

"If this doesn't smoke out Sfozra, he's unsmokeable," Mosko said. "But are you a little bothered by the way Avignon got onto this tub without us knowing?"

Donovan nodded. "I'm also bothered that he didn't check in."

"He's not following the script."

"Throughout his life he never did."

"Which is why you like him, right?" Mosko said.

"Let's just say I don't hate him as much as I did yesterday."

Acting very much the role of an activist eager to capture every aspect of a crime against nature, Avignon panned from the men to the cruise liner and then down into the inky blackness that separated the two ships. Then Dennis and his partner looked over to Donovan for direction, who waved them into the gangway door. Avignon followed them, taping all the way, using the small camera that Donovan caught him with the night before.

"How'd we do?" Dennis asked as he trooped down the stairs, the others following.

"Good," Donovan said.

"This is exactly what we did the night Sforza came over and threatened me."

"Let's hope he was watching," Mosko said.

"I think he's always watching," Dennis said.

Bringing up the rear, Avignon pressed a palm against Donovan's shoulder and said, "I added the Rainbow Warrior sign as a value-added. What do you think of it?"

"Nice touch."

"So are you and I okay now?"

"Not yet."

"Come on! I didn't kill anybody this time. I didn't harbor any fugitives . . ."

"Even though the harbor is the place to do it," Donovan said.

"I didn't do anything but what you asked."

"If you wake up in the morning in your own bed and not in Riker's Island maybe that means we believe you, pal," Mosko said.

Once down below, Dennis led the procession into the backstage area and the storage room, with Donovan noticing that it was, indeed, possible to walk that route without becoming aware of events on the dance floor. Mosko and he waited outside the door while Dennis and Lachaise got their equipment. It took but five minutes for them to pack up their rudimentary sampling gear and begin to head back topside.

"Keep to the schedule," Donovan said.

"This is how we always do it," Lachaise reported, pausing only slightly to rub his lower back after the strain of picking up a bucket.

"What happened to your back?" Donovan asked.

"Your wife happened to my back."

"And sleeping in an abandoned gravel silo had nothing to do with it?"

"I'm comfortable there. Besides, I like to stay mobile. There's an issue I mean to tackle in the Indian Ocean next year."

"What's there?"

"Radioactive waste dumping from the Pakistani nuclear weapons program," Lachaise replied.

"This is how it's going to be for the rest of your life?" Donovan asked.

Lachaise nodded, then yelped slightly in pain while hefting the bucket, which was filled with sampling lines and collectors.

The procession proceeded back to the deck. When they got there, Donovan scanned the side of the *Trinidad Princess* and noted that two adjacent portholes were now illuminated from within. Staring hard, he thought he saw some sort of figure within; faces, perhaps, hovering near enough to the portholes for breath to condense on the cool glass. And then they were gone, but he couldn't be sure if he imagined it.

Dennis and Lachaise went forward to where the sound of a bilge pump could be heard over the background of harbor noise and general New York City buzz. Avignon followed, taping all the while. Donovan led Mosko through the internal maze of corridors on the freighter until he found another exit, this one just below the wheelhouse and accessible to it via a short set of stairs. They watched from that hidden spot as the two men went about the business of sampling the water, casting several collecting devices into the water and then hoisting them up, to pour the water sampled into a variety of vessels. They worked silently, as was their rule, and the task was done within fifteen minutes.

They packed their stuff back up and headed aft along the port railway, meeting Donovan and his colleague back at the original spot.

"That's it?" Dennis asked, as he went into the safety of the ship's core.

"Take your stuff back down below per usual, and then we're done," Donovan said.

Dennis nodded and once again led the way down below. As Donovan followed along, noting that after a while he could see quite well in the famously dark port gangway and that it wasn't really as crud-encrusted as advertised, he heard Mosko get on the cell phone and say, "The bait is set, boys. Stay sharp."

When the group had returned its stuff to the storage room, Donovan said, "That's it? Do you run tests now?"

"We only do it every few days," Dennis replied. "At the moment, I need to pick up a battery for the unit. Why, do you need to see how it's done?"

"Nope. Just curious."

"Collecting is the most important part," Lachaise said. "Especially if you make the bad guys aware that someone is watching."

"And if the bad guys turn murderous?" Donovan asked.

"We try not to let it go that far. But if it does . . ."

"It's good to have it on tape," Avignon replied, patting the camera.

"Can you put that thing away now?" Donovan said.

"Do you want me to?"

"No. I just said that to see if my lips still work."

Avignon put the camera away.

"As my colleague here noted, we set the trap. Now let's see if the target organism shows up."

" 'Target organism'?" Dennis laughed.

"From what you tell me," Donovan said, "Sforza only takes human form on occasion."

"I hope you can protect us from him," Dennis said.

"*Mrs.* Donovan can if he can't," Lachaise added, rubbing his back.

"I'm proud of my wife," Donovan said.

"We got enough cops hiding around this ship to arrest a tidal wave," Mosko said.

"So let's party," Donovan said happily, leading the way to the dance floor.

Dennis said, "About my dad . . ."

"Is he coming?" Donovan asked.

"It's hard to tell. Probably he'll show up close to dawn, per usual. Hey, you know what? Something funny happened."

"Like what?" Mosko asked.

"I stopped by that Chinese restaurant where he takes his nickels and dimes to buy food," Dennis said. "I thought I'd pick something up and put it in the fridge for him. The owner told me that someone came in and put down a couple hundred bucks on account for my father's meals."

"Whaddya know," Donovan said. "Can we go to the party now? I have my eye on some smoked cheddar I saw back there."

When he got back to the party, the captain found that the group had adjusted itself into knots: McCann and Mrs. Bennett arguing in a pair of chaise longues carried down from atop the cabin, Caren and Marcy talking about fashion in the middle of the dance floor, standing atop Ingram's chalk outline and the now-thoroughly-crushed rose petal, and Veronica Cascini hovering nervously at the end of the buffet table nearest the door leading to the port gangway.

The arrival of the new batch of guests reshuffled the conversational deck. Before too long, Lachaise had engaged Valerie Bennett in conversation about her husband's environmental policy and Caren was flirting with Dennis (Mosko having fallen out of favor, a development that, as a married man, he appeared to welcome). Mosko paced back and forth, talking on the cell phone while plucking black olives from a bowl. McCann had gotten himself another whiskey and was looking over Dennis's collection of old junk.

Donovan had taken an interest in what Veronica Cascini was up to, and, under the guise of rummaging through the buffet, watched her while munching smoked cheddar on Wheat Thins. His interest level rose when she looked around to see if anyone was watching, then suddenly plucked her purse from the table and disappeared up the port gangway. She was gone for five minutes, after which she reappeared, smiling broadly and looking as if her feet floated an inch or so above the floor. She sashayed across the dance floor to Caren, who smiled broadly in return. Then Caren took Veronica's purse and sashayed off toward the port gangway and up it, singing "Happy Days Are Here Again."

Donovan's eyes glazed over. He went to Marcy, who had been talking to a now-bubbly Cascini, and said, "Sometimes I'm so goddamn dense. Or maybe it's just been *so long!*"

"What, honey?" Marcy asked, giving him a quick hug.

Cascini giggled.

Scowling, Donovan grabbed Cascini by the arm and

dragged her across the floor and up the port gangway. "Hey, where are we going?" she laughed.

"The same place the profits of the Cascini Agency are going—up your lovely nose!"

She laughed. "Do you really like my nose?"

"Yeah, but the current version with two nostrils! Cocaine! Christ, how retro!"

With that, Donovan yanked open the door of the supposedly hideous port bathroom to find a not-too-bad little room, barely big enough to stand or sit but containing the requisite and fully functional porcelain appliances as well as a convenient, chest-high shelf upon which Caren had just inhaled a line of cocaine.

Her face flashed shock and amazement. She was about to scream when Donovan clapped a hand over her mouth and held her until she relaxed.

"Don't scare the pigeons," he said.

"What *pigeons?*" she asked, in a whisper.

"The target organisms. Oh, never mind." Donovan pulled Veronica into the bathroom with the two of them and closed the door.

"A threesome!" Caren said.

"In your dreams. Look, girls, so maybe I was a little slow figuring out why the two of you were so fond of this side of the boat but claimed otherwise. So maybe Dennis had a reason for lying about the condition of this facility. This is the drug room, and the reason I didn't see any drugs at the party."

"We were just having a little fun," Veronica said.

Donovan said, "Well, while you were doing it, and I'm talking to you, Veronica, and I'm referring to the time *just as you were going home* the night of the murder, did you hear anything?"

"You mean, while I was in here with the door closed doing a line?'

"Yes."

She sighed. "There was someone on the stairs."

"Going up or down?"

"Down."

"A man?"

"Yes."

"Was there anything in particular about the sound?" Donovan asked.

She thought for a moment, then said, "Clump *clump*, clump *clump*."

"Like a man with a limp?"

"Just like that," Veronica replied.

Donovan thanked them for their help and released his grip on the bathroom door. Caren brushed the remaining cocaine off the shelf and looked at Donovan and said, "You're a cop. What about *this*?"

"Ask your doctor if it's good for your body. Ask your accountant if it's good for your career. Hey, it's your choice. Just leave me out of the decision. Let's go back down below, but don't make noise."

The two women bobbed their heads up and down. Donovan's cell phone, which he had set on vibrating mode, went off. He brought the instrument to his ear and listened for a moment. Then he said, "Okay, lights out," and put away the phone.

Donovan pushed Caren and Veronica back into the head and once again pulled the door shut.

"Hey!" Caren protested.

"Showtime," Donovan replied, pulling out his Smith & Wesson and flicking off the room light.

Caren suppressed a scream, but then grabbed both Donovan and Veronica and wrapped them in a gigantic hug from her long arms. The three of them were pressed together, their breath roaring in the tiny, iron-walled room that was, after all, a functional seat-and-sink for one in an old working boat.

"Breathe quieter," Donovan whispered as the sound of feet . . . four of them, he was sure . . . echoed through the hull. Donovan listened intently as the owners of those feet paused by the gunwale, doubtless to look over the side at the spot where the sampling took place. Then the feet picked up again and within a dozen seconds were coming down the port gangway.

Donovan felt Caren suck in her breath as if to scream again, so he put his hand over her mouth again.

The intruders were on the stairs.

Clump, clump, clump, clump.

And, clump *clump*, clump *clump*.

"That's him," Veronica whispered.

And then Donovan heard a man's deep voice, older and born of whiskey and machine oil and tobacco and salt air and the inexorable weight of the years, say, "Can't do nuthin' right. Have to do it all myself."

The noise became different when the two men reached the foot of the stairs. Donovan let go of Caren and pushed the door open again just as one of the men below knocked over the old ashtray stand. Caren went to scream, and this time he let her, and the sound of her shriek was drowned out by the yelling of cops—"Police, freeze! Hold it right there!" And then came the inevitable and unmistakable voice of Brian Moskowitz, barking, "You don't put those arms up and I'm gonna rip 'em off and feed 'em to my goat!"

"Who's *that*?" Caren asked.

"Who do you think?" Donovan replied, and led the two women back down the gangway.

Sforza and Greave were being searched for weapons, their faces pressed against the cold iron of the walls by four detectives supervised by Moskowitz. The lights were back on in the dance area. Several of the guests—Dennis first among them, peeked around the corner at the proceedings.

Donovan ushered the two women in his charge back among the group on the floor; Marcy took them in tow to make sure they didn't stray. As she urged them back to the party, Cascini kept gesturing at one of the men and whispering, "That's him! That's him!"

"Harley," Donovan said.

"Yes!"

Donovan walked over to where his men had the two suspects under control and had determined them to be free of weapons. They were quite a pair—one tough old wharf rat and one slender kid who did, in fact, resemble Brad Pitt.

Sforza was built like a bull and gave the impression he was similarly tempered. His jeans seemed to have been welded onto his thick legs, and were held up by a broad leather belt that also supported a belly that appeared to have been bricked in. Greave, on the other hand, looked enough like a model to be one, were it not for the complete lack of demeanor. He, too, wore jeans, but tight-fitting ones. Donovan was certain that he saw the insecurity of a country boy in the big city for the first time.

Donovan looked the two of them over for a while before settling his gaze on the young man. Donovan said, "Brad Pitt, I presume."

"Huh?" Greave replied.

278

"I heard all about you, and I did some research on my own, some of which just came in this afternoon. And . . ."

Sforza was getting red-faced holding his temper and his tongue. He shouted, "What's going on here? You want to talk, you talk to me!"

Eyes afire, Mosko grabbed the man by the shirtfront and hurled him back against the wall hard enough for Donovan to feel the vibration through the steel floor. "Whatsa, matter, English a second language for you? You stand there and shut up until the captain gets DGFR to talk to you!"

"What's that?" Sforza asked.

"Damn good and fuckin' ready."

In the corner of his eye, Donovan saw a grin of vengeance break across Dennis's face.

Donovan continued his cut-short conversation with Greave, saying, "I heard you like Starbucks and Manhattan Boardroom Suites. You're clearly a man of wealth and taste."

"I, unh . . ."

"Walk to the other wall and back," Donovan said.

Greave did so, and the slight weakness in his right foot was apparent. It wasn't a huge impediment, just something that caused the young man a certain inconvenience.

"How'd you get that?" Donovan asked.

"Oh, my foot? Something fell on it a few years ago."

"What?"

Looking a bit sheepish, the man said, "A transmission."

"Really? That must have hurt?"

"I'm all right now, sir."

"You're a mechanic."

"Yes, sir. I used to work in a gas station back home. Now I fix things aboard the *Trinidad Princess*."

"And off it, too. Does that limp give you trouble going up and down stairs?"

Nodding, Greave said, "I got to take them one step at a time."

"Which is what you did the night Rob Ingram was killed," Donovan said. "I have a witness who heard you clumping down the port gangway . . . those stairs you just came down . . . just before Ingram was killed."

"Sir, I . . ."

"Was up on the cabin roof pretending to be asleep. But the second you were left alone you came down here . . ."

"Grabbed a knife and stabbed Ingram to death," Mosko added. "Then you ran back to the roof to establish an alibi of sorts."

"No!" Greave stammered. "No, I wouldn't do that. Mr. Ingram was good to me. He got me this job and then he . . ."

"Paid you extra to spy on the *Sevastopol Trader*. Or, rather, to slip in here and destroy whatever evidence Dennis and Peter had gathered."

"Mr. Ingram was worried they had found him out," Greave said.

"*We* found *everyone* out," Donovan said. "At least, we're working on it. Here's another piece of the puzzle. At first, Mighty Joe Young here"—Donovan hooked a thumb in the direction of Sforza—"tried to bully his way aboard, but Dennis warned him off with his big knife. So Ingram hit on the idea of setting up a pretty boy like you as a 'model' and getting him aboard the night of Veronica Cascini's well-publicized party. Ingram was sharp enough to figure out that being great looking is enough to get you in lots of doors, at least for a start. Ingram set you up in Manhattan Boardroom Suites to distract attention away from *Trinidad Princess*, but he didn't know that we can pull fingerprints off money. You left George McCann's business card in a desk drawer—a typical Ingram dirty trick—and came down here for the party."

"Mr. Ingram was my friend," Greave protested. "I was trying to help my friend."

"But Ingram lost confidence in your ability to get the job done," Donovan said.

Sforza snorted, and Mosko pointed a finger at the man to return him to silence.

"And he decided to crash the party *himself* after someone who shall go nameless . . ." Donovan cleared his throat, which made Marcy smile. ". . . brought to his attention the fact that Caren Piermatty was here."

Donovan noticed then that Caren had joined the ranks of those pressing in around the scene of the interrogation. In fact, *all* the guests were unable to resist moving within earshot. An exception was Valerie Bennett, who stood back by the exit.

"Ingram came here the night of his death to make sure the damaging evidence was damaged beyond repair. But he decided to have one final fling with Caren . . ."

"And didn't realize I knew that's what it was, and didn't care," she added.

". . . Underestimating her severely," Donovan added. "Anyway, they came down here to get it on a little, after which Ingram figured to shoo her off and do his dirty work, having been blessed with a perfect excuse to be below decks in case Dennis caught him. Then, however, something unexpected happened."

"He got killed," Mosko said.

"Yeah, basically," Donovan said.

"By this guy," Mosko continued, pointing at Greave.

Donovan offered the palms-up gesture of "could be." Then he *said*, "It could be."

"Whaddya mean it could be? This guy scooped up the knife, which was laying on the floor just outside the storage room door. Remember, Avignon kicked it out there."

"I kicked it out there, remember?" Avignon offered.

"And ran up to Ingram and stuck it in him."

Mosko looked proud of himself.

Donovan said, "Ingram was getting it on with Caren in the middle of the dance floor. They were standing there. Backstage, Avignon knocks over the ashtray stand. Caren screams. Chops grabs the knife off the shelf. He screams. Then he recognizes Avignon and throws the knife down. Avignon kicks it out the door and closes the door."

"Told you," Avignon replied, obviously happy to have Donovan believe something he said.

"Ingram chases Caren topside and goes to investigate," Donovan said. "You see, he thinks that the noise was made by his spy, Brad Pitt here. But *he* comes down the gangway and goes to the storage room, hears people talking inside, and chickens out of going in. He sees the knife on the floor and picks it up. Then Greave hears another voice from a different direction—Ingram telling Caren to leave."

"He goes out onto the floor and stabs Ingram," Mosko said.

"You're a bright guy, I keep telling you that," Donovan said. "It could have happened the way you say. But first let's take a look at everyone who might have wanted to kill Ingram."

Several of those looking on wished they weren't and shuffled around nervously.

"Caren Piermatty. Ingram put her in the hospital."

"I put *him* in the hospital, too," she said back.

"Nonetheless, you had a reason to kill him. He nearly derailed your career, and he cost you a lot of money. You ain't exactly a Roller Derby girl who can make a living with a banged-up face."

Caren smiled in a silly way, and Donovan was reminded that she was mildly whacked.

"Caren has no effective alibi for the time of the murder. On to Veronica Cascini," Donovan continued. "Full disclosure—my wife's friend. Had a good reason to kill Ingram. He cost Caren and her money once, and all of a sudden here he is again, and just at the point where her career is going up her . . . up in smoke."

She gave him a wry sort of look.

"Caren is Veronica's alibi. It won't work for either of them," Donovan said. Then the captain called out, "Howard, was there blood on her jacket?"

"Nada," was the reply from Bonaci, who loitered by the food.

"Nada," Donovan said. "Now, on to Dennis Yeager . . . or Hickey, or . . . Dennis, what are you calling yourself these days?"

"I'm sticking with 'Yeager,' " he replied.

"Full disclosure . . . Dennis is *my* friend. He has no alibi for the time of the murder, but his motive is silly. Nobody I know of kills someone because his ship is dribbling cleaning fluid into the water. And as for Ingram's politics being very different from Dennis's? Dennis is smart enough to know that Ingram wasn't going anywhere in the electoral process. Third-party candidates are an occasional amusement in American politics, but never a real threat. Sorry, Mrs. Bennett."

She shrugged, and Donovan wondered for a moment how much she really cared about her husband's future.

"On to Peter Lachaise. He has no alibi, but his motive is about as good as Dennis's. Besides, he was on his way to getting Ingram in a more conventional way—by revealing him to be the proprietor of an environmental hazard. It seems to be much more delicious a victory to watch your victim squirm while alive. Lachaise is a little strange, but what the hell: This is New York. Sergeant Moskowitz, have I left anyone out?"

"Avignon," Mosko said.

"Michael Avignon," Donovan said, with a grin. "The man means so much to me I forgot for a moment he's involved in this. Michael Avignon was actually *here* when the murder took place, sitting on the floor in the storage room shooting footage of Dennis's father. You may ask, how did he not know it was happening? Avignon is self-absorbed to the point of tuning out everything but this stupid video documentary he's been working on for a dozen years."

"Seven of which I spent up the river, where you sent me," Avignon chimed in.

"Allowing him to feel victimized, which is the last thing he is," Donovan said. "Avignon also is a voyeur. He doesn't *do*. He watches. In this case, while Ingram was being stabbed to death Avignon watched an old man eat Chinese food."

"What about the old man who was eating Chinese food?" Mrs. Bennett asked, edging forward. Now she seemed to be interested in the proceedings.

"That would be Dennis's father, who turns out to be the reason . . ." Donovan looked over at his friend, and asked, "Okay to talk about this?"

Dennis said, "Yes."

"Who turns out to be the reason that Dennis has been dock-hopping around the waterfront," Donovan said. "His father is emotionally on the edge, homeless, and adamant about it. But he likes to have a place to come inside in the early morning hours for reasons that are too elaborate to go into. So Dennis managed to dock *Sevastopol Trader* where his sad old dad can hop aboard when the mood strikes. He was here the night of the murder, with Michael Avignon dutifully chronicling him as a symbol of . . . of . . . of . . . Okay, Avignon, let's hear the ten-second summary."

"Of the coexistence of incredible wealth and wretched poverty in New York City in the twenty-first century," the man replied. "And furthermore . . ."

"That will do," Donovan snapped. "So Dennis's father was here . . . there, in that little room about which so much has revolved"—Donovan pointed at it—"being immortalized on videotape. He and Avignon alibi one another, which is to say neither of them has an alibi you could trade in for a handful of Good & Plenty."

"They could have done it together," Mrs. Bennett said.

"It's possible," Donovan acknowledged.

Mosko stared at his boss, as if to reply, *What are you saying?*

"Dennis's father *has* a motive," Donovan said. "He thinks that an invading force is about to storm ashore. He could have thought that Ingram led the first wave. And Avignon is just twisted enough to let him do it just so he could capture the carnage on camera. When I sent him up the river for seven years it was for doing exactly that. *But* . . . we have been in and out of every aspect of Avignon's life and property holdings, such as they are, an apartment above the Starbucks in Williamsburg, for the past several days, and if he shot footage of such a murder we are unable to find it."

"It don't exist, babe," Avignon said.

The crowd of interested parties had pressed in closer, perhaps sensing more drama. Donovan said, "You might ask, what about Valerie Bennett?"

"What about me?" the woman replied, looking surprised, then stern.

"I can't think of a reason you might want to kill Ingram except, maybe, his going over to Caren Piermatty and, in so doing, jeopardizing your husband's candidacy," Donovan said. "And lately I've been getting the impression you don't care so much about that."

She didn't reply, which Donovan took as a reply.

"What you *did* have was opportunity. You were the one who heard Ingram leave the *Trinidad Princess*. You might very well have realized that this was your chance to get rid of Ingram *and* have it blamed on Caren."

"Hey," Caren protested.

"Or on a host of others," Donovan said. "Don't tell me you didn't know she was here. Anyone who looked over the rail of the promenade deck could see her. And don't tell me you couldn't have sneaked down here. We know how easy it was."

Mrs. Bennett looked away. Donovan could feel her anger rising.

Donovan sucked in his breath and said, "A lot of you could have killed Ingram. But only one did. You, Greave."

The young man went absolutely white.

Mosko smiled.

"It was dark, but Greave is accustomed to working in the bowels of a ship," Donovan said. "He picks the knife off the floor outside the storage room. He goes out, just like my partner said. And he plunges it into Ingram's chest."

"Why would I do that?" the young man wailed.

"Yes, why would he do that?" Valerie Bennett asked. She had moved closer yet.

"Mr. Ingram got me my job on the *Trinidad Princess*. I was just a volunteer in the Virginia campaign office, and he got me this great job. Who was I, a mechanic in a gas station in . . ."

"Hemlaw, West Virginia," Donovan added.

Greave looked blankly at Donovan for a moment, then continued: "I had never seen the world, and Mr. Ingram gave me the chance. And then he paid me great money, *great money* to do some spying for him. Why would I kill him? He did all these things for me . . ."

"To get you out of the Virginia campaign office where there was a very good chance you would figure out that he raped, brutally beat, and permanently damaged Dawn Huckins, daughter of the guy you worked for at that gas station in Union, West Virginia, and who you were going to marry," Donovan concluded. "Problem is, you knew that already. What you needed was a chance to get him alone."

The silence that descended upon the gathering was thick enough to cut with a knife, an old knife, an especially long and brutal knife once used to mince whales.

Greave was even more silent, and Donovan swore he saw the boy grow into a man in that very instant.

"Give up the hick act, kid," Donovan said. "I've seen it before. Once, for reasons even I have forgotten, I found myself hanging around the U.S. Monopoly Championship at the Sheraton New York Hotel. In the finals, a couple of really bright and very obnoxious college kids from New York . . ." Donovan pronounced it "New YAWK." "Were playing this supposed hick from West Virginia. This kid looked like he rode the hay rake all the way up Route 1, and they were making fun of him—his clothes, his accent, his intelligence. Well, to make the story shorter, he took them to the cleaners . . . twice. First he took them to the brink of losing, and they became silent and grumbly, and then he let them win most of it back, and they started mak-

287

ing fun of him again. So he won everything again, this time going all the way until he owned not only all their money but all their game pieces. When they had slunk off, I went up to him and said, 'You did that on purpose. You didn't just want to win . . . you wanted to *destroy*.' And he looked at me with this goofy phony innocence and said, talking just like you do, 'I'm afraid I don't know what you mean, sir.' "

Greave looked into Donovan's eyes and said, "I'd like to speak with an attorney, sir."

"Get a good one, kid. You killed Ingram and then went back to your fancy hotel room to telephone your girlfriend's father to brag about it. You're under arrest. You have the right, et cetera and so forth . . . my colleagues here will read you the rest of it."

"Can I ask a question?" Sforza asked.

"What?" Mosko growled.

"If this kid killed Ingram, why'd he stick around? He wasn't no good to me. Worst mechanic I ever saw. I only kept him 'cause Ingram said to."

"I don't know," Donovan said. "To make a return trip to ensure there was no evidence pointing to him. Maybe it was arrogance. Maybe a desire to return to the scene of his one and only triumph in life."

Then Donovan looked at Greave and said, "Am I getting close?"

The young man looked up at the ceiling.

"Maybe he wanted to dance on the grave . . . the chalk outline, I mean. After all, it seems to be a popular idea."

Greave looked back down and at Donovan, and their eyes met.

"That's it," Donovan said.

"You're never going to be able to prove any of this, are you?" Mrs. Bennett asked, stepping up closer. "He'll get a good lawyer . . . a rich, liberal lawyer from New York City will represent him just because he killed Rob Ingram."

"I have a new business card," McCann chimed in.

A few seconds after nearly all eyes homed in on him, looking aghast, McCann said, "That was a joke, people. Have you not heard of a joke before?"

"You'll never convict him because your case is all circumstantial and because he killed to avenge what Rob did to his girlfriend," Valerie Bennett said.

"It's an imperfect universe but we'll do our best," Donovan said. Then to his men he repeated an old and favored phrase, "Haul him off—kick the shit out of him and cuff him to the radiator in my office."

Mosko said, "It's been six or seven years since you had an office with a . . ."

He was interrupted by a shriek of female fury and a flurry of limbs. Valerie Bennett reached into her purse and pulled out a small automatic and was leveling it at Greave's chest when Marcy's foot came up, out of the shadows or nowhere, really, Donovan only being subliminally aware that she was that close, and the gun went flying to the ceiling and then clattered to the floor harmlessly.

"Jeez, Louise," Donovan said, borrowing a phrase from a gay colleague.

Two detectives pounced on Mrs. Bennett, who was struggling and breathing the word "no" over and over, and dragged her back and away from the others.

"Attempted murder," Donovan snapped.

Now crying, she stammered, "Rob was a hard *man*, but he was a *man*! My husband hadn't even slept in the same bed with me for ten years!" Then the detectives pulled her away and out of sight.

"I was wondering if that wasn't an issue," Donovan said.

"Are you okay, honey?" Marcy asked, standing by her man and slipping her arm under his.

"I'm fine."

"My husband takes care of things," she said proudly.

19. DONOVAN PUTS THE CHICKEN BACK SAFELY INTO HER NEST.

It was a fine Sunday and Donovan and Marcy sat under the canopy on the aft deck of the *Sevastopol Trader* watching their son as he sat on a blanket moving the plastic cows around his red-and-white toy ranch. The tide and the wind were heading upriver, propelling a fleet of small sailboats past the *Intrepid* and the *Sevastopol Trader*, past the gaping hole left in the waterfront by the departure of the *Trinidad Princess* on a trip to Panama. His flirtation with Caren Piermatty having gone, predictably, nowhere, Dennis was busy trying his lines on Mary O'Connor, Donovan's cousin from Ireland and Daniel's nanny.

Donovan felt reasonably certain that this new flirtation was doomed as well. But it was fun to watch, holding hands with his wife and spending a calm Sunday afternoon enjoying the pleasures of the harbor.

"It's so bright and airy here with the *Trinidad Princess* gone," Marcy said after a time.

"Mmmm," Donovan said.

"You're purring," she said, and rested her head on his shoulder.

"It was a pretty good week, all in all," he replied. "We caught one cold killer and killed one reactionary political career. If Pete Bennett's presidential hopes survive the murder of his campaign manager and the arrest of his wife for attempted murder of the suspect, Bill Clinton's Teflon career will look like George McGovern's in comparison."

"What I don't understand is why Ingram would make such a big deal out of Dennis's spying on their dumping a little dry-cleaning fluid into the water. Wouldn't it have been easier to just fix it?"

"No. The fact that the *Trinidad Princess* had dry-cleaning fluid in the bilgewater was probably indicative of a huge systemic problem—bad pipes, all-in-all weird infrastructure—that would . . . will . . . cost millions to fix. They were looking at a complete overhaul and the attendant loss of income while it happened. It could have ruined them. Plus the bad publicity."

"I see. My honey is so smart. And Sforza?"

"He no longer has reason to harass Dennis. And Brian made it clear to him what would happen if he did."

She nodded, then said, "Veronica says she's going into a program. She's going to get straight before her entire agency goes up her nose."

"How many times did we hear that in the eighties?" Donovan asked. "Look, I don't care how people kill themselves as long as they don't make a mess that I have to clean up."

"That's very practical."

"I'm a practical guy. Messing with people's private morality causes nothing but trouble."

"I think she means it, though."

"And Caren?"

"Who knows?"

Donovan got up and walked to the aft rail and stretched. "Want to go up to City Island next weekend and rent a sailboat?" he asked.

"Sure, honey. I should be done with my paper for the

law review by then. By the way, my seminar leader wants to know how the *Daily News* got ahold of the information about Ingram having been violent."

"An unfortunate leak that every responsible person in the NYPD deplores," Donovan said, rolling his eyes.

"One that nonetheless compensated the *News* for having run the thing about Paco, the Brazilian model," Marcy said, making quotation marks in the air with her fingers.

"I suppose that's how it worked out," Donovan said. "Come on, let's go to City Island next weekend. Let's see if I still remember port from starboard after the week I've had. I want to teach Daniel how to sail."

"Daddy, play with me," said the boy, in a soft little voice.

The sound of his son's voice in the cool harbor air made Donovan go misty.

"Play with your son," Marcy said, and that's just what Donovan did, sitting with the little boy on the blanket and picking up the plastic chicken that had found its way, on its side, dangerously, into the corral with the cows, and putting her safely back into her nest.